Brody

THE FOUND BY YOU SERIES: BOOK THREE

VICTORIA H SMITH

BRODY: The Found by You Series: Book Three

Copyright © 2015 by Victoria H. Smith

One

BRODY

I SAT at the counter of the old diner I always stopped at on my route. I could have driven longer, but when I got close to Mae's, my foot instinctually hit the brake. She had my apple pie ready at the counter like clockwork. She knew I'd stop too. She had my schedule. Two a.m. and pie just went together, and if I was going to have it, it might as well have been at the best twenty-four hour diner in Arkansas. And believe me, I'd been to quite a few of them to be able to say that.

The middle-aged black woman made sure to scoop a good-sized portion of vanilla ice cream right on the top. A la mode done right.

I grinned at her, forking in a few bites before she went to serve two others that came in, a girl and a guy. They sat at a booth, taking my attention a bit. I might not have paid them any mind, but the guy had a few years on the girl and she didn't look to be his daughter; him being white and her African American. I couldn't see her face with her head down and long hair covering her cheeks. The strands streaked with some kind of magenta color and I found that pretty unique. She piqued my curiosity, this strange woman hiding behind her hair, but the guy took his place beside her, hiding her from my view. His hand slid over the tops of her brown shoulders. He squeezed her. I looked away. The two weren't really any of my business.

Settling into my spot, I went back to enjoying what I considered the fourth meal of the day—the one between dinner and breakfast. Since I started truck driving a few months ago, my schedule was all messed up. I ate when my body needed it and right now, it needed Mae's pie.

Finishing up my dessert, I gazed over my shoulder and realized the couple that came in after I arrived, were gone. It was just as well I hadn't noticed. I didn't allow myself to have many breaks when on the road so when I did, I was in my own little world.

I wiped my mouth with my napkin and gave Mae a tip the equivalent of the cost of my tab. It was damn good pie and I wanted to support her small business. Through previous chats, I knew the diner to be family owned. You always took care of family. That I knew.

Picking my ball cap up from where I'd previously placed it on the counter, I slipped it on top of my mop of blond hair. That shit got all over the place when I knew I had nobody to impress. The hat had become a permanent part of my daily wardrobe outside of work.

Sliding away from the counter, I made my way to the bathrooms to wash my hands. This was the final stop before I drove into the night. I had to get back on route, back home.

The door was closed when I got back there. I poised my hand to knock and verify no one was inside, but a shrill scream on the other end raised the hairs on the back of my neck and raced my heart into overdrive.

I tugged on the handle immediately, but it was locked.

"Someone's in here!" drummed a male voice from inside.

"Shut the fuck up and pull your underwear down. I paid for this you fuckin' tease so give me what I want."

I didn't need to hear anymore.

I took a step back and kicked the door in on nothing but sheer adrenaline. The hinges were rusty and old like the rest of the diner and the door caved easily.

The scene before me turned my stomach. The man from before, the big one who had come in with the girl earlier, had his pants down with his back to me. The girl was there, too, her hair long and colorfully streaked. I could see her eyes now between the strands. They were doe-like orbs, big and brown and glistened like starlight. They also had tears. They slid down a face covered in thick makeup. She sat on the floor before this man, her arms around a set of legs covered in black fishnet stockings. She had bruises on those arms and she stared at me wide-eyed with strong terror etched on her face.

Her aggressor whipped around and red welts on his face told me the girl fought back. She fought, but he didn't stop.

I'd make him stop.

He came at me and I didn't waste the advantage I had to assess the situation beforehand—my position versus his. I was sure my age and all those years I spent in construction with my dad and brother helped as I grabbed the guy's arm. I tugged him to the side, slamming him head first into the tiled bathroom wall.

He fell to the floor, groaning with his hand on his head. Blood seeped between his fingers and the red smeared across the wall let me know how hard he hit. Despite that, he got up with wobbly steps. He charged for me.

I socked him in the gut and he went down again. This time, I joined him and let my fists fly. I gave this fucker a choice to stay down. He wasn't getting another.

"She wanted it," he called out, an old fuck who I could

now see was at least thirty years this girl's senior. "The cunt asked for it. She can't say no after I paid her."

I sent another blow to his face. "If a lady says no, that means no, motherfucker. It don't mean shit if you paid her."

He let out an *argh!* as my hand came away from his gut. I stood, feeling he had enough, and when he didn't attempt to get up and come at me again, I knew he had. I didn't hit a guy just because I felt like it. If I punched a dude, I had a damn good reason. Only tools continued to hit a guy when he was down.

Tired and breathing heavily, I glanced over at the girl. She blinked back tears, staring at the filth on the floor. Her small body shook under her hands. She looked to be in shock.

Shit. I probably scared her more than this guy with what I did to him. I lifted my hat, pushing my hand over my sweaty brow and head before putting it back on. Cautiously, I stepped forward, treading lightly. I didn't want to scare her more.

"Are you okay?" I asked her.

She jumped. Her eyes made a beeline up to mine, hers still sparkling in tears. She gripped her legs. Tensing, she didn't say a word.

I raised my hands, letting her know I wasn't a threat. "I ain't gonna hurt you. I just want to know if you're okay."

Her brown eyes searched me, hesitance in their gaze. She had these eyes that made a guy want to stand up straighter and be just a little taller if only to make her feel more protected. That's what I wanted her to feel—*protected*, and that she was safe with me.

Slowly, she released her legs, but pulled them to her chest again when the guy on the floor moved. He stared at her, pushing up on his hands.

"You little bitch," he spat behind busted lips. "Give me back my money."

I grabbed him by the back of his shirt before he could get closer to her, giving him a swift kick to the gut.

He held his stomach with a grunt, rolling to his back. I pulled out my wallet. I was unsure what money she'd accepted from this man, but I hoped what I had was enough to keep him from coming after her.

I threw money at him. "Now, she doesn't owe you shit, so stay the hell away from her." I looked at the girl, her glistening eyes laced in terror. "You coming? We should get you out of here."

Two

ALEXA

I FOLLOWED HIM ON AUTOPILOT, hardly able to keep my footing steady with my shaking legs. He kept checking behind him, this man, as if to make sure I was still with him while he escorted me away. Away from my latest nightmare...

I curled my arms around myself, tight against my chest, and focused on the man. His shoulders broad and his body wide, he left a trail in his wake. A scent, so masculine, it was woodsy yet sweet and reminded me of an orange candy. Like the citrusy kind I ate at the movies as a kid.

We walked swiftly across the front of the diner, the pots and pans clacking in the kitchen. He drew a jacket off a seat at the counter, covering his large body.

"Mae, I think you better call Hank to take out some trash in the bathroom," he said, shrugging the jacket on. "Dick back there tried to attack this girl. I got him down enough for you to remove him."

"This girl" meant me. I shied behind him. The black woman who served me at the booth earlier tonight came from the back. She put her hands on her hips, frowning at me.

I hid more behind this stranger. His head turned my way when I moved. He shifted, covering me more.

I wonder why.

"Thanks for handling it, Brody," she said, wiping her hands on her apron. "We got some real monsters rolling through here."

Lowering my head, I gave a small smile. His name was Brody. The woman let out a "Hank!" cupping her hand around her mouth and my smile left me. I nearly jumped out of my heeled boots and immediately looked for the exit. Brody was directly in front of me, so I couldn't move though.

"We got some trash for you to take out in the bathroom," she continued, staring back into the kitchen. "Bring your bat. He's a live one."

Now, I really wanted to leave. Like he knew, Brody started walking away, lifting his hand to wave at the woman. "Thanks, Mae. And sorry about your door back there. I can fix it next time I roll through town. I had to bust it to get the guy down."

She waved him off. "Don't worry about it. See you next week."

We were almost to the door when I eyed the booth I sat at before. My bag still tucked in the corner where I left it. I grabbed the handle and a pair of blue eyes met mine when I looked up, deep like sapphire stones. Brody grinned at me and the chimes of the diner's door rang as he opened it.

Averting my eyes, I slid past him. The fresh air and the gravel under my feet, let me know I was out. Free. I immediately took off running on instinct. I had no idea where I was heading, but I had to get out of here. I had to keep going.

Now.

Brody

The girl sprinted off like she was on fire. I'd never seen someone so skittish, but after what happened, I couldn't blame her.

I didn't want her to think I was chasing her so I stayed behind. In a last ditch effort, I cupped my mouth to call to her. "Hey, you don't have to run! I can call someone for you. A cab to help you? There ain't nowhere for miles out here."

I didn't know if she heard me at first, but when her tall boots slowed down on the rocks, I assumed she had. Slowly, she turned around, her small body moving up and down with quick breaths.

I drew closer to her, but not too much, stopping within several feet. That was enough to see her. The streetlights surrounding the diner caught her, spotlighting her willowy frame before me. She wore a leather skirt with lacy straps crisscrossing up the sides. Her shirt was tight and low cut, revealing her chest like the short skirt exposed her legs. Like her makeup, she was overdone and I could see she didn't need it. She was so pretty.

I lifted my hands again like I did inside, not so high this time. I wanted them in front of me so she could see them and she did watch them at first, but eventually gazed into my eyes.

I didn't waste a moment. "Look. I don't know you or your story. I know I'm a stranger, but I genuinely want to help. Like I said, I can call someone for you. I'd just rest easier knowing someone came to get you and you weren't out here wandering by yourself."

She was still curled up, locked up into herself while she held her sparkly bag. She eyed me over, staring at me with hesitance. The way she stared, it was almost like she'd never seen a person before. Maybe it wasn't that, but that she generally just didn't trust people.

I didn't know what to do to show her I meant no harm and that it was okay for her to let her guard down a bit, but I was sure the amplified ruckus that suddenly shot through the air didn't help. We both whipped around from the sound to see Hank, Mae's cook, dragging a body out of the backdoor of the diner. Neither the girl nor I were far from the diner so I didn't need to squint to see who he had in his hands.

Hank threw the son of a bitch out on his ass. Dude was definitely getting his beating in tonight. Shit was more than deserved.

"Don't you come back here, ya hear?" Hank shouted. The burly black man would scare the hell out of me if I wasn't on his side. "You do and we won't be calling the cops. Mae calls *me*."

The guy could only grunt, rolling to his side while Hank went back in. He slammed the door behind him and the guttural moans of the guy rang in the air. He attempted to get up and I suddenly went tense. I didn't want a round two with this guy, but I would if he came at the girl.

"Can I go with you?"

Her voice came out of nowhere. I turned. A set of brown eyes stared at me, pleading. If I hadn't heard her not two seconds ago, I would have thought I imagined her voice. It was light, vulnerable, and her expression was just the same. She needed help. She wanted *me* to help her.

Her eyes flashed to the guy. He was getting to his feet, but he wasn't getting any closer than that.

I made a step toward her, only one, and her eyes went back to me. I waved toward my eighteen-wheeler parked in the wide lot. "Of course. Come on."

Lowering her head, she went with me. I kept to the side of her, but kind of behind. I ended up being close enough to shield her, but far enough away to give her space. She started picking up, moving double time as she gazed behind her sporadically at the groaning man in the back of the diner.

I stiffened. If she was keeping a visual on this guy, perhaps he was more dangerous than I thought.

I was the one moving quickly now. I got to the passenger side of my green rig, opening the door for her. She hopped inside with quick steps. By the time I closed the door behind her and turned back to the diner, I lost a visual on the guy. It was like he vanished. Gone completely.

Shit.

I got going, moving quickly to the driver's side of my rig. I opened the door and the girl jumped, shaking on the passenger side of my truck.

Since I had no idea what I was dealing with, I knew what I had to get before we even took off.

"Hey," I said to the girl, strapping myself in, then getting my truck fired up. "I need you to buckle up, then grab the box underneath your seat."

My order seemed to fluster her, but she acted quickly, handing me what I asked for after she got herself strapped in. She watched me open the box with wide eyes. They'd only get wider when she saw what was inside.

Three

ALEXA

He had a gun. A real gun. I not only got in a truck with another stranger, but this time, the stranger was armed.

I think I'm going to be sick.

I slowly maneuvered my hand to the truck's door handle while he got the thing out of the box. I gripped the handle like a vise. The truck wasn't in motion yet. I could still get out...

He cocked the handgun and I jolted. Letting go of the handle, I suddenly felt faint.

"Who's that guy back there to you?" he asked, lifting his shirt to slip the gun into his waistband.

My mind whirled by the situation, the potential danger of this man with his gun, and then he inched his shirt up, my head spinning more at his cut abs. The tight skin stretched over them...

My mouth dried and I blinked when he lowered the hem. Cocking his head, he found my eyes, that grin from the diner on his face. The expression brought my anxiety levels down, but that didn't make sense. I didn't know this man. How could he calm me so easily?

"You gotta give me something, darlin'," he said, a strand of blond hair moving over his blue eyes. Some of it had fallen from his hat. "I need to know what I'm up against. Is that guy dangerous to you? Do I need to worry about him?"

He'd gotten his gun out to… protect me? Not hurt me? I couldn't help but question why. Why did he step in at the diner? Let me go with him now? Call me… darlin' in such a nice way?

"Would it be okay to hear your voice again?" he asked, his own quiet. It was almost as if he feared being too loud around me. "A yes or no if he'll follow us or not? I would just like to be prepared if I have to pop a cap in someone tonight."

He said this so light-heartedly, that grin strong, and I let a smile escape my lips. I found myself liking his humor… as well as his voice. He had an accent. It drawled lightly on every syllable he made, the tone so deep.

I shook my head, pulling my bag to my chest. "No. No, he won't follow us. I just met him not too long ago." The man had scared me was all, the way he cornered me, but now, I didn't find myself so scared.

Brody grinned wider. He faced the road, getting his truck into gear. "Well, all right then."

Brody didn't say much after that, though he'd yet to tell me his name. I had a feeling he might have been too scared to carry on a conversation with me considering how the night started with my hesitance. He remained silent, his large hand massaging over his steering wheel, and the bill of his hat covered his eyes in the darkness.

Words tickled my mouth so many times. I wanted him to talk to me. I liked his voice…

"Um," I said lightly. He didn't even turn. I had to speak louder. "I, um, need to go to California."

He panned my way, those eyes of his shining. He faced the road with a nod. "I can get you as far as El Paso. That's where I'm from. It's my last stop."

El Paso... Texas? That was a step closer. I could do that. And now, I knew the origin of his accent—Texas. He was from Texas.

That silence hit us again, lingering like a large elephant in the truck.

"I'm Brody, by the way," he said, his words so sudden they caused me to jump. They also made my heart flip flop in the large seat of this truck.

He glanced my way, but didn't linger like he was expecting a response. He simply glanced, then his gaze went back to the road.

It wasn't good to give up too much information about myself, but a name might be okay. I swallowed, dampening my mouth. "Alexa. Some people call me Alex, though."

What friends I still had. Family... Why did I tell him that?

"Can I call you Alex then?" he asked, again, not staring expectantly.

As of now, he seemed to be an ally. I wouldn't use the word friend, though. He glanced at me again and I nodded awkwardly under his gaze.

I looked away quickly, staring out the window and listening to the eighteen-wheeler's hum. Sleep dragged down on my eyes, days of uneasiness and my body on edge for so many reasons, but I wouldn't succumb to it. I knew better than to sleep in front of strangers. Men in particular. I knew better.

Pushing my hands under my arms, I curled up against the door, trying to stay warm. Tonight had been chilly.

My lashes fanned when heat from the truck's vents suddenly warmed my face. I turned slightly, catching Brody pull his hand away from the truck's heating and cooling buttons. I didn't think he intended on being caught. He didn't acknowledge what he did at all, simply adjusted the bill on his hat before placing his hand back on the wheel.

I lay my head against the window again. This stranger was sure surprising me.

~

Brody

The heat helped. She finally allowed her eyes to close, her head of wavy hair lying against the door. I'd been watching her for a while. Not directly, but with stealth. She'd been fighting sleep for miles. I was glad she finally allowed herself to give in to it.

I didn't judge folks. It wasn't my way, but I was ninety percent sure this girl was a prostitute. All the signs were there —on the outside anyway. There was the way she dressed and presented herself with her physical appearance, then of course, the incident at the diner. That ten percent that she might not be was really buggin' me, though. She didn't... *act* like a prostitute, if that made sense. She completely back-pedaled from that guy and looked absolutely mortified on that bathroom floor by what was happening. Sex workers didn't do that. "Lot lizards" as some of the guys in the other rigs called them. Was she a first timer? I didn't know. All I did know was that her name was Alex and Alex was trying to get to California.

A couple hours later, I learned something else about the girl riding with me. She wore a watch and its alarm went off like a shot clock at a basketball game.

The beeping pulled Alex instantly out of sleep, startling me as well. Again, another odd thing about her. Who made their watch go off at random times like that? It was well after midnight. And if someone needed to do, it they usually set their cellphone. Did she not have a cellphone? The whole thing all seemed off to me.

Alex shut the sound off immediately. After she did, she gazed around frantically, her fingers clutching her chest. Her other hand pushed into her hair and she had a far off look in her eyes like she was lost or something. Shit, maybe she was. She seemed so disoriented.

"Alex?" I asked, trying to make solid eye contact with her.

Her eyes flashed my way, body breathy and shaking.

I raised my hand, patting the air gently, soothingly. "It's okay. It's okay, you're safe. It's me, Brody. We're just driving, traveling together."

At my words, she seemed to come out of it. Relief swept her face. Pushing the bright hair away that matted to her sweaty brow, she swallowed hard. I'd managed to calm her and bring her down a bit. I was glad.

"I'm sorry," she said, letting out a breath. She let her head fall back against the seat, crossing her arms. "I didn't mean to fall asleep. I guess I forgot where I was for a second."

I wondered where this woman had been and if she woke up in a new place every night. I wanted to know her story, but I didn't want to push her or risk overstepping my boundaries. In the end, I smiled at her. "I figured you might be disoriented. And you can sleep. It's all right."

Though, she did turn her head to look at me, I lost her gaze just as easy. She stared upon the road before us and I knew she didn't feel sleeping was all right. She was so closed off. She had a large seat in this truck, but she curled herself up into a tight pocket of it.

She raised her wrist, studying her watch for a moment as if she had some place to be. But saying it was late was an understatement and the girl was clearly a wanderer. Her needing to be somewhere at a certain time didn't make sense.

She lowered her wrist, biting her lip, and I quickly gazed away, back to the dark world ahead.

"Will we be stopping at a motel soon? You know, to rest?"

She really was nervous to let herself sleep. I had a feeling people before me messed that up for her. I glanced over at her, tapping the steering wheel. "I don't usually do motels. The company doesn't pay from them. I have a bed in the back. I usually sleep in my truck."

She gnawed her lip at that and I quickly said, "You know what? Never mind. I can look for one. No big deal. I haven't seen anything in a decent amount of miles. We're bound to come up on one soon."

Dishing out funds I knew I wouldn't get back didn't sound ideal. Especially, after I pretty much cleaned myself out of cash with that guy at the diner. But I would so she could be comfortable. I wanted her to trust me. We had a lot of miles together and I didn't want her uneasy during them.

"I... I can't ask you to do that. Spend more money after what you..." She bit her lip. "Do you usually stop at a truck stop or something? I'm sure I can find a bench to lie on and stretch out. I don't want to be a bother to you."

She'd actually rather sleep on a bench than in my truck? Again, seemed odd. She had been so hesitant to sleep around just me, but had no problems doing so publically. Was it because more people would be around or something else? "Yeah, I usually stay at a truck stop, but you wouldn't be inconveniencing me. I can stop if that's what you need and don't worry about before. I was happy to step in. It's just money, and well, that could have been your life."

My words sent a light shining behind her eyes, another sparkle, except this time it wasn't because of tears. A full smile graced her face, one that sent my heart soaring that I put it there.

She reached into her shirt and when she pulled out several twenty dollar bills, I raised my hand in protest.

"Keep it," I said. She needed it more than I did.

Nodding, she slipped the money back into her shirt. Setting her hands on her lap, she turned my way. "I want you to stop at the truck stop. I can sleep there."

"How about I do, but you sleep in the truck. I'll pull some blankets and stay up here, and you can use my bed."

Her mouth parted and I realized exactly how forward that sounded. I'd broken ground, and now, I was stomping all over my work. I lifted my hands. "Nothing funny, I swear. You'll have complete privacy. There's a curtain separating here from the back and everything. You'll know if someone tries to open it, too. The hooks creak like a bitch on the bar. Hell, I have a padlock too to keep it closed if you feel that's necessary—"

She laughed and the sound reminded me of wind chimes. She shook her head. "I think it's okay to do without that last part and thank you."

In a few miles, I got us to a truck stop I'd frequented before. It was one of the nicer ones and actually had a nice little restaurant there. Perhaps Alex would like to get breakfast in the morning. Maybe I could get to know her a little better. She'd checked her watch several times during the drive, and the minute I parked, she was unbuckling herself.

"I'm just going to go use the bathroom," she said, opening the door.

I unbuckled mine. "You actually don't have to do that. I got a small one in the rig. I recommend it anyway. You never know the conditions of their bathroom and I always keep up on mine."

I was convincing her more for myself at this point. Images of earlier sent flashes in my mind. Her in the bathroom... on the floor and crying. I wanted to be able to keep an eye on her. She seemed like she needed me.

Her gaze left me and went to the door handle in her hand and my heart thumped, bouncing around with unease.

Please stay.

The anxiety left instantly the moment she dropped her hand from the door. She nodded, standing when I did. I tried not to look too relieved that she decided not to go. I didn't want her thinking I was weird for wanting her to stay.

I led her back the few steps to the back of the rig. The bed was collapsible to make room for seating at my small table. I ate there and played cards sometimes. I lowered the bed for her, getting out fresh blankets from the above cubbyholes.

She sat curtly on the edge of the bed, checking for springiness when she bounced on her heels, and the entire image peaked in cuteness. I handed her the blankets and she took them.

"Bathroom is in there." I pointed to the right at the door separating the back from the front of the rig. "It isn't much. More like a port-a-potty with a sink to wash your face and brush your teeth, but it is clean, I assure you. I got a spare toothbrush in there, too. It's unopened and there's soap in the cabinet above the sink."

She nodded. Her eyes flashed away and she smoothed her hands across the bedding I gave her. I got to see another one of those smiles when she did.

Brown eyes looked up at me from under dark eyelashes. A smile touched there with their soft creases, too. "Thanks, Brody. For everything."

Four

ALEXA

His sheets smelled like him; masculine with that something sweet.

I pushed my cheek softly against the pillow, my nose, then my lips lightly next. Is this what it felt like to be close to him? The comfort and ease of him...

I waited about an hour sleeping in his sheets, wrapped up in the scent of him. I told myself it was because I needed to be sure. I needed to be sure Brody had settled in for the night up front and that sleep had taken him so I could sneak away. I'd waited too long already and I had to go. I knew the real reason I'd stayed rested against his pillow was the same reason I didn't leave his truck in the first place, though.

I liked that Brody wanted me to stay here tonight. I liked being in his bed, which in itself was just incredibly stupid. He was most definitely one of two things. One, a pervert like most men I found myself around lately, or two, had a wife; a pretty one who was real nice and the two had made an even more perfect child between them. The latter made more sense.

I turned my face away from the pillow, mentally kicking myself for my thoughts of him. I couldn't put him on some type of pedestal because he helped me. My guard still had to be up. I couldn't afford for it not to be.

I pushed his bedding down, checking my watch.

Past time to go.

I never undressed into the spare t-shirt I had or washed up for bed like Brody said I could. Being fully dressed, all I had to do was slip my boots back on and grab my bag. I did so quietly. I couldn't wake him up.

When I stood to my feet, the tied curtain ahead worried me. Brody said it creaked on the bar above. I had to take the chance.

Untying, being careful, I slipped through the drawn curtains, bending my body easily like a choreographed move.

I wouldn't let my thoughts linger on the fluidity of that move or that it *had* been rehearsed to be that easy at one time in my life. I got to the truck's door. I didn't want to look back at Brody, but I had to for a visual so I could escape unseen.

He sat in his chair, large body curled up in such a small space. He was quite large, big. I'd probably mistake him for a laborer, a man who worked with his hands all day if I didn't know he was a truck driver. I assumed he was asleep. He had his head leaned back against the window, the bill of his cap pulled down over his eyes with his arms crossed over his chest.

I reached for the handle and pulled, and with only a click, the large door opened with ease. The internal truck light that came on wasn't bright but I needed to extinguish it quickly.

I was out and into the parking lot within seconds with the truck door closed behind me. Once I was out, I didn't look back. It wasn't because I didn't want to. I couldn't. I had no time.

The truck stop felt cold in its emptiness. A woman inside swept and looked up when I opened the door. She had messy blonde hair and seemed tired with the light bags under her eyes. It was late.

I approached her. "Do you have a pay phone?"

Her gaze went back to the floor, her hands sweeping. "In the back. Near the bathrooms."

My heart jolted at the location. What happened tonight was still too fresh. I pushed past the feeling, heading back there. I was actually willing to sleep at this truck stop, on a public bench when I knew better than sleeping around strangers, just to have access to a phone. I could get over being near the bathrooms for a few seconds. I had to.

The pay phone hung on the wall where she said. I pulled the receiver down to my ear, listening for a dial tone while I wrestled with my bag for a few quarters. I didn't hear anything on the other end of the phone and my stomach dropped, my heart thudding.

In a panic, I flicked at the metal piece on the box, trying to prompt a dial tone. I did so several times before I tugged the phone from my ear. When I did, the telephone cord pulled out of the phone box completely.

My heart sunk even more.

I slammed the phone back onto the box, the tears of frustration watering my eyes.

They fell as I leaned on the phone box, my body defeated and spent. All the things I'd done, *made* myself do, and I couldn't even call...

My eyes blinked down more tears and I caught my reflection on the box's silver plating. Red rimmed eyes stared back at me. I had cried so much tonight. I'd been crying a lot lately, nightly. Leaving California had been nothing but a mistake. I knew that now. I was paying for it every day.

Why had I been so selfish?

I thought what I was doing was for the best, that I was doing right by creating an opportunity. It was one that wasn't just for me, and look how that turned out?

I shook my head, pushing my fingers underneath my eyes.

The black mascara that coated my fingertips disgusted me, how it hid me and made me something I wasn't.

Rubbing my arm across my lips, red lipstick smeared on my dark skin. The girl in the reflection could have tarnished the metal with her broken image.

I gazed away from her, charging off. The lady who swept met my eyes first. She was behind the pay counter now, leaning on it. I approached her, a clear shake wavering my body.

"The phone back there is broken." I didn't mean for the snap in my voice, but the frustrations weighing down my life made me erupt. My anger only blazed more when the woman looked up, eyeing me briefly before casting me off.

She grabbed her cellphone off the counter, clicking on it. "You asked where the phone was. Not if it worked."

My jaw clenched hard, but seeing the woman with the one thing I needed kept me sane, calm. I swallowed to make sure my voice came out right for the request.

"Can I use yours?" I asked her.

She gazed up again, but again made it only brief before going back to her phone. "I ain't no pay phone, doll."

"You can use mine, baby."

Chills covered my skin at the words. I didn't recognize the voice, but the tone... The suggestion of it... I recognized all too well.

I turned on my heel slowly, hesitantly. A man stared at me holding a case of beer. He was older than me, but not by too much. Maybe late twenties, early thirties. He had dark skin like mine and the way he appraised my body wasn't lost on me.

He reached into his pocket, drawing out a black phone, and I could only stare at it, then back at him. I was fully clothed, but this man's gaze blazed a nakedness over me. It was like I knew what he was thinking about and envisioning. This man wasn't just presenting his phone. No way he was. What was fucked up was I knew how I looked. Mascara runny, lipstick smeared. Despite that he wanted me anyway. He wanted to...

I forced myself to give him a smile, no matter how his suggestive gaze made me feel.

Casually, I turned back to the woman. "Can you send out a text for me?"

She rolled her eyes. "Sweetie, he just said you could use his phone."

I curled my fingers on the counter, my eyes watering again. I didn't do it on purpose. I couldn't stop it if I tried. "Please."

She finally gave me her full attention, looked into my eyes, and suddenly she didn't seem so distant, cold.

She rose up. "What do you want it to say?"

Breathing in, I gave a small internal prayer of thanks. "Not much. Just that this is Alex and I'm unable to talk tonight, but I'll call tomorrow at the scheduled time. I swear I will."

I wanted to say more. I wanted to say so many things more. The words this woman was allowing me were limited, though. I knew that.

"Number?" she asked.

I told her quietly. I didn't want the man behind me to know. I stood there, watching until I knew she sent the message. I faced the man and he looked insulted like he wanted to say something or *do* something. I breezed away from him before he could, not looking back. He still had to pay for his beers. That bought me time to get back.

Get back to Brody.

I headed to the truck quickly, silent. The ease I felt as I got closer, didn't make sense to me. But the moment, I opened the door, slipped back in, and closed it behind me, I understood. That guy inside the truck stop made me feel naked, violated, but with this truck's door closed behind me, I no longer felt that way.

I stepped up the stairs.

Brody's mouth had parted, his broad chest moving up and down as he rested.

Biting my lip, I held in a smile. I maneuvered my way around the truck's seat and made it into the small bathroom Brody made a big deal about keeping up on earlier tonight.

I touched the mirror above the sink, studying the reflection of the girl in front of me. Bright hair and heavy make up attracted that man to me. That had been the point. That was always the point.

Slipping my hand into my hair, I tugged, pulling the wig off, the illusion.

I think I wanted to wash up now.

Five

BRODY

DAMN. I should *not* be staring at this girl right now. I lied to Alex. I did. I told her the curtain that divided the back from the front of the truck creaked on the hooks. Truth was they didn't make a peep when they moved. I fibbed a little so she'd stay and I'd readily admit that if she asked me about it—and apologize for the initial lie of course. I knew she'd be safe here and I couldn't trust she'd be okay if she chose to leave. Despite the fact she said she'd stayed in the truck last night, I was still a little paranoid that she would be gone when I woke up. The thought had me up early today, my body aching as I unfolded myself from my chair. This body and that tiny seat didn't mix well when it came to sleeping, but I would do it again for the girl in the back of my truck, the one sleeping in my bed, the one I checked on now through a crack of the curtain to make sure she'd stayed and was okay...

Damn. I *really* shouldn't be staring at her right now.

The urge to do the appropriate thing, close the curtain and walk away after now verifying her well-being, poked at my brain. I couldn't make myself do that, though. Close the curtain and walk away.

She had short hair, not long, but damn if that look wasn't more becoming than girls I'd seen with the longest hair. It swept just a little bit over her closed eyes, reaching her lashes but nothing more, and not every girl could pull the shortness off. I had seen something similar only on actress, Halle Berry, and Alex... she rocked it something crazy. The length let me see her face more and exposed it in new ways to me. She must have washed her make up off before she went to sleep; her full lips looking so soft. The girl didn't have a stitch of makeup on, not an ounce, and my earlier thought that she didn't need it rang true. I idly wished she'd open her eyes so I could see the whole package of the girl I wanted to shield; stare upon those eyes I wanted to keep fear out of. I didn't understand the need for the heavy make up or the wig I could now see as a few of the magenta strands of it peaked from inside her sparkly bag on the floor. I needed to know more about this mysterious girl I was riding with. So much more.

My phone buzzed in my jacket and I realized I couldn't take the chance of waking her up. If she saw I looked in on her, she might run, misunderstanding why I checked in.

After tying the curtain closed, I left my truck to take the call. The name on my phone had me sighing before I picked up.

"Hey, Gram," I said, trying to sound cheerful, happy that she called.

There was silence before she spoke. "Brody, you sound funny. Are you not happy I called?"

Never could fool my grandma. I pushed my hand behind my neck, rubbing at the tension. "Of course I'm happy, Gram. What's up? You doing okay?"

"I'm fine. Fine. You on the road, sweetie pie?"

Nah, but I should have been now that I thought about it. I'd gotten up on time to head out and meet my deadline for my delivery. I had a drop off and pick up at one of my company's locations a couple hundred miles away. I hesitated leaving first thing because I wanted Alexa to be able to sleep. She looked so exhausted last night. I wanted to have breakfast with her this morning, settle down, and get to know her, but I supposed it was too late for that now.

I headed toward the truck stop, opting to get her coffee and doughnuts instead.

"I'm about to be," I told Gram on the way. "I just woke up not too long ago. I got a deadline to make on some parts that need delivering before I cross the state line home."

The line went eerily silent. I knew exactly why, but I didn't dare break it. Gram hated me on the road and that I took this job.

"Brody, I don't like you traveling for work."

I lifted my eyes to the heavens. I called that one. Opening the doughnut case, I grabbed a couple of cream-filled dough-nuts and a cake one with sprinkles. I wondered if Alex liked those.

"It's not safe. You could get robbed or something."

"I haven't yet, Gram," I told her, selecting more dough-nuts with tissue paper. "And you know I can handle my own."

Not only did I grow up in a house full of men, one in which all of us boys were rowdy as hell, but I'd been in a bar fight or two. I blamed that on my stupid days. All of which occurred in my late teens and early twenties. It was back when I thought the girls I met in bars were worth fighting over. I was twenty-five now and didn't have time for that shit. In more dangerous situations, I had my firearm. Gram knew that. Fuck, she showed me how to use it. My pop could shoot like the best of them, but my gram, she knew a gun like the back of her hand. She had to. It was just she and my Aunt Robin living out on a small ranch by themselves. My grand pop died a few years back and since then, it'd been only the two of them out there besides the ranch hands.

"I know you can; that doesn't mean I want you to," she continued.

I closed the box of doughnuts. I'd gathered a dozen or so inside. I wanted Alex to have choices, as I didn't know what she liked. I was filling two cups with coffee when Gram spoke again.

"Don't you think this is silly? You could just be working for your dad."

I gripped the cup I'd just sealed with a plastic lid. My gram made a mistake. I wouldn't be working for my pop. His name might have been on the construction business he just launched late last year, but it wasn't his. Not really. Besides, I didn't need the handout. I took care of myself. I always brought in money and put it back toward the family when it was needed; whether it was a fence that had to be mended on my Gram's ranch or even just a utility bill to make things easier on my pop. I worked the most out of all us kids growing up, even more than my older brother, Hayden, when we worked with Pop all those years at *Carter's Construction*. Working was something I was good at and took pride in and I liked the feeling it gave me to give back to the people who raised me. I'd always been able to do that. I'd always been able to help out.

That was until earlier this year.

I sealed the other cup with another lid, placing both coffees in a cardboard cup holder after I did. "I like what I do, Gram. And I'm safe doing this job. I promise."

I was only mostly sure on both things I'd said, but I couldn't worry my gram. Mostly was enough in this case.

"I hope so. Are you coming to dinner Friday?" she asked.

I smiled, walking my items to the counter to purchase. "Of course."

"Good. Your pop will be there."

I held my smile like she was here to put it on for. "Perfect."

Gram filled me in on the list of grub she was making for

Friday while I paid for the coffee and doughnuts. I ended up using my debit card, as I was running low on cash after last night. The list of food on my Gram's agenda had my mouth watering by the time we finished up the call. I was actually happy to come home for a bit and relax a minute between routes to see her and my aunt.

I exited the truck stop and the sight of Alex sent an unexpected jump into my heart.

She stood outside my truck, her hand pushed into her short hair. She'd been wrapped up in my sheets earlier so I missed the image of her in a shirt way too large for her, framing only the most developed parts of her body. The shirt was so long it nearly covered, what I assumed, were tiny shorts. I could see the hem of them just below her top. No fishnet stockings covered her legs, her feet bare on the parking lot concrete, as she wandered outside my truck with her hand in her hair. This was a different girl in front of me. Like the one last night had vanished. One thing that hadn't changed was the expression on her face. There was an uneasiness there while she gazed around.

I stepped toward her, coffees balanced on top of the box of doughnuts. "Alex?" I called to her. She was still a fair distance away from me.

Her eyes flickered in my direction and I got to see the image I wanted to before. I got the whole package with those large eyes on me. She said a single word, "Brody," before dropping her hand from her hair. Something I also noticed: she didn't seem so worried anymore.

ALEXA

OF COURSE he was in the truck stop. Of course. And he brought doughnuts with two cups of coffee.

That was so sweet.

I could mentally kick myself for worrying about him. When I got up, he wasn't there in the front cab. I peeked in on him behind the curtain and the first thing I did was panic like an idiot. He wouldn't just take off and leave his truck with me inside it.

God, Alexa. Get it together.

My attention redirected to his hand when he lifted it from his side. He placed a black smart phone I didn't know he had on the doughnut box next to the coffees.

The air left my lips in small breaths. He had a cellphone. Of course he did. Most people had one. Maybe I could use his tonight....

"Look at you."

My eyes flashed up to his sapphire blue ones. *What did he mean?* "Sorry?"

Those eyes twinkled at me and I found myself grateful for

my confusion as long as they continued to do so in my direction.

He gestured to me. "Trying something new with your look?"

My body went ramrod straight, my toes—my *bare* toes—curling on the concrete beneath my feet. Shit, did I really come out here in my sleep clothes? My hair most definitely a mess, as I didn't check out a mirror before I panicked that Brody was missing?

I backed toward the truck, pushing my hand into my short hair like that would hide my lapse in judgment.

"Sorry," I flubbed. The door hit my back in my backward steps. I reached back for the handle, opening the door. "Let me just go fix..."

"I actually like it."

His words came out just as I faced the door. I turned back slowly. "You... like it? My bed clothes?"

Or was it my bare feet? My mess of hair? What exactly did he like? I wished he'd say.

He blinked instead, rubbing his hand behind his neck. "I guess I meant to say... I mean I don't *not* like them. They're great. But I just meant, uh..." He dropped his hand from his neck and presented the doughnut box. "Breakfast? I got us something for the road. You drink coffee, right?"

I couldn't help my smile. This big strong guy flustering. I reached for a coffee, tipping it to him. "Thanks."

He nodded, his gaze drifting off, and I stood there awkwardly, trying to come up with something to say. He just complimented me... I think. He looked nice too. He always did. I wished he didn't wear his hat so much, though. I wanted to see his eyes without the shade of the bill casting over them and his hair that looked so soft.

I cleared my throat. "I uh, like your look, too."

Before he could say anything, I brought the coffee up to my lips and bolted up the stairs of his truck.

Brody

Hell, what did that mean?

I tore my shirt off in a frenzy, knowing I didn't have a lot of time to change while Alex changed her own clothes behind my curtain divider.

Her comment couldn't have referred to my shirt. Could it? Not this old work shirt handed down though the turnover of new employees for the company I worked for. No way did she compliment that, which was why I was rummaging through all these godforsaken cubbyholes in my truck for a clean one. By the grace of God, I found a t-shirt tucked away behind a bag of beef jerky I had. Laundry day was when I got home, so options were scarce these days.

I slipped the shirt on, jetting into the tiny bathroom. Pushing my cap off, I looked for a damn comb. When I found one, I tackled the mess on my head.

Maybe she was being sarcastic, I thought, getting my hair semi-manageable.

After clicking off the light in the bathroom, I took a seat in my chair, breathy from all the quick shit I did. Alex didn't seem like the type to be sarcastic, though. The girl seemed real as hell. She probably had to be with what she'd most likely seen.

I pushed my hand into my hair. Did she mean she liked how I looked generally? I shook my head. I guess I had to pass this off as another mystery that was her.

The girl was so damn quiet I nearly rocketed out of my seat

when she made her appearance up front. With the coffee I bought her to her lips, she took an even quieter seat. Her look from last night returned. She wore her short skirt and her revealing top, but the fishnets were gone, her makeup as well. She also left her wig behind and I smiled studying her. I really did like her look.

She pushed a short strand of her hair behind her ear, lifting her eyes to me. "Are we going to go, Brody?"

Yeah, if I could just stop looking at you... Staring and trying to figure you out...

I turned, grabbing the box of doughnuts off the dashboard so we could go. I slid my phone off the box, slipping it into my pocket. I caught Alex watching me. More so my hand as I put my phone away. I gazed down and realized my gun was exposed. I had to lift my shirt a bit to get my phone in my pocket. I had it tucked into my waistband as I strapped up this morning. I was still a little paranoid after last night.

I pointed at it. "Does this bother you?"

She blinked. "Oh, no. I was just..." She shook her head. "No, it doesn't bother me."

I wasn't so sure. I gestured to the bottom of her seat. "Go ahead and hand me the box again. I can put it away. No biggie."

She lowered, gathering it. "You really don't have to. I was looking at—"

"It's fine," I told her, taking the box. Having the thing on me just meant my paranoia piqued anyway. I put it away, then got us moving, pulling my truck out onto the road.

Alex sat quietly, her cup of coffee pressed to her lips. She eyed the box of doughnuts I set on the console, but seemed apprehensive to help herself.

"You can have some if you like. There's plenty," I said, glancing at her once before staring back at the road.

When that lowly box of doughnuts stayed stationary, I reached down, lifting them up to help her out. Finally, she took one, thanking me lightly before nibbling even lighter on the frosted cake doughnut. I'd have to remember that she liked those.

"How um," she started, nibbling a little on her doughnut. Her hand swept up, brushing away that dark hair from her lashes. "How old are you?"

Blinking, I sat back a little. She wanted to know something personal, personal about me. But what was more interesting was she actually asked.

I smiled a little. "Twenty-five," I said placing the doughnut box down. I tipped my chin once my hand returned to the wheel. "You?"

I wondered at first if she'd even answer me. I mean, I knew she was the one to ask initially but still. She was so closed off.

A light, "twenty-two," left from her lips and something soft, something beautiful, pushed into her mouth. Damn, this girl could smile.

Eating her breakfast, she didn't dare seem to want to ask anything else and what I wouldn't give to get her to talk a little more and open up.

During my casual glances at her, I noticed I wasn't the only one doing it. I'd catch those lost eyes every once and a while. This last time I decided to acknowledge that.

"What?" I asked her, keeping my voice teasing. "I got something on my shirt or something?"

I damn well *made sure* I hadn't. Finding this shirt was a bitch and I wouldn't dirty it up in front of this girl.

Her head of short hair lowered like she was going all shy. "Nothing. It's just..." She smiled even shier. "You took your hat off."

I pushed my hand over my hair. Did she like my hat? Hell, I'd put that shit back on.

"I can pull over and get it out of the back." I said this mostly joking but if she wanted me to, I probably would. My comment got me another one of those laughs out of her that reminded me of chimes in the breeze. Mission completed.

I studied her hair. "Looks like someone else left something in the back."

Her eyes flickered up like she could see her own hair. Chuckling, she put her hand to her head. "Want to pull us over so I can get it out the back?"

I had to laugh myself at this point. She had humor, too, by playing off me. I liked that. I tapped the steering wheel. "It's definitely different. Shorter, but that's not a bad thing."

I wondered why she hid it. That hairstyle definitely wasn't bad on her. Before, I ached to push the magenta locks away, to see her dark eyes and the soft features of her face better. Now the same feeling tugged at my fingers. Not to push away, but to touch and thread lightly through.

Shrugging her shoulders, she viewed the road. "I prefer it this way. It makes it easier to..." She bit her lip and I was left hanging on her sentence.

What was she going to say?

She didn't finish the statement. Shaking her head, she said, "Never mind," before bringing her arms around herself. The mood in the truck went awkward again, filled with a familiarity from when we first met. I feared we were headed back to square one and the urge to keep that from happening tugged my lips to say something else. Laughing seemed to open her up. I headed that route.

"So is she your alias?" I asked.

Her gaze went to me first before she turned her head. "Who?"

"That girl in the back with magenta hair." I pointed behind with my thumb, keeping my eyes on the road. "Is she your other self? Your alias?"

That smile returned, starting slow at her full lips before brightening her whole face. "I guess you could call her that."

"Kind of like that girl where I'm from. The singer from Texas? The one married to Jay-Z?"

She eyed me with a short laugh. "You mean Beyoncé?"

"Yeah, that's her name." I knew I had the right one. That girl was a household name in my state. I didn't follow her music, but I caught Jay from time to time. I flicked between him and my man Blake Shelton. Many miles on the road, I enjoyed all types of music.

I looked over at Alex. "I heard she's got an alias, one she breaks out when she's on stage with the lights on her and the crowd's screaming her name."

Before, Alex couldn't have looked like she wanted to withdraw more, but as she brought her legs up and hugged them, grinning over her knees, I knew I got her back. She was going to play along.

"Sasha Fierce," she said with a smile.

I nodded. "Sasha Fierce. So who's your Sasha Fierce? What's the name of the girl in the back?"

She glanced away, chewing her lip as she stared at the road. The silence in my truck worried me at first, afraid maybe she wouldn't continue, but then she turned and said one word, "Valentine."

A word associated with the heart seemed so fitting for her. Alexa, not the alias. Yet, she used that to represent her other self, the one she kept hidden, and I didn't understand why.

Keeping up with the game, I played along, smiling. "Valentine it is then. You'll let me know when she comes out? I want to be able to brace myself in case she's as crazy as Sasha Fierce."

Again, Beyoncé was huge. I'd seen her in interviews on T.V. and the girl on stage definitely didn't match her soft-spoken demeanor.

"Promise," Alex said before turning away. She reached down to the console and got herself another doughnut, a long john this time, and it sat well that she felt comfortable to do so.

I didn't know this girl at all, why she wore the mask, or felt the need to hide. Alex was definitely a girl with some reservations, but she intrigued me more and more with every word she allowed me to hear and I wanted nothing more than to peel back more layers.

Seven

ALEXA

"You like blue gum balls?"

I gazed up from playing with my fingers. I did that when Brody was making his way back to the truck from inside a rest stop. It kept me preoccupied while he made those lengthy strides back to the rig, but even still, he caught my gaze sometimes. He spotted me watching him come back. He'd always smile and not make it too awkward. He was just that way.

Sliding inside, he opened his hand, and like what he said, he had a blue gum wrapped in cellophane paper in his large hand. He grinned. "Got an extra one."

"You always have an extra one," I told him, but didn't reach out cautiously like I had before. He always seemed to bring something back for me whenever we stopped, even though I told him he never had to. Sometimes it was a bag of chips or other times, candy like this gift, and every time, I let him know he didn't have to. I went there again.

"I told you I didn't need anything," I said, trying not to smile while I popped it into my mouth. Because even though I meant what I said, I enjoyed it every time he did. Perhaps, it was the thoughtfulness of it. That's what I kept telling myself anyway.

He returned his hat to his head, sliding it on tight. He only wore it when the sun went high. I noticed that as he kept taking it off and on through the day. He shrugged. "Eh, it was only twenty-five cents, Alex. It's not like it set me back or anything. I bought two instead of one. No big."

"Yeah, but still."

"But still," he paused, swinging those bright blue eyes of his my way. He waggled blond brows above them. "It's not a problem."

Frozen in place, I simply nodded. That's all I could do under that gaze. I was able to relax again when he released me from them and strapped back in, but then I thought about something while I chewed the blue raspberry flavoring in my mouth.

"Where's yours?" I asked him, strapping back in as well. "Your gum ball?" He said he got two.

Like he remembered, he slouched back, reaching into his pocket. Out of it came a shiny red gum ball, as well as something else.

The plastic ring sat tiny in his large hand, a sliver one with a clear stone in the center. It was pretty.

"A mood ring," he said, those eyes managing to find mine again. That hat came off when he pulled it from his head. "You don't want it, do you? It came out with my gum ball and can't really do anything with it."

He smiled a little on the end there, and like before, I took this gift too, my belly doing weird things when I did.

"Thanks," I told him. I had to keep my face from splitting wide in a smile.

He said no problem and his hand returned to the wheel. He drove then, no other words about it said.

The miles went long after that moment in the rig, but not in a bad way. It fact, it was more than the opposite. We sat quietly sometimes, but other times neither one of us could shut up. We talked about the casual banter of nothing, but it felt like everything all at the same time. He'd tell me about his job and life on the road. Though singular work, it wasn't without a story and that's what Brody always seemed to have: a story. He could make the smallest things funny and every time, he got me. I'd get swept away in it and happily break from life because of it. And that's what he did for me, made me forget about everything else. I got to just sit there and be with him and even though I didn't really contribute much to the conversation with my own funny stories, that was okay. He let me be. I could *be* there with him with nothing else expected from me. He had a story for every minute, every hour, and those occasional moments when I did comment on them, he made me feel like what little I had to say *did* matter. Maybe it was the way he listened, focused on the road but slightly turned my way and every once and a while, that jaw of his would shift. His eyes would find mine and crease in the corners before facing the road again. He was engaged and that kept me going. I really did talk about nothing. It would be about something I saw while we drove or something he said, but he seemed interested with every word. And then there were the smiles. His lips pursed sometimes, then ticked up in the corner after I said something.

I liked those the best.

Before I knew it, we had been in the truck over three hours. They'd been three hours of talking, three hours of laughter, but most importantly, three hours with him. I didn't want to admit how much I enjoyed them, but I couldn't help with every passing moment. His incessant stops only added to that. Though, we'd been in the truck three hours, we had actually been traveling longer with the added times of his stops. I found that odd at first, how often we pulled over. He didn't seem to drink an unusual amount of liquid or anything that would warrant so many pull overs. It seemed to be a normal amount, and each time, he never returned empty handed. Like with the ring he gave me.

I clutched that ring now, smiling at a cool tone of green in it. It was in moments such as those stops, that I believed he enjoyed spending time with me. He wouldn't give something to a someone he didn't like, right? Though, he did say it came out with his gum ball. But was it in my head, how I'd catch him glancing at me just as much as I glanced at him while we drove? Or how he always seemed to know just what to say to make me smile? Like he enjoyed making me smile.

"I'm picking up some parts here," he said, pulling me out of my thoughts. Turning the wheel, he pulled the truck off an exit. The sign off the highway mentioned a small, populated town in Oklahoma. He glanced my way. "Once I do, the drive's a cake walk to Texas. I drop off there. It's my last stop, and today's pick up shouldn't take too terribly long."

I found myself wishing it would as I nodded, turning away to the window. If that was his last delivery that meant our miles of driving had almost wound down, and also, that I'd be alone again. I'd be alone until I figured out a way to get home myself.

I curled my fingers around the stone again, but this time no joy came from it. I couldn't get into my head about this; him. Things like his little gifts at the stops, this ring, and even all the attention he gave me while on the road had to be nothing more than his character. He was a genuine guy. He was a *nice* guy, and no doubt all the gestures he made toward me had to do with how we met. I couldn't deny the situation in which he found me. Maybe his kind gestures were nothing more than that—*kindness* and a sensitivity to the situation he put his own self in. He was handling me with kid gloves and being nice because he felt he had to. I would too if the roles were reversed.

My stomach turned a bit as I laid my hand in my lap, feeling naive.

Of course he's being nice. Of course.

"Is that okay, Alex?"

I looked up at those deep blue eyes, making myself smile a little. Usually it wasn't hard to do around him. He always seemed to allow me to find a brightness inside myself I couldn't contain. But now, finding it actually felt like effort. Smiling felt like effort.

He rested his arm across the steering wheel. We must have stopped sometime in my wandering thoughts. He tilted his head, studying my face with his lips turned down. "Is everything all right?"

I nodded, releasing the hold I had on the ring he gave me. I let my hand settle to the side. "Yeah. Sorry. I guess I just missed what you said before."

His smile came back. I was glad. "I asked if you were going to be okay here?" He pointed behind himself. "I'm going to open up the back and let them load. I just wondered if you'd be all right sitting in here for a bit while I did. Since you'll be by yourself and all."

Wow. He really *was* handling me with kid gloves.

He feels sorry for me....

I brought my arms in, holding myself. "I'll be fine."

This made his smile grow. "All right then. I'll make it quick. After they do what they need to, we'll head out and cross the state line home."

His home. Not mine. I nodded and he left me alone in the truck.

A few men in coveralls came out of a large garage-like door

directly behind Brody's rig. I watched them in the side view mirror. Brody went back with them, talking for a second with one while he spun his keys around his finger. But suddenly, he stopped spinning the keys. He palmed them, lowering his hand to the side, and all the while, he still talked to the man in front of him. I couldn't see Brody's face while they spoke, as he was facing the man and not in my direction, but I did notice his shoulders raised and dropped like he sighed.

The man in front of him pointed in a general direction to the right and Brody gazed that way. Before I knew it, he was handing off his keys to the man, then heading in the direction he pointed. I found that odd. He'd said he would let the guys into the back then come back to me. But he didn't do that. He was walking away while the man he gave the keys to opened the truck and unlocked it.

I didn't expect the leap that jumped my heart as I whipped forward, watching as he moved farther and farther away. I gripped the door handle, preparing to get out and see where he was going, but I stopped when he turned around. He stared directly at me, past the distance between us and the glass of the windshield separating us. It was like he was still in the car with me, telling a joke, and making my heart happy with his humor. Tilting his head, he smiled at me, and I felt my hand lower from the door. I sat back in the chair, and like he knew I was okay, he turned again. He went inside the building, and I watched as he let the door close behind him.

I placed my hands in my lap. Breathing hard, I realized I wasn't doing it before; breathing. I didn't like that. I didn't like that—at all. How had that happened? How had *this* happened? My connection to him? My dependence on him? Brody and I were temporary travel companions. Anything more than that... Anything *deeper* than that just...

Just couldn't be.

I twisted the mood ring on my hand between two fingers.

Somewhere along the line it turned a deep blue. I had no idea what that meant and maybe didn't want to know.

I gazed up. Brody hadn't come out yet. I wondered how much time I had.

Turning the ring, I twisted it until it came off. I couldn't think as I stood and grabbed my bag from the back, my wig next. If I did stop to think, I would hesitate. I knew I would. I gripped my ring in my palm until it came time. Time was when I passed the dividers between our seats. I left the ring in my own seat, squarely in the middle. Maybe he'd think I dropped it on my way out and didn't leave it on purpose.

I hoped so.

Brody

Mr. Michaels, my boss, was in his office like his shift manager outside said he was. I wasn't going to act like I didn't know what this was about, but I made sure I was confident when I entered the room. I stayed professional, calm.

"You're late, Brody," he said, barely looking up at me when I came in. Once I sat, he immediately wrote something down on a clipboard. He was probably writing me up.

I knew what would happen today. The minute I crept past my deadline hours ago, I knew. That still didn't stop me from doing what I wanted. I had dragged my feet. I dawdled. Every unnecessary stop I made and the time I wasted by making them, I knew would result in certain consequences. I made some choices and I'd own up to them. There'd be no reason to shy away from them. They were probably pretty dumb and definitely incredibly selfish. That last one took me a bit to real-ize: how selfish I was being. There was no denying that now. I knew.

I pushed my hand over my hair, restless, while Mr. Michaels continued to write. He looked up and I settled my hand down so I didn't look so uneasy. "I'm sorry, sir," I said to him. "It won't happen again."

And it wouldn't. I didn't want to be known for dicking around. I was a hard worker and had been showing that since I got this job. I wasn't going to mess it up and be stupid like I had been. I could only hope Alex didn't realize what was happening around her. If she did, she wouldn't trust me anymore. I told myself I was doing it for her by making all those extra stops. I was making sure she had time to rest from the relentless driving. Long durations of travel not everyone could handle and I only wanted her comfortable by being conscious of that. It was only in the last couple hours or so I realized exactly what I was doing, which was why I plowed through the last hundred or so miles of our trip. Those stretched out moments in the truck with her, those stops, became more about me than her. They become more *for* me than her.

They'd become about her wind chime laugh and how her body gently vibrated from the force of it. I only got her to do it with my crappy jokes. And they'd also became about her smile whenever I'd come back with things for her from a stop we made. She always said she didn't want anything. But that smile of hers read otherwise. Despite the other things, I was well aware of what really made me say the hell with my delivery deadline. It was the pure joy I got from every minute and every second of her unease going away. The tension faded. The worry melted away from those once scared eyes, and I... I loved doing that for her. She was starting to trust me. She *did* trust me, but she wouldn't if she knew what I let happen.

She wouldn't if she knew I took advantage of our time together.

I tried not to think about that as I waited for Mr. Michaels to finish what he was writing. He did. Looking up, he made a steeple with his fingers. "You know I had to write you up for this. We got a three strikes policy around here and that's one."

I nodded, understanding.

"I'm also going to have to dock your pay."

My heart charged behind my chest. He was... *docking* my pay. Why? I rose up. "I'm sorry, sir. I don't understand."

Leaning forward, I knew he was about to make it clear. "I know you're new, Brody, but this is in your contract. I lose money when deliveries are late. This is why deadlines are set. Money I lose as the result of late deliveries must be replenished. All drivers around here understand that, which is why they make sure they're never late. They are the ones penalized if they're at fault. I advise you to take a look at your contract. You'll see it's all set out."

I didn't consider myself a slow person. I wasn't dense. I wasn't stupid. I'd read the freaking contract and I didn't recall seeing anything like this in it at all. It didn't feel right what was happening. Not at all.

"You'll be seeing the difference in your next paycheck, Brody." He said that so matter-of-factly, so dry and cold, I had to fight my jaw from clenching. To this guy, I was just a number, just another employee who fucked up and now he was collecting what was his. Maybe he wasn't too far off about me. I felt more and more like a fuck up every day I forced myself to drive away from home. I felt it when I had to leave my family and friends for weeks at a time for a job that had once seemed like the right plan for me.

Things didn't seem so clear now.

Before I left, I asked my boss for a copy of the contract. He even highlighted the part about the wage garnish. I had to laugh, trashing it before I exited the building. There was a line there. A single line filled with so much legal jargon, a guy would need a lawyer to even decipher the shit. On top of that, it was an amendment, a *recent* amendment I briefly recalled he made a bunch of us sign before we could even get our last paychecks. The bastard lied about it being normal company policy. I wasn't surprised and with all of us employees hurrying to get paid that day, I bet I wasn't the only one who overlooked the new policy. Crazy thing was, I couldn't even get mad. This was my own lapse in judgment. It was *me* that signed something I didn't fully understand.

I was understanding a lot of things now.

Heading out to Alex, I considered what made me late in the first place. This thing with her... I had to remember what it was. She was a girl. She was a girl who needed a ride and I couldn't get attached to her. We couldn't...

We couldn't *be* anything but what we were: me giving her a lift. I could only blame whatever attachment I created because of my job. I had to admit, I was by myself a lot. I guess it was just nice to have someone around for a while. I wouldn't let things be that way anymore. I'd get her to where the line ended for me and let her go.

I'd let her go.

Holding on to that notion completely made sense. It made sense until I exited the building and looked up from my strides. Looking for a familiar face, I realized it wasn't there. *She* wasn't there, at least not at first glance through my rig's windshield. I picked up my pace and the closer I got to my truck, I knew it to be true. She wasn't in my front seat. She wasn't where I'd last seen her.

I didn't let myself panic as I opened the door or even when I went inside and didn't see her in the front or the back of the truck. But when I saw the ring I gave her, the plastic mood ring sitting in her seat, the twisting in my gut now had merit. She left. Why did she leave?

I jumped out of the truck even quicker than I entered it. I whipped around, not even knowing where to look or where to go. Pushing my hand in my hair, I tried to think. She seemed fine when I left the truck. She said she'd be fine. I thought she was, but my hand dropped at a brief moment of recollection. Before I went inside to see Mr. Michaels, I turned, and when I did, Alex didn't seem so okay. In fact, the last time I saw her eyes that way was this morning. It was this morning when I left her to get doughnuts. I looked at her before I went inside the warehouse and I know I saw that look go away. With the way it did, I figured the unease I believed I saw in her eyes at first was just my imagination. Maybe I wasn't imagining it.

The shift manager handed me back my keys when he passed me. Before he could go, I touched his shoulder.

"Hey, have you seen a girl?" Panicking, I took a moment to breathe. I had to so I could describe her. "She's kind of tall, but not as tall as me. Her height's mostly because of her shoes. They're these tall boot things with heels. She's also pretty, real pretty, and has these eyes. They're deep and dark and gorgeous like her skin."

I didn't say it would be a particularly *good* description, but as frantic as I was it, was the best I could do.

The seconds in which it took this guy to think I thought I'd lose it. "Does she have like a purple-red hair thing going on?"

Oh, God. She put her wig back on. I nodded.

He pointed across the street and my heart sunk. It was a park, a park full of people.

"She went in there," he said, before leaving me.

Shit. How was I going to find her in there?

Eight

ALEXA

Keeping my head down, the magenta strands of my hair framed my eyes as I strode through the park. Dusk; it was getting late in the day. Despite that, the park was pretty active and that was only a good thing. I blended in amongst the people playing Frisbee and exercising, and all the while, I kept my feet moving. I forced myself to go forward and not look back. The further I moved, the further I got away, my anxiety levels rose. It wasn't because I had no idea where I'd be sleeping tonight. In fact, not knowing where I was or even how I could travel out of this town ebbed it. It was knowing with each step I made, the odds of me seeing the man that saved me again grew smaller and smaller. That had been the point, though. Cutting ties now meant I didn't have to do so later. No more emotions could get involved. No more ties or connections could be formed and no more feelings could develop.

If they were even real feelings at all.

I had one goal and one goal only. I had to get home and right some wrongs that needed to be fixed. I had to correct some mistakes—*my* mistakes.

I continued to move through the park quickly and like a lifeline was needed, my saving grace came in the form of a bus only a few paces from me. It pulled to a stop near the sidewalk, letting on passengers, kids and their parents, that filtered from the playgrounds. I didn't know where this bus was going, but I did know it would take me away. I could figure out my next move once I rode it to the end of the line. I had a little money, but didn't know if it was enough to afford a train or long distance bus ticket. If it wasn't, I knew I was left with little options to get more, one of which I couldn't even stomach to do the last time. How I let things get that bad disgusted me. I'd done some fucked up things before to get by, but that... I didn't even want to think about it as I got into the bus line.

Standing there, thinking about what little money I did have and why, I couldn't resist looking behind me for a set of deep blue eyes. He wasn't there, though, and wouldn't be there anymore. Stupidity reared its head when I let my thoughts linger on him. I thought about how I didn't even get to know some of the most mundane things about him. Like some of his favorite things to do or his favorite season. Heck, even his last name I never found out.

Ignoring the tug at my heart, I turned to look forward and move with the rest of the line, but my gaze stopped on a little girl still standing in the park near the four square lot. She looked ten or so and I knew exactly what caught my attention about her. She wore a pink tutu, spinning on the tips of her toes in a circle.

The vision warmed my heart. She was so carefree as she twirled. Her hands above her head, she was lost in her dance. Why can't things be that simple always? Why couldn't things be that beautiful always?

Dropping her form, she ran over to a ring of boys and girls. They all varied in age, but didn't seem to be that much older than her. They looked to be twelve to early teens and surrounded a couple other boys dancing. Free styling in the middle of the circle, the kids didn't need any music at all. They just danced. They had *fun* while the group around them chanted them on.

When a couple were done, others moved in, showing their stuff as well. They all did various forms of hip hop, hitting anything from breakdancing to various popular moves in music videos. The young girl on the side in the tutu watched, her eyes wide in fascination. Before I knew it, she was attempting to make her way into the circle. I was glad she wanted to show her stuff. I doubt she had any formal training at all and was just playing around before, but all kinds of dance should be represented in that circle.

I almost made it to the head of the bus line, but couldn't help letting my gaze linger in that direction. I wanted to see her start. Turns out, she never got the chance. The moment she tried to break into the circle, another girl a little older than her, stood in front of her, eyeing the young girl's tutu.

"You can't dance here," she said to her. "Ballet isn't real dancing."

Now, I knew this girl was a kid and didn't know any better, but frankly, her comment couldn't have pissed me off more. Who was she to say what was *real* dancing, but apparently her words were enough for the little girl in the tutu. I should have let it go. I needed to, but as I watched that young girl, walking away from the dance circle with her head hung, I couldn't help being affected. This girl's enthusiasm, her passion, was crushed all because of one comment, all because one person said she couldn't do something.

"Hey, little missy. You getting on?"

I looked up at the bus driver, the one waiting for me to board so he could leave. I held the handle, but found myself looking back to that little girl. I didn't know how strong this girl felt about her style of dancing, or if she even wanted to dance professionally at all, but what I did know was we all deserved a chance to live for our passion. No matter how naïve those passions turned out to be.

Brody

When I didn't see Alex at first glance, I just started walking. I stayed along the perimeter of the park. She no doubt went in deeper, but I figured she wouldn't stay there. She had to leave the area eventually and the odds of me coming across her would be better this way. The urge to stop my search, give up before it barely began, tugged away at me. What if... what if she was *trying* to get away from me for some reason? What if I did something wrong and put her off? I realized what I'd done by taking advantage of a situation when she trusted me to get her to Texas. Maybe she realized that, too.

Thinking about that, my stomach turned and I did stop, gazing down at my hand. Opening it, a plastic ring met my eyes and I ended up shutting my lids.

I acted inappropriately with her and should have known better considering the way I found her. I gave her things, things like this ring and even money at one point. At the time, these things seemed innocent enough, but in hindsight, they were something I probably shouldn't have done.

Looking up, I gazed across the park one last time. I never wanted to confuse Alex or make things unclear about my intentions, but with the things I gave her, I no doubt did.

My hand lowered and I turned to walk away. I turned to end things hoping for the best for her. I hoped she found that safety she needed. What that meant for her, safety, I didn't know the extent of, but for me personally, I hoped she would gain some kind of freedom. She'd be free from her stresses and everything else that seemed to be weighing her down. I had no idea what that relief looked like for her, but when I finally spotted her over on a painted foursquare lot with people surrounding her, I believed I got an inkling of what that freedom might look like. They cheered her on. They cheered her on because she danced for them.

Spinning on her toes, hell, the tip of her *boot*, she made a 360-degree rotation, but once she completed the spin she didn't stop. She kept going, doing another and another. She spun forever, and though, what she was doing fascinated me, yes, what had me entranced was *her*. With the fluidity of her body during her movement, she looked like a bird cutting through the sky and a strong passion illuminated her face that made those eyes, so uneasy before, bright. This was a different girl out there, one I'd only caught glimpses of when I was fortunate enough to be let in through her laughter. I'd never seen her so free before.

I'd never seen her so alive.

～

Alexa

The chants of the crowd shot a pulse through me. Their cheers rooted me on, amped me up, and I continued to spin with the charge of them. This always happened. It always did when I did this, danced, no matter how long it had been. I was a slave to the movement in the best possible way. Doing this was a mistake, dancing. I knew that, but it didn't feel like a mistake now. It never did. It only felt right.

I ended in the proper position as if I did this only yesterday. The body never forgets. Looking out to the crowd, I
displayed my arms and form proudly and the kids pumped
their fists in response. I loved it, but in the end, I didn't do this
for them or their encouragement.

Standing tall, I looked at the young girl ahead of me, the
one in the tutu. She was more excited than all of them. In fact,
her excitement was tenfold as she clapped her hands for me. I
smiled, picking up my glittery bag. I doubt she expected me to
come over to her and her jaw dropping as I approached, told
me that.

I stopped in front of her, noticing a girl had made it over
to her side. She was the same one who discouraged her style of
dancing in the first place and stepped ahead of the girl in the
tutu.

"That was so cool. Where did you learn that?" she asked.

I didn't look at her, only the girl at her side with so much
hope in her eyes. "Dance school," I said, shouldering my bag.
"In ballet class."

The girl in the tutu's eyes flashed brightly. I gave her a
wink, then excused myself from the pair. From behind me, I
heard the girl who bullied ask where the little girl got her tutu,
and I could only smile as I walked away. I wanted to head back
to the bus stop, but the bus from before had gone. I could
always go to the bench and wait for the next one. I guess I was
going to have to. It was getting late, would be dark soon, and I
needed to get off the street before that happened. Being in the
dark only gave permission for the darkness to come out on the
streets. Maybe I could ask someone about any local shelters in
town, then see what happened in the morning.

I checked my watch. I still had a while yet until my alarm
went off. I wondered if the shelter would let me use their
phone when it came time. Dropping my wrist, I knew

someone who probably would have let me use his phone had I asked. I hoped he was okay and didn't worry about me. I was going to be fine. I could take care of myself. I just wanted him to be fine, too.

"You told me you'd let me know when Valentine came out."

His voice actually caused a shallow breath to escape my lips and I never... I never thought I'd hear it again, but I did. He found me. He found me again.

I turned and his proximity I didn't prepare for. He was right there. Only an arm's reach out, he was a touch not so far away and managed to get even closer when he stepped forward, his large body enveloping the space around me. It kissed the air with his woodsy, citrusy-sweet scent. In fact, he got so close to me most people might have stepped back.

I didn't want to step back.

He tilted his head, a stand of blond moving over his eyes, and a ghost of a smile highlighting his pink lips. "Valentine?" he asked, his voice light, joking like he always was.

Smiling myself, I slipped off my wig. "It's just Alexa. Sorry. I can't control her sometimes."

His gaze moved over my face, my eyes, my lips. "Maybe you shouldn't."

I couldn't stay looking at him. Under Brody's eyes, it was easy to lose myself to shyness.

A low cough hit the air when he cleared his throat. I looked up and he had stepped back like he remembered himself. He slid a hand into his pocket. "You like to dance?"

I wished that was the word good enough to describe it. Rubbing my arm, I shrugged casually. "Yeah. Yes. I like to dance."

"Just ballet or...?"

"No, not just that. All kinds really. I like all kinds."

He nodded. "You went to school? I couldn't help hearing what you said to those girls."

Chewing my lip, I acknowledged that, too. "I used to. It seems like forever now."

In that moment, I had never felt such mixed emotions before. I wanted him to keep asking me things and to *keep* pushing me. It would give me an excuse to finally let someone in, to finally let *him* in, but at the same time, I wanted him to back away from his questions entirely. I really was a mess. Seeing his hand clench at his side, I denied him the ability to do either. He had something there, something he squeezed that made his knuckles white, and though I didn't mean to pry, I couldn't help it when I reached out.

I touched him.

His beautiful eyes followed mine to his hand as I moved my fingers delicately over his warm knuckles, then to his fingers that were so much bigger than mine. His mouth parted and he turned his hand over when I guided it to do so. His fist remained clenched, but slowly, he let me open it. I got to see his palm then, and there in the center was the mood ring he gave me. I'd never seen it this way before, though. It was a yellowish-orange.

"You, um," he said, swallowing. "You left—"

"I dropped it," I finished for him, chewing my lip again. "I dropped it."

He looked at me for a long moment, studying me. Eventually, he nodded again, and I was happy to see that full smile of his return.

"You dropped it," he confirmed, holding me hostage to that wonderful gaze. He slid his hand out of his pocket and reached down, surprising me when he was the one to engage a touch between us by grabbing my hand. I thought he'd put the ring in my palm but he didn't. He put it on me, sliding it on naturally, as if this was supposed to be. It was as if this was always supposed to be.

All too soon, he let my hand go and both hands went into his pockets this time. "Look, Alexa. If you were leaving for whatever reason, going out on your own, that's okay. You can do that you know? Anytime."

Though, I knew that were true, I didn't want to admit that to him. I didn't want him to know I left because things felt too deep. I didn't want him to know I *felt* and it... it scared me. I was embarrassed.

Sparing both his feelings and mine, I remained silent.

"As long as you know that," he said, nodding. He gazed around and I wondered where we'd go from here. He found me again, but was that good for either of us? He had places to go and I did, too. Being together again would only make that worse once the trip concluded. That's why I left in the first place.

He faced me. "You said you like to dance, right?"

That's not what I thought he'd say next. I almost thought his next words could possibly be parting ones. I had run after all. He had to have known that. I pushed my bag up on my arm. "Yeah."

He chewed in the inside of his cheek a moment, rubbing behind his neck. He seemed nervous, and really, I'd never seen him so cute. Brody was so huge, wide, and powerful, so it was different seeing him looking vulnerable.

Dropping his hand, he let out a breath. "Would it be weird if I took you out some place?"

I blanched the words came out so quickly. Despite that, he continued.

"There's this place I think you'd like a few hours away," he said, though a bit breathy. "This place after we reach Texas. They got dancing and stuff. I don't know. You probably don't have time and it's probably even weird that I asked, but I just thought you'd get a kick out of it. Nothing funny. I just think it would be fun. I don't know, is that weird?"

He got a laugh out of me at his sudden awkwardness. He's the only one who'd been able to get me laughing so much in a while. "No," I told him, and his eyes flashed, but then the smile came back. It came back after I told him it wouldn't be weird at all.

Nine

ALEXA

Brody was right. The place he was talking about wasn't far away at all. An old barn-looking establishment, the building was bustling with people. They both came and left in clusters and my heart charged at the sound of amped up music, lights flashing from the inside out. This looked to be a bar at first glance, but they definitely had a dance scene and I surprised myself by how excited I had suddenly gotten. Brody told me he wanted to take me dancing, and really, I had been amped just because it was him and he asked. I didn't know what this meant for us.

But I also didn't want to fight whatever it was either.

Brody ended up parking the rig by several others in the far dirt lot. This spot must have been pretty common for fellow truckers. He pulled the parking break and we sat, the bodies filtering in and out of the building before us.

"This is it," he said, smiling a little before facing me. We'd shared few words up until this point and part of me figured that had been due to really not knowing what to say. As far as myself, I had no idea what to make of him asking me here or it if meant anything for me to wonder about at all.

I placed my hands in my lap. "Yeah, it's real cool."

"Yeah?" His eyes showed genuine interest before facing ahead. He tipped his chin in the general direction. "You wanna go in?"

I did, but an awareness of a problem I had suddenly flashed itself before me as I eyed cut off shorts and cute tops. I gazed down at my revealing blouse and leather skirt. What if he wouldn't want to be seen with me? I didn't necessarily look like the type of company he'd keep.

"What's wrong?"

I touched my shirt. "I don't know about my clothes. I want to dance, but I..."

I didn't want to say it, but I looked like a whore. Before that had been planned, but that wasn't okay now. I didn't want him to have to be seen with me like this.

His gaze appraised me, and coming back up to my face, his eyes softened. I think he got it that I felt uncomfortable. He put his arm around the back of my chair. "I'll see what I got," he said.

I watched him go to the back and out of one of his cubbyholes he retrieved a plaid shirt, a button down with long sleeves. He held it up. "It's not much but..."

By this time, I had come over and the gift more than warmed my heart. I slid it out of his hands. "Thank you. This will be perfect." He was quite bigger than me, but I could more than make do.

This seemed to please him. He left the rig so I could change. I tucked away my purse tightly inside, not wanting it to get in the way of dancing, but did take all the money out and carried it with me. I came out and had fashioned Brody's shirt into a form fitting top I tied at my waist. The sleeves I ended up strategically bunching and I had to say, it looked all right. Brody's lashes flashed when he turned and it seemed I might have been correct on that.

"You make it look way better than I do," he said, but as soon as he did, his gaze traveled away. I noticed he was being rather cautious. Perhaps, because he was confused like I was about what this evening meant.

He gestured toward the building and I flanked him, telling him thank you for the compliment as the rocks crunched under our shoes. He didn't have to ease into saying something nice to me. I more than liked it and I think acknowledging that made him feel better about what he said. He smiled, easing up, and got us both into the line of the bar. The place was more than packed, and in all honesty, I wondered if there'd be room for us to make our way in. A buzz hummed over the crowd and I knew they were just as antsy as I was to get inside. That rebel beat was charging the air the closer we made our way to the front, and the excitement inside me grew. It had been so long since I could just dance and have fun. I was more than ready.

"I think you really will like this place," Brody told me, his hands in his pockets as he took another step forward. With his height, he made an excellent driving force through the cluster of folks outside the door. They seemed to part for him.

I played with my fingers. "Is there a deejay or a sound system—"

The words left as an altercation broke out directly ahead of us between two guys who'd clearly been pre-gaming on the drinks before coming here. A large one shoved the other and that's when Brody stepped in, raising his hand. "Guys, cool it," he said, but they didn't listen. Soon the shoves turned into hits and the already buzzing crowd rumbled in response. They clustered in on them for a piece of the action and I was shoved from behind.

Brody turned, his eyes wide. "Alex!"

Someone grabbed me, but that someone didn't strike any fear in me.

Brody's arms came down on both sides of my body, bracing my shoulders before backing me against the wall of the barn. Once my back touched, his arms surrounded me, his hands flat on the wall while own his back took the brunt of the hits from the random fists flying around us. I should have been terrified, but I wasn't. It was hard to be when I felt so protected.

Facing away, Brody cringed at a hit to his side and I both hated and loved that he was using his body to keep mine safe. Eventually, some of the bouncers came out and got the crowd under control. They dragged the guys who started the fight away and that's finally when Brody's large shoulders loosened. Muscles in his arms twitched and he turned, his gaze taking inventory as they scanned me down. He could have lowered his arms then as I was okay, but he didn't.

My heart charged and a lump the size of the state formed in my throat when his gaze redirected. It settled right on my mouth. A sheen covered his bottom lip when he stroked his tongue just slightly over it, his chest moving up and down under his thin t-shirt.

Kiss me. Please kiss me, I thought because I wanted him to. I wanted him to so badly.

Stepping back, he didn't, though. His arms lowered and he breathed deep, pushing his fingers over lengthy blond strands.

"You okay?" he asked, and I nodded, trying not to be disappointed.

Blue eyes left and I followed his back into the crowd that now seemed under control enough to filter inside. He glanced my way and gestured, his hand out. I thought he'd take mine, but he didn't. Like he thought better of it, he pushed his hands into his pockets.

Holding my arm awkwardly, I let him lead me inside. We

remained silent, making it into a dark foyer among the cluster of people who sought access to the bar like us. Once there, I believed our next stop was to go inside, but that Brody... he continued to surprise me.

His hand came down my arm, but this time, it wasn't any way a touch of protection. He touched me. He touched me *to* touch me, his fingers feeling their way down to my wrist. He backed me up out of the crowd again and when my back touched a wall, my heart thumped clear through my skin to beat against it. I couldn't see him. Not clearly anyway in the dark foyer, but I could feel him. His hands started on my shoulders, but eventually, they came to rest on my cheeks. His chest pressed against mine, I could feel his own huge heart jabbing, pressuring toward my own, and I could feel his mouth. I could feel his lips, finally.

A sound hummed from them and his taste followed suit. He bit my bottom lip, so gentle before taking his own taste, his tongue softly doing things to mine. When he stopped and backed away, I felt so warm. I couldn't stop the liquidly heated feeling and his forehead touched mine. I could make out a smile on his lips.

"That was me saying fuck it," he said, laughing gently.

I chewed my lip. "You should do that more often."

His fingers touched my cheek, eventually finding their way down to my wrist to hold my hand. If there was any confusion about what this was, being here, that seemed to be gone now.

I was glad.

A set of well-worn jeans led me inside, the view of which had me distracted momentarily from the vibrant room. Neon lights with beers on tap lined the back wall behind the bar and a dance pit in the middle of the room was directly ahead of it. And a pit it was. Folks were giving it full use; spinning and vibing with each other in a group. Brody brought us to the wooden railing that sectioned the seating level off from the pit. Taking it all in, my tapping feet had me ready to dive in.

A hand went to the small of my back, resting, and my heart went into overdrive.

Brody.

He leaned in. "Do you like it?"

Even in here with all the music, the boisterous depth of his voice fought through. I nodded, gripping the railing.

He smiled at me before his breath touched my ear again. "Food first?" he asked.

I shook my head, going to his ear this time. "Beer?"

And the grin he gave me when he pulled back had my gut going all wobbly again. "I think that can definitely be arranged, darlin'."

God, I could not handle him and that accent and that word. Nope, I could *not*.

His hand sliding down to mine, he gestured for me to come with him, but I told him I wanted to keep watching the pit. I fed off it. He let me stay, but only after making sure I was okay. I actually was. I loved the environment here and the bar was only about ten feet away.

He left with a chuckle, pointing to where he would be. After he left, I shook my hips, swaying to the latest Hot 100 track. They really played everything here. This place had a hometown country feel, but a spin on it with an urban edge. I couldn't help but get into it. Perhaps, that's why he brought me here, understanding my style. He'd been so absorbent our entire trip, getting to know me in all that despite how little I gave back, so that shouldn't surprise me.

Turning, I watched Brody, his hip leaning against the bar. He was waiting his turn like everyone else, but then he wasn't alone. A girl came up to him, a Hispanic girl, pretty, with a flurry of ultraviolet hair. Her arms covered in a full set of tattoo sleeves, she waved at Brody, which he returned with a smile. He was always smiling. I thought she'd be on her way, but she wasn't. Instead, she chose to cross in front of him and lean back on the bar. Her position, arms rested back with the tip of her boot out, had her breasts pushed way up over a top that didn't strike me as super revealing at first. Now, I could definitely see, and my sight didn't fail me as she reached over and squeezed his thick arm. One I hoped to at least touch tonight when I danced with him.

My heart dropped like a stone when she moved in and got closer. It definitely seemed like Brody knew her since he didn't pull away. He actually smiled at something she said before the expression immediately left his face. He's the one who put his hand on her arm this time, but only to increase some distance between them. Holding up his hand, he shook his head at her and...

Turned her down.

She pouted, a joking way about it when she touched him again, and again, he put some distance between them, politely moving away. She gave him a hug, which he kept friendly before finally stepping away. Brody sat back against the bar again. He proceeded to wait his turn to order and I turned to the pit, unable to help my smile.

The music changed, a more classic, country hit this time, and the pit transformed. The room hooting and hollering, they formed into a line dance. The whole thing was something out of a movie and I loved it. Eyeing the bar over my shoulder, I could see Brody wasn't any closer to being done. He had his arm on the bar, still waiting to order.

I'll stay near the railing so he can see me.

Going all in, I joined the group. I hadn't done these particular steps before, but I was a fast learner. I moved my hips, falling into the beat with my steps, and my black boots gave me my own personal edge to the traditional dance. A girl next to me started showboating a bit, breaking formation, and added her own spin to the dance. She went sharp with every move and quickly got the attention of the rest of the pit.

I guess I couldn't help what I did next.

Getting to her side, I fell instep with her. She smiled, and together, we kept all eyes on us. Eventually, I mixed it up a little, offering a little alternative dance as well as some hip-hop. My partner stopped dancing entirely and clapped above her head, giving me the floor to do my thing. I couldn't stop even if I wanted too. I fed off every step, took in each beat like I had at the park. Music and dancing were my life.

By the time the song ended, I had just gotten going, but I stopped as a guy in a set of well-worn jeans got my attention. He also wore his strong grin and had a matching set of glasses with foam on the top in his tight fists.

The perfect image.

Brody came into the pit. He found us a set of high top tables off to the side and we took up station there. He set the beers down. "If I'd have known that's what you were working with, I would have said to hell with the beers and stayed with you."

For the first time, I felt bashful by what I'd done, pushing my hand into my hair as he slid a beer toward me. He took a sip himself, then watched me with a soft eye as I had a sip from mine.

He shook his head. "Where'd you come from, Alexa?"

I didn't think he was actually asking me. It was more of a fleeting thought I imagined by what he saw me do. I knew because he never pressured me before.

I played with some dried foam on the side of my mug. "New York," I found myself saying to him. "But originally from California. That's where my hometown is."

He swallowed what was left in his mouth of the gulp he'd

just taken, blinking. I didn't think he expected me to answer what I was pretty sure had been a rhetorical question. Still, he got it back though, wiping the shock from his face as he set his glass down on the table.

"New York, huh?" he asked, tapping his large finger on his glass. He didn't push this. I was absolutely positive he was scared to and I'd given him reason. I had been so withdrawn from him before.

But I think I could trust him.

His finger left the glass with a smile. "I haven't been. I got a brother in Miami, but that's the closest I got."

I giggled. "That's not very close."

My amusement lifted his lips, his hand going to rub behind his neck. "I'm a small town guy, I guess. I don't even live in El Paso. Just outside of it. I've only really gone where my truck will take me."

I had a feeling about that, him being more small town, but I liked it. I liked him.

"Well, it's wonderful," I continued. "The shows. The dancing. That's what I went for, to dance."

He didn't look the least bit surprised, smiling. "It suits you. I can tell it makes you happy."

He had no idea. The lights, the action, and excitement of the city, I had no words for how great and magical it was. I'd went there with a dream, but came out with a harsh reality.

I tried not to let that reality reflect upon my face, my failures. Instead, I lifted my head, agreeing with what he said. "Yeah, it does. There's so much life there. It's amazing. I just loved looking at it every day and being there in the city."

"I can see that," he said, his eyes shining. He took a sip of his beer, wiping his mouth after. "It doesn't sound like you ever wanted to leave. So what's got you traveling? You just headed home for a while?"

I was headed home for a while. But the thing was, I

wouldn't be going back to New York. My priorities were in California...and magical New York? Well, in the end, it had just been too big for me, but he didn't want or need to hear all that.

I shook my glass before sipping around the foam. "Mmhmm. I'm headed home for a while, but what about you? Small town guy? How did you find yourself in a job like driving for a living?"

The question caused him to laugh, a light sound that warmed my ears. "I guess in the end, you gotta make money."

"Yeah, but you could have worked closer to home. It has to be more than that. You must like driving."

His gaze escaped to the moving crowd. He watched them, no words on his lips. He seemed to have something resting on his mind, but whatever it was, he didn't share it. He simply tipped back his glass, taking down the remainder. He stood, holding his hand out to me. "Dance with me. The crowd already got their turn with you."

He didn't know it, but he could dance with me any time he wanted. I finished my beer and let him guide me away. We went into the pit, but by the time we did, a slow song had started. It was almost as if the deejay knew my silent plea.

Brody brought me in, taking me by the hand. His other hand to my waist, he tugged me, close, and I pressed my body against his, his chest hard and unyielding. I rested my cheek there, loving the way he smelled and the feeling of his hair at the nape of his neck. I worried I was getting too personal, moving my fingers there, but he was doing it, too. His cheek to the side of my hair, he played with my short strands sending small charges throughout my entire body. He wasn't doing anything I wasn't doing myself and the feeling both thrilled me and scared me. We didn't have a lot of time together.

What we had was borrowed, but in those moments, that didn't seem to matter. He played with my hair and I played with his and we both allowed ourselves to forget. I guess they called that living in bliss. I brushed my lips against the collar of his t-shirt, that place right before shirt met skin. He breathed in and I knew I hadn't done so discreetly. His hand bunched the back of my shirt, bringing me closer. I believed he didn't want me to stop, so I didn't, pressing my lips harder. Eventually, I touched skin, his, and the feeling warmed me down to my toes.

His head rubbed against mine and I continued, kissing him, breathing him in, and with every kiss, I just wished he'd take me away. He made things so much better. He made me feel... *safe*. I didn't deserve that. I didn't deserve him because I was selfish. I knew because my selfishness was what had kept me away from home so long, my stubbornness.

"Hey, buddy. Quit hogging her. Why don't you give the rest of us assholes a chance?"

The voice immediately sent my back up and when Brody swiveled us around, it stayed there. A guy in a dark Stetson hat stood to our side and he smelled so strong of whisky, my nose burned. He appraised me, a smile on his lips, and his swaying let me know I wasn't far off about the alcohol in his system.

Brody brought me back to him, ignoring the guy. He attempted to dance us away without confrontation, but the drunk's hand touched his arm. Brody's hand left my waist and I immediately wanted it back. He stepped in front of me. "I think you should take a step back."

The guy got into Brody's face and I seized up, gripping Brody's waist. The guy lifted a finger at Brody. "And I think you should chill out. I just want to dance with her."

He slurred every word and Brody wouldn't relent. He gestured to the side, calmly, but I didn't know how much of that was an act. I'd seen him obliterate a guy. He'd done so for me.

"Imma need you to take seat," he said. "I won't say it again."

"And I will. After I get a dance with the lady." He stared around him at me. "Hey, baby girl. You wanna dance—?"

Brody initiated the first shove, but he didn't step back. Not this time. Moving me to the side, he looked to charge right into the guy on the crowded floor.

"Brody!"

And he stopped. Just like that. Turning, he glanced my way briefly before facing the guy again. His face red, Stetson hat snorted like a bull.

"Just fuckin' let me dance with her," he growled, his jaw clenched.

Brody shook his head. "She doesn't want to dance with you."

"But you haven't even fuckin' asked her! You speak for her or something?"

His hands shaking, Brody brought them together, cracking his knuckles, and I knew what would happen next. I'd seen him in action first hand. If I didn't do something, he would and I had a feeling if it weren't the right something, Stetson hat would instead. He was clearly drunk, a loose canon...

I put my hand on Brody's arm, not wanting to take the risk. "I want to dance with him."

Like before, he came to a full stop. He stared over his shoulder, his own face red now. He pushed a hand through his hair. "You, what?"

"She said," came Stetson hat, pushing around Brody. Stetson put his hand out. "She wants to dance with me."

The guy didn't allow me to come the rest of the way. He simply grabbed my hand, yanking, and I faced Brody, my feet dragging underneath me.

"Just be cool," I told him, going with the guy. It was my

last ditch effort to talk him down. I wouldn't risk him getting hurt over this guy. It wasn't worth it. It was just a dance. "It's not a big deal."

Brody let me go, his fists releasing, and he disappeared within the crowd when I was pulled away. Whipped around, I was pressed against a chest I didn't want to be anywhere near and forced to slow dance with someone I wanted nothing to do with. Grabbing my hips, Stetson forced me against him and I choked on the fumes from his breath.

"I told him you wanted to dance with me," he grunted, sliding a hand on my ass. "Don't you, sweetness?"

I fought the bile from raising, nodding. I had to let him think I wanted this. If I fought, it would be worse. This guy was all hands like most were who felt fit to touch me, only one guy hadn't been in so long, only one, and I tried to find him during the dance. I needed to keep him in sight, not for protection, but to make sure he was okay. I couldn't find him though, and the dance continued on without relenting. And the whole time a stiff erection pressed firmly against my stomach.

I wanted to vomit.

After it was finally over and the song changed, Stetson leaned down, brushing a kiss on my cheek. I cringed.

"Thanks for the dance, darlin'," he said. He turned a word, so nice and special, into something horrible. He turned a moment into something horrible.

He looked to leave, but I grabbed his shoulders, forcing him to bend down to my level. He did so with nothing but a grin as I went to his ear.

"Don't call me darlin'," I whispered. Raising my leg, I kneed him in the balls.

He grabbed himself with a grunt, moving away, and I didn't waste the opportunity. I left him on the dance floor and went to find the only person I wanted to be near.

The only person who could make how filthy I suddenly felt, go away.

I knew I didn't deserve that from him, but I sought him out anyway. I didn't find Brody in the pit, though, or even at our table. No, he was at the bar. He had another beer in his hands. The glass full, he didn't chug it, just nursed it, and I settled in on the barstool beside him. He didn't even move when I had, nor did he look my way.

My stomach sank. "Hey."

He lifted and lowered his chin, so cold as he played with the perspiration on the side of his glass. I guess I deserved nothing less, for leaving, letting that guy dance with me, but I didn't regret it. I couldn't have Brody fighting again for me, *that* was something he shouldn't have to do no matter how willing.

I felt the need to explain myself.

"About that guy," I said. I wanted to tell him I knew he wouldn't stop. I wanted to tell him I knew exactly the type of guy that was, and the only way to keep him away was to give him what he wanted. Guys didn't stop unless you did, the bad ones anyway.

I couldn't risk Brody getting hurt once again for me and I had to explain that to him, but the look those blue eyes gave me at only my three words kept me from continuing.

Brody raised his hand from the bar, his lips so tight. "Not a big deal, right?"

My own words felt like a slap and shook me down to my core. His gaze left before I could even give an attempt at explaining myself, and by then, I no longer saw the point. I just sat there with him in silence, a silence I think we were both far too used to. It reminded me of those early miles together, two strangers tossed into a pairing of the unknown. And we were strangers. We were.

And then my watch beeped.

It sounded at me with a fury and Brody turned, staring at it while I kept my eyes on him.

I pressed a button and the noise stopped, but even still, my watch remained present between us. Brody stared at it as if it still rang and I watched him, my gut twisting with every passing moment. It twisted because as we sat there, the two of us with so many unspoken words between us, the reason *why* my watch went off waited for me. The beep represented the sound of priorities and stood for all I lived and breathed for.

That little boy who expected my call.

It pained me to ask what I had to next, but I dampened my mouth, making myself speak anyway.

"Do you think..." I asked Brody, pausing. This was so hard to do, ask him for a favor now. I pushed through. "Can I borrow your phone? Make a call?"

His gaze found to me, but only remained for a few seconds before facing the sticky bar. He didn't move and my heart did a full rotation in my chest. Not because he didn't let me use his phone, but because I was no longer present to him —clearly.

His big body lifted when he let out a breath and raising his hip, he pulled out a familiar black phone, setting it on the bar.

Slowly, I reached for it. "Thank you. I'll be right back. It's quieter over..."

A raise of his fingers from the bar told me he didn't need or want to hear it. I walked away before I made the situation even worse. I found a quiet place to talk by the bathrooms, and dialing the phone, I pressed my hand to my mouth. My throat had closed up. My eyes burned...

"Hello?"

But that voice made some of it go away. I smiled through cloudy eyes. "Hey, baby. It's me."

Silence settled for only a moment. "Aunt Alex? Aunt Alex, is that you?"

The tears clouded more. I nodded. "Uh huh. It's me. I'm sorry I didn't call yesterday. I had a hard time getting to a phone. I got a text out to you, though. Did you get it?"

"Mmhmm, but…" his watery voice whimpered through the phone, clenching my heart. "But I was so scared when you didn't call. You always call, Aunt Alex. You always call."

And I did no matter what. I always did. I called the same time every night. I wiped under my eyes. "Everything's fine," I said, sniffing back my tears. "I'm good. Everything's good."

"You promise?"

I gave a light laugh. "I promise."

He sniffed into the phone this time. "When are you coming home? You're still coming, right?"

"I am, baby. I've been traveling for a few days now ever since I got your call."

I dropped everything that day, what little I'd built, and in doing so, that told me how selfish I had been. After all these years, I had nothing to show for the time away from home, and staring around a rundown apartment in Brooklyn told me that. That apartment had been the product of my dream in the form of a tower of bills and no work. Those bills sat next to my dance shoes, and those shoes sat next to the ones that actually paid the bills.

I breathed into the phone, trying to forget.

"I'll be there in the next few days," I told my nephew now. "Three tops." I still had the money situation. I hitchhiked to get this far, some traveling situations worse than others, but that was something he didn't need to know. I didn't tell him a lot of things for good reason. He still had hope in this world, his own pipe dreams. The ones I'd lost long ago.

"And then you'll take me away?" he asked, showing me that hope in his small voice. "Me and mommy? You'll take us away from him? If you talk to her, she won't stay with him. She left last time. We moved."

I knew exactly the *him* he referred to. It was the one that made me leave New York immediately and come for my nephew and my sister. She had a habit of blurring the lines between love and pain and my nephew was right, I was the only reason she left last time, but the real reason, he had no idea why. The real reason he wouldn't be able to handle at his young age and I hoped he never found out, for his sake.

I forced a smile into the phone, hoping I could make it reflect in my voice. "Of course. I got a little money saved and picked up some along the way. It will help us."

I lifted my head and tattoo sleeves met my eyes. About ten feet away, the Hispanic girl with purple hair eyed me in the hall, the one I'd seen earlier with Brody. She chatted with two friends, a silver piercing in her nose.

She wasn't being shy about watching me on my call.

Turning, I bowed my head and snuck into the bathroom for more privacy. I leaned on the sink. "We'll head out on the road for a while. It will be fun. A vacation."

"Really!" he asked, excited.

I smiled. "Really, and after that, we'll figure everything else out. Now, go to bed and don't worry about me." He wouldn't now that I called. He just had to hear my voice. It kept the nightmares away. Always.

A few more words and my nephew was finally at ease. I sang to him in those last few moments, a lullaby I made up with his name, Aiden. Once he let me go, I hung up the phone, sliding it into my pocket.

I finally let the cries leave my throat after that, the frustrations at being so far away, the feeling of helplessness and anxiety of not knowing how to correct that. Because after I got back on the road with Brody and arrived in El Paso, I would be stranded. I would have no means to get to Aiden, and nothing to offer when I finally arrived. What's worse was the unease I felt at being stranded combatted that of the sinking feeling I got thinking about traveling without Brody. I'd have to let go of him eventually. I couldn't hold onto him forever.

I splashed water on my face, trying not to dry heave at the unknown. I was dabbing my face with a paper towel when someone else came into the bathroom. She went to the sink, leaning back against it, and her breasts bulged over her top once again when she took a deep breath.

"Hey," the girl said, eyeing me behind her violet locks. The silver piercing in her nose glistened under the bathroom lighting and she didn't leave me alone after I tilted my head, acknowledging her. She continued to leer at me, though, stare, and not knowing what was up, I decided to avoid the situation completely. I went to leave, but she grabbed my arm, pulling me back. I wiggled out of her hold.

She simply smirked, finding that amusing. "You sure are a pretty little thing," she said, reaching to finger a strand of my hair.

Turning away, I sneered. "Sorry. I don't swing that way."

A shrug of her shoulders and she crossed her tatted arms over her chest. "You wish, sweetheart."

I had no reason for this foolishness, so I stepped away, but stopped when she called out to me.

"You fucking with Brody?"

I spun on my heel, eyeing her. "What?"

Using the sink as leverage, she pushed off, approaching me. "You heard me. Are you *fucking* with Brody? I heard you on your little call and it sounds like you're fucking with him. Then there's you dancing with other guys and shit like he ain't even there, so if you're fucking with him, you better step off. He's good people, Brody Chandler, and he don't need whores like you messing with him."

She didn't need to tell me that. I knew I wasn't good enough for him just as I knew he was too good for me, but I didn't have to take this from her.

Whipping around, I maybe took one step before she cut me off and got up in my face again. Her hands shot out, hitting my chest and I swiveled down, grabbing the black handle out of my boot.

A shine of silver hit the air and I raised the knife, something I'd acquired from one of the many truck stops Brody stopped us at. After that john in the bathroom...

I wouldn't let myself go unprotected again.

The girl stepped back, but instead of looking scared she only shook her head. "Pretty little thing's got some claws."

Extending the blade, I tried not to shake. I'd never stabbed someone before and a wavering of the knife showed that.

The girl noticed. Her hand came out of nowhere, slapping the handle from my palm. It hit the floor and her chest hit me, backing me up into the sink. She tipped her chin, grinning at me.

I tried not to cringe as she touched my cheek, her finger flicking my hair.

"What you got on you?" she asked, appraising me. "I'll tell you what? You give me everything you have and I'll consider forgiving you for the knife thing."

I swallowed the thick, heated ball in my throat. "And if I don't."

She tugged a strand of my hair a little too hard. It seared, jolting through my entire head. Her curly lashes flickered up. "You end up on the floor and poor anyway."

Breathing, I tried not to look threatened by that. The girl had maybe twenty pounds on me, thick in the places where she'd need it. Despite that, I thought I could hold my own.

But at what cost? My thoughts flashed to Aiden.

Looking away, I reached into my bra, finding my twenties.

"Pull the cup down," she said, and I faced her. She lifted her shoulders. "Wouldn't want you hiding nothing."

I'd been humiliated and violated, and what started out as such a special night left me nothing more than disgusted with myself. The girl left after she got her money, made me *show* that she got all the money she could possibly get from me, but before I could go back out, I found a toilet. Gripping the bowl, I lurched yeasty beer until there was nothing left but bile. I wiped my mouth, cleaned myself up, and managed not to get anything on Brody's shirt.

I found him at the bar moments later, and he had a visitor with him that had just taken everything I had to get me on the road with my family.

Tattooed girl sat on the barstool next to him, talking to him, and something told me it was nothing good. Her eyes lifted to me, a grin on her face when she did. Sliding off the bar stool, she squeezed Brody's shoulder before walking my way. She passed me, winking, and I turned my head in the other direction.

I joined Brody at the bar, setting down his phone. He reached for it and I couldn't keep my mouth shut.

"Who's your friend?" I asked him like I had a right.

He pocketed the phone, glancing back to where the girl left. "Chloe. She's a local girl. I roll through town a lot."

Meaning, he saw *her* a lot and something told me if I wasn't here that's exactly what he'd be doing tonight. I looked away and when I felt eyes on me, I raised my hand, covering my face. Funny how before I wanted nothing but for him to look at me, but now, I couldn't bare it.

He rested an arm on the bar, leaning in. "Alex? You all right?"

I closed my eyes. "I think we should get on the road." It was time to end the ruse, him and me. Chloe had been right about something. Brody Chandler was too good for me.

I left the barstool, telling him I'd be out at the truck. He asked me to wait, that he needed to pay his tab, but I wasn't hearing him out. I wasn't hearing anything. I was in my head, scared, ashamed... and heartbroken, even though I had no right to be. I set myself up with Brody. I put myself in a place, in a mindset, where I could see myself in his, and now, I was paying the price with reality.

I walked out into the chilled air and nearly passed his truck, thinking I would be better off by myself from here. But in the end, I couldn't do it. I headed in the direction of the rig, but a flash of brown leather met my eyes. I bent down, and picked it up. Cracking the wallet open, I found credit cards. I found money. How easy it would be to take whosever wallet this was. I desperately needed the money. Aiden and me needed the money, but my conscience wouldn't allow me. Aiden would never want me to do that—*steal*. That's something I hadn't had to do yet and I decided I wanted to keep that part of my soul.

I went to close it when I heard my name, then saw blue eyes.

Brody's.

His gaze was on the wallet, the one in my hands, and mine caught a name, a face I hadn't noticed before on the trucker license inside.

I closed it, going to him. "I was just checking whose this was," I explained, not knowing what else to do. I knew exactly how this looked. I held that wallet for a long minute before I ultimately decided to turn it in and I didn't know how long he'd been standing there watching me.

The look on his face, I couldn't explain exactly, but it wasn't the same one he came in with. It wasn't the one that lined his face when he danced with me, kissed me. He pushed a hand in his pocket. "I didn't ask, Alex."

"I know but..." I didn't know what else to say. I had considered taking it even though I didn't know it was his and I couldn't lie even to myself about that.

He let out a breath, raising his hand. "I gotta pay my tab. I know the owner. He trusts me to come back."

The way he emphasized that word, *trust*, made me want to vomit again.

I handed him back the wallet, let him go, and once he left, I knew this was done.

I knew this was over.

Ten

BRODY

Alex didn't sleep that night, and to be honest, I couldn't really either. Up front in my truck's seat, I lounged in silence with Alex tossing and turning on my pull out behind me. She did that all night, moving about at the rest stop I got us to about fifty miles outside of town. I considered driving all night, pushing through those last few hours into El Paso, but I got over myself and my pride. Knowing my limits, I took us here to get whatever sleep we could.

Turned out it wasn't much.

I pushed an arm behind my head, adjusting, thinking, but most of all regretting. I just couldn't get the images out of my head, her in the bar, her in the bar with *that guy*, and then her again, those other images not so bad. They were the ones of her in my arms, her lips bruised after I kissed her.

I thought I knew her or at least had a feeling about her. Honest to God, I didn't think she was capable of stealing from me, but that desperation in her eyes I couldn't forget. She had a hope behind them at what she found, and really, that should bother me more. It should but...

"She was calling someone 'baby' on the phone, Brody,"

Chloe had said at the bar. "Said she came into some money for her and... well, whoever she was calling her bae."

That hurt more. Not that Alex was stealing or could have possibly taken advantage of our situation together, but that I let feelings come into this and fooled myself into thinking the two of us had something going.

I can't believe I kissed her.

Opening my eyes, I leaned my head back. All the hours I spent with Alex, all the minutes, replayed through my head and I couldn't stop them. I couldn't *deny* what I felt and still felt about her, but if what Chloe said was true...

A sniff caught in the air, somewhere behind the curtain within the confines of the back of my rig and I tilted my head with it, listening to the faint sound.

Swallowing, I turned away as the announcement of rain dotted my windshield. It picked up, got harder, but that didn't matter. Alex was in the back crying, I could still hear her.

I guess I found something that hurt more than deceit.

Early morning saw me up with the day and not to my surprise, Alex rose as well, neither one of us choosing to catch up on that lost sleep. She came up front. Her glittery bag on her shoulder, she was dressed back in the clothes I met her in, her wig back on.

"Mornin,'" I said, surprising her, and I guess myself a little, too.

Holding her arms, her eyes found mine and her bright hair didn't do much to hide the darkness under eyes. Passing me, she murmured, "Good morning," her eyes to the floor before taking a seat up front. I had doughnuts stacked up there, fresh coffee from the stop as well, but she didn't take either. She simply sat there. After strapping in, she moved her bag to her lap and stared out at the pattering rain that wouldn't seem to let up.

Turning, I finished folding up my blankets from the

cramped night. I shoved them into the cubbies in the back when my gaze caught my shirt. She had it folded up all nicely and placed squarely on my pull-out like she'd never worn it.

I put it away with the rest of my stuff.

The trip out of the truck stop reeked of the familiar; me in my seat, her curled up in hers with her arms folded over her bag. Driving, my hand on the wheel, I acted on something I decided during that restless night. I kept myself in check, my emotions and everything else, and just drove. I did so every hour and every mile that passed. I wasn't cold to Alex. No, I'd never be that way, but I wasn't entertaining certain thoughts or feelings that had been exchanged between us either. I made sure things stayed neutral between us, nothing but respectful. There was no more laughter, no jokes, and no more... just no more of what had been. I drove her and she sat beside me. I drove her and she let me, quiet as bird wings. I think, when I pinned it down, that sucked the most about this new approach. She wouldn't share her voice with me anymore, but I guess I wasn't trying to really talk much either.

We'd driven so long in silence I almost forget she was there, but then suddenly in my peripheral I'd catch sight of her. I couldn't lose her, my awareness wouldn't let things be another way. I dropped my last bit of cargo off in a neighboring town and then mine came quickly, and with it, a reminder of what was to come and what I had to make myself do.

The rain had stopped and Alex's eyes found their way ahead to the first signs of city. Through the drive, her gaze had drifted off during the many miles, but not to sleep, no. She wouldn't do that. She didn't let herself again. Turning, her brown eyes found all movement, every building and landscape until we traveled out of it and on toward the outskirts where I lived.

Home.

Like I'd told Alex, my family and I didn't live directly in

the city, but a small town just outside. Either way, I wouldn't be taking Alex there. Doing that wouldn't make sense.

Her hair swayed over her cheek when I turned the wheel. I took that right to make a single stop before our last. She blinked, clear wonder behind her eyes but not enough to voice it.

"Got a stop to make," I told her, knowing she wouldn't ask me. I didn't want her thinking anything was up. I tipped my chin toward my company building we were coming up on, and as I parked the rig along the others, I supposed my purpose here became obvious. I glanced her way anyway. "I gotta switch out the rig for my truck. We'll be on our way after that."

I didn't say to where because I didn't know. Technically, we had come to the end of the line. I got her to where I told her I would and had no other obligations really, but just because there weren't any didn't mean things had to be that way. I turned off the engine and she followed me as I stood. Gathering her bag, the look on her face told me everything I needed to know. I hadn't known Alex long, but one thing I wouldn't forget was the way I found her. How the fear looked on her face and how the worry drained it and made me want to reach out and do anything to fix it. She had that now, that fear of the unknown.

Opening the door, she left with it and I let her. I gathered a few things before I headed to do the same, my laundry and a small bag of trash. I never left my gun in the truck, so I took that, too, tucking it in my waistband. By the time I got out, I noticed Alex had started walking, but I caught up quickly, flanking her until I was alongside her. We kept silent, my bags on my back and hers over her own. I made steps toward my pickup, anxious with every step I redirected that way. I didn't know if she'd follow me and take that last bit of help. I wanted her to. Even with all that had happened, I did. Taking a chance, I went that way, and was grateful to hear rocks crushing just behind me under her feet. Maybe she followed because she didn't know what else to do. Maybe she followed because she felt she had no other options. Either way, she chose to stay with me just a little bit longer.

She couldn't hide from me so well here. My truck was spacious but nothing like the rig. She had to stay close. I had so much to say to her, but then, really not so much. I just wanted to know one thing: Had it all been fake? Had it all meant nothing at all to her? Did she go around doing this all the time, traveling with a guy and embedding herself so deep or did she just choose me for some reason?

Maybe I did have a lot to say after all.

The train station came into sight and the moment for questions passed. Parked in the lot, I didn't even realize I intended on coming here. It had been instinctual for some reason. I sat there, arms on the wheel with the engine still running. I had so much bottled up, so much I wanted to get out. Bumping my fist on the wheel, I decided to man up and let it all out. I needed answers from her and the quiet just wasn't good enough for me anymore.

The dinging of the door ajar raised my head, but the sight of her little body leaving my truck tore me up, tore me up something terrible. She got out and slammed my door, but didn't leave. She just stood there almost like she was in limbo.

I rolled down the window and I caught sight of her when she turned, that gorgeous face staring back at me as she pulled her hair away. Those nut-brown eyes still had stars in them, sparkle despite how sad.

I knew I didn't have long, so I swallowed, trying to make every word count.

"Just can you..." I paused, my mouth nothing but dry. I went on despite it. "Take care of yourself, all right? Don't trust anybody that shouldn't be trusted. Can you do that for me? That's all I ask."

She stared at me, her lips closed so tight. And then those eyes had shimmering in them again, glassy. She moved a hand over her face, blinking it away, and when she nodded, that bright hair slid over her cheek.

I wanted so much to touch it, but she stepped back, pushing her bag up her arm.

"Thank you," she said, nodding once again. "Thank you so much for everything."

She continued to nod even while she said it, the words thick and hard to make out. Adjusting the strap on her bag, she turned around, and then walked away.

∼

Alexa

I walked for what seemed like miles, my boots cutting into the soles of my feet. I didn't feel I had much choice but to just walk and move on. I entertained the idea of getting a train ticket to get me as close to California as I could before the ticket lady reaffirmed what little I did have for a one-way trip down the line. Chloe left me with pretty much nothing at the bar. I had enough for a couple meals and not much more than that. I either had to hitchhike to Cali or walk. Walk...

Really, the walking was helping me to get it together, helping me to settle the guilt with my strides and remove those final images of Brody's face from my head. Those ones of sympathy, remorse, that turned his mouth down and sent a hot strike through my chest. But then, I felt bad for that, for trying to remove his image from my head. I didn't want to forget him and his kindness. My heart burned just thinking about that possibility, so I walked, removing him to no avail. This was both a relief and agonizing defeat in my head.

That first night, I managed to find a shelter on the far side of town. They had warm food, water, and I filled up not knowing where my next meal would come from. Despite being grateful for the food, my saving grace came in the form of a phone. They had one for residents to use, so as soon as my watch beeped I shut it down quickly and called Aiden. I sat there on a chair by the phone, listening to him with a warm heart. He had school today, loving his fourth grade year. I listened for any indication, any tell of fear or anxiety, but he never had that talking to me. I made him better. He made me better.

Baby, I'm almost home.

I talked to him as if nothing about my situation changed. I was still coming for him come hell or high water and being stranded wouldn't hold me back. I'd figure out how to get to him. I didn't live in NYC so long without being resourceful. There might be some things I'd have to sacrifice. There might be some things I'd have to do, but I'd do them. I needed to get to him. I couldn't fail him.

I held my bag to my chest moments later, lying under the covers of a blanket that kept warm so many before me. The soft snores of others in bunks around me became something of a lullaby and I closed my eyes. My hand found its way inside my bag as I rubbed on it with the pads of my fingers, a nervous habit I guess after Chloe. My hand caught on something and I pulled it out.

Pushing the blankets off my lap, I sat up and leaned forward into the soft light of room. In my hand was some money, two twenty dollar bills and a note paper clipped to it.

For food and anything else. Take care of yourself.

He didn't even sign it. He didn't have to.

Eleven

BRODY

I PULLED up along a long stretch of road Friday night, nothing but gravel crunching under my tires. A few cars were already in the driveway, my brother Hayden and his wife Karen, and of course, my Aunt Robin's SUV and my gram's truck. I had to smirk at it. The little lady had the biggest ride of all of us. Even bigger than pop's, his last in the line. Gram did say he'd be here, didn't she?

Parking, I brought up the rear, sitting for a second. Pop had a decal on the truck bed, that matched the ones on the sides. Business owners usually had those.

Reaching over, I punched my glove compartment open. The thing always needed a little jimmying. Out popped various papers, receipts, and an orange bottle. I had several there, but just one that needed to be taken in the evening. I had the others this morning. Cracking open the prescription, I dry swallowed two of the tiny pills inside. I'd need a refill soon and was grateful I hadn't run out while on the road and traveling with Alex.

I closed my eyes with the swallow, trying to think only

positively. Nothing stressful. Just positive. She was a strong girl. She'd be all right.

She had to be all right.

Not allowing myself to think any other way, I made my way to Gram's house from the side. She wanted me here. She wanted me present so I'd be here. The side of my Gram's ranch home had fine wooden panels that never ended. I'd never get over what my grandpop put into this place before he died. It was the only standing home I had ever known since Pop raised my brothers and me in a trailer park. That had been all right for us though. That had been all right.

The very man who'd brought me up surprised me when I went to open the side door of the ranch house. Stepping away from the door, I caught my pop's burly frame. He was flipping some meats with a spatula over a large grill, thick smoke rising up above his dark Stetson hat.

Now or never was my thought as I redirected, heading that way to say "hi" to him. I hadn't seen my pop as often as I should. Lately, it had just seemed easier that way. He, like most, had assumed I didn't want to be a part of his new business, the one he started alongside my brother Griffin. A loan from my pro-athlete brother created a means for my pop to leave his previous job in construction and start his own just last year, a small crafting business. Right in the heart of the city, *Chandler & Sons Furniture Co.* would soon take a small piece of the business pie. They'd open this fall, but they would be minus one son in tow.

Bracing myself for battle, I approached the man behind the business, knowing good and well we'd have words here. We had in the past over my decision.

He turned slightly, a phone in his hand, and my pace slowed. He was on a call, his voice low into the phone, and I decided to delay the inevitable for just a bit longer.

"Uncle Brody!"

Closing the side door, I grabbed my niece Sarah off the floor before she could crash into me. She had a habit of running. Spinning her upside down, I smashed a kiss on her face. That elicited a giggle and when I pulled away, I noticed the half eaten cookie in her hand, as well as a ring of smeared chocolate around her mouth.

"Didn't know you were growing out a goatee, kid," I said, pointing at that chocolate 'stache. I leaned in. "You sneak that or somethin'?"

She knew good and well she couldn't have cookies before dinner. And though, I could smell the warm chili moving through the air, my gram had a strict "no eating until everyone is here" policy.

Sarah lifted her little finger, giving the *shh* sound and I could only laugh at her. I brought her on my hip; the girl getting way too big too fast. It seemed to be just yesterday she was in diapers.

"Where's Grammy and your mama?" I asked her.

"Kitchen," she said, nibbling on her cookie. "They're makin' pecan pie."

Damn, was it good to be home. Sarah pointed the way, her cookie gone before we could even hit the kitchen. The room was a heaven of warm smells and hard working women, the back bone of my family. To my surprise, my cousin Marlene was in town from college, cooking away beside her own mama, my Aunt Robin.

I set Sarah down, letting her lead the rest of the way. She tackled Karen's leg, slamming her face into her thigh and begging if she could finally have a cookie. She was an ornery little thing. Karen said no and Sarah left the room pouting. The exit sent the entire kitchen looking my way as Sarah had to pass me to get out. And so, the tsunami of hugs and kisses began. I got told everything from I was looking too thin to asking where my laundry was so they could do it. Always trying to take care of somebody, these women.

I gathered my aunt under my arm as she'd been the one who asked about my laundry. I lowered, kissing her cheek. "I can handle it." They didn't raise me to be independent for nothing.

She patted my chest and I made way for Gram. She got to me and I squeezed her with both arms, having to squat just to do it.

"I swear, Brody. You're gonna break this old woman," she said, laughing as she warmed my back with her hands.

She was wrong about that; me breaking her. This woman could never be broken. That wouldn't be possible.

I went to pull away from the hug, but she didn't let me at first, holding on for what seemed like just a moment longer. I let her, not minding, but it did worry me a little. My gram... nothing really could get past her, and that... yeah that did have me worrying. She let me go eventually, looking none the wiser, and I thought maybe the extra long hug had been in my head. By the time the hugs wrapped up and initial hellos passed, Sarah had made her way back into the kitchen. I gathered her up and took her out, knowing the women were working in there. We got into the living room and I set her down, letting her run away and another member of my kin appeared in the next room; Sarah doing a good job of announcing my arrival. My older brother Hayden sat on the couch by himself, turning his head.

I pulled off my ball cap, tossing it on a table behind the sofa, and slapped his hand. I had to do so kind of quiet as he had a sleeping baby in his hands. Crissy was only a few months old now, Karen giving birth to her over the summer.

He fist bumped me after. "So you do exist."

I'd call him a fucker if he didn't hold an infant. I let that one slide and crossed in front of the couch to sit beside him.

"Just lay off with that, Hay," I said, settling in. I knew my job kept me away for weeks at a time. Gram reminded me of that every time I talked to her. I moved my hand behind the couch. "You ain't ever handling Griff like this." He was younger than us, a couple years behind me.

Hayden smirked, watching what I could now see was a ball game, basketball. My family was really into the game. Especially, since Griffin went pro and all that. He was in Miami getting at his game while the youngest of us, Colton, was training to do the same at Texas State.

Hayden turned my way. "Last I checked, Griffin has to be where he is. If he had it his way, he'd be here."

He didn't have to voice it because we both knew that. Griffin had a place for home, family, like the rest of us and his wife, Roxie, seemed to really love being here too when the pair of them came back home to visit. Shit, they'd even had their wedding here on Gram's property in the end. But the thing about Hayden's statement was I saw it for what it really was. He wasn't getting on me for not being home, not really. He was doing it because of the reason he felt I wasn't, that being my denial of the family business.

I wished it were that simple.

I ran my fingers through my mop of hair, resting my arm on the top when I realized I was doing it. "I didn't come here for all this," I told him.

He nodded. "But Pop's here and you're going to have to— deal that is."

I sighed, knowing he wouldn't lay off with this. He hadn't in the last few months of the development, since my decline. I had still been working at *Carter's Construction* then, the company me, him, and my pop used to work for before the business came along. That, in itself had confused them all, working for someone else instead of helping with development of the family business, and even more when I left *Carter's* abruptly, deciding to branch out on my own.

"He's out back if you're wondering," Hayden said. "Cooking on the barbecue."

I folded my arms over my chest. "I know. I saw him, but he was on the phone."

Hayden acknowledged that, lifting his chin. He laid a hand on Crissy's head, placing it on blonde hair so thick already. Hers was curly though, much like Colton's in that way. Hayden turned to me. "Do what you want. You know I don't care and Pop... he'll be okay. But just don't distance yourself from the family. Gram won't say, but I know it scares her, you being gone. I think it reminds her of mom. You remember how dismissive she was in the end, right? Just before?"

God, how could I forget? She made up any excuse, anything she could to be away from my brothers and me; my dad. And when she was around, she wouldn't even hug us or show any kind of affection toward us. I remember that being weird, even then, despite being so young. Then she was gone. Just like that. Not even a goodbye. I only remembered the thought of her now. She'd been gone so long.

I didn't want my gram feeling that way or any way close because I chose a different path. I would have to talk to her about it, set her mind at ease. Me not being around had nothing to do with not wanting to be here. It was just something I needed to do for me.

Something I had a feeling they wouldn't understand.

"Soups on, fellas!" came Aunt Robin's voice from the kitchen and I smiled. She always said that.

Bracing himself, Hayden rose with my niece, his hand on her back.

"I'll handle it," I said to him and he turned around, nodding in understanding. I'd make sure Gram knew what was up, all of them eventually, but for now, I would have dinner.

I had my hands on my knees, getting up myself, when the doorbell rang. Hayden went to turn that way with Crissy, but I told him I would get it, heading toward the door. A woman stood behind it, pretty with dark skin and a large hat blocking the sun. She also had a white casserole dish in her hands. The clear lid on it let me know it was some kind of dumplings.

I widened the door. "Can I help you with something, ma'am?"

She slid off her hat, revealing large curls that swayed wildly in the wind, and gave me the largest of smiles. "Yes. Are you Brody? Or maybe Hayden?"

My brow rose. "Uh, Brody. I'm sorry, but I don't think I know—"

"Ann?"

Pop came from behind me, out of nowhere really, and approached the woman. He drew forward with his hat off, lowered in his hands, and when he arrived, he touched her shoulder, guiding her in for one of those friendly hugs, which said something in itself. My old man? He wasn't a hugger really. He never had been.

"Blake." This woman grinned, pulling away. My pop still had his hand on her shoulder from when he brought her in, but he didn't take it back. He simply redirected to her forearm, holding underneath it and cupping it.

"I'm glad you could come," he told her and then I froze in place when he turned to me.

Forgetting myself for a moment, I removed the slouch from my back. I made sure I carried myself well when he was around. Still, I didn't think that would omit my recent history with him though. He wasn't really talking to me as of late, since my decision.

I braced myself for that. "Hey, Pop."

I prepared for the worst, even in front of this stranger at the door. What I didn't prepare for? Was a damn pat on the back.

He passed me, squeezing once, while he brought this woman inside, his hand still on her arm. "Hey, son. How've been? All right?"

I blinked. "Yeah?" I couldn't help the question really. Who was this fella I thought was my old man?

He nodded, then faced the woman. Ann, I believed her name was as he said it before. "This is Ann, Brody," he said, not looking at me. Only at her. "Ann, this is one of my boys. Second in the line of age. Brody, Ann was one of my nurses when I was in the hospital."

And then her face appeared in my mind, the one who checked in the most, who'd been there when Pop had gone through the rough with his heart attack last year. Reaching over, I shook her hand, wishing I could do more. "I remember. Thank you for everything you did."

This seemed to please her, her hand slipping from mine but only to slide on top of Pop's still on her arm. "This one had all the fight. I only helped him find his way."

He smiled at her. "Let me take you to meet the rest of the family. Brody, can you take Ann's hat?"

I ended up getting that, her wrap, and my pop's hat when he gave to me. Hurrying, I placed them in the closet, trying to get to the kitchen. Pop brought a woman, a real woman to my gram's house. Hell, this was crazy. But when I got in, I seemed to be the only one surprised. This Ann was greeted with hugs and even a cheek kiss from Gram. They took her in, took her dish, and the Chandler ladies brought her under their wings. The whole scene reminded me of the day Griffin's wife, Roxie, had been introduced and Karen before that. The difference was, we all felt like we knew them before they even came. Griffin and Hayden wouldn't stop going on about the women they were dating prior to them being introduced. We were all close that way. But I didn't know this Ann.

I felt like the only one.

Even Hayden gave her a hug, sliding Crissy into her arms when she asked to meet her, and Pop stood close to her side, his hand settled on her lower back while she cooed. Hayden stepped back and I grabbed him, walking out of the fray a bit. I just tipped my chin toward the scene, wondering what was up, and he shrugged, not understanding.

I decided to break it down. "You know her? You know Pop and... her?"

To this, he crossed his arms, looking up at me slightly, me taller despite being younger. He frowned. "Maybe you should start existing more," he simply said, before rejoining the group.

And I stood there, taking in the scene, the scene I wasn't a part of. I agreed with him all the way about that, what he'd said. I should exist more, be here more.

But maybe, at least right now anyway, I couldn't be.

Twelve

ALEXA

"Please. I'm only twenty minutes late," I said, shrugging my bag up my shoulder. My chest rising and falling, I tried to catch my breath from the sprint over several blocks, but the woman in front of me kept me from reaching that goal. It was her eyes. Her eyes told me all I needed to know about my answer.

Please. I have nowhere else to go.

The woman at the shelter's door sighed, leaning against it. She had just seen me coming when she went to close up and lock down for the night per the shelter's protocol. I stayed at many who'd had the same policy. She shifted her weight on her hip. "I'm sorry, sweetie. But you're going to have to find another place to stay tonight."

Swallowing, I looked away.

"We have rules here," she continued. "You're here by eight or you don't get in."

"But it's 8:20," I said, showing her my watch. "Can't you just make an exception? It's my job. I had to stay late or I wouldn't get paid." A decision I decided to make for a little extra cushion, but now seemed like the most foolish thing. I picked up three jobs today, odd ones in cleaning that I'd found posted at the library. Brody's money allowed me to get a decent outfit and some tennis shoes. Each job paid between fifty to seventy-five dollars a pop. I figured I would need that. It would get me a one-way ticket back home with a little left over to help with my family. But now, it was costing me a warm place to sleep tonight. I knew that as the woman in the shelter went to close the door.

"No exceptions," she said, inching it closer. "Now, you're gonna have to go—"

"But I have nowhere else," I pleaded. "I just need one more night. One more and that's it." Because after that, I would be gone. I could finally leave Texas, El Paso, and head home.

She laid her arm on the door, tilting her head. "You and everyone else, dear," she said, nodding. "You and everyone else."

I sat at a diner that night, watching the cars cruise by the windows until they got so dark behind them. Then those cars became few and far between, later and later into the night. By that time, my coffee had gone cold, the only thing I could make myself sacrifice a little money for. I had to stay awake. I couldn't sleep just anywhere. Anywhere made me vulnerable. Eventually, the owner of the diner realized I wouldn't be ordering anymore or leaving. He came over to my table, remorseful, polite, but in the end, he still made me leave.

I went by foot after that, just walking and trying to stay out of sight. I held my arms, wondering how I let it get this bad. Homeless, alone. At least in New York, I had managed to get myself to a place where I wasn't on the streets, however little I had. I should have come home sooner.

I should have never left.

I made the mistake of thinking I could make it and that I could make change happen for Aiden. I could take him and my sister away. I could take care of them. I smirked behind a tear-streaked face.

I couldn't even take care of myself.

A car pulled up to my side, cruising along slowly. Shielding my face, I kept on moving forward, ignoring it, but it wouldn't stop or drive away. I braced my feet to run, not knowing what else to do when the window went down.

"Hey!" A male voice shouted. "Hey, I'm interested, honey."

My back up, I dared to glance his way. He looked like some business guy. Caucasian, in a dark suit. He also drove one of those nice rides, a Mercedes Benz with the windows rolled down. One more thing I noticed was his left hand on his steering wheel. He had a gold band wrapped there.

I stopped. Looking at him, I didn't say a word.

Was he...

"Twenty for the front," he continued. "Forty for the back, right? Those still Wayne's prices?"

Wayne?

This guy grinned. "I want the deluxe package. I'll even give you an extra hundred if you let me eat that pussy."

He was looking for exactly what I thought and the very notion of it returned a similar feeling I wanted to never experience again. My throat closing up made it hard to get air either in or out, the acidic bile burning in a rapid rise up from my stomach. They'd been things I felt in an act of desperation to a familiar situation. In fact, the same situation I found myself in currently. Things got so bad. I'd gotten so scared that I...

But things were different this time. I didn't have a Brody to save me if I changed my mind. No, I had lost him. I lost the only good thing.

I stepped toward the car, giving up, and choosing anything but the fear. But then a voice across the street came, and a girl, she raised her hand. Dressed in fishnets and a tight,

busty top, she strode over to the car. This got the guy's attention. She was definitely dressed sexier than my shorts and
tennis shoes. She leaned down, grinning at the man through
his open window.

"This girl don't work for Wayne," she said, tipping her
head my way.

He frowned. "Damn, I wanted the good girl thing today,"
he responded. Turning, he gave me the once over, clearly
liking what he saw, but the girl got him back, pointing over her
shoulder.

"Well, we got a new girl. Piper. She'll hook you up real
nice across the way."

The girl redirected his attention just that way and another
busty girl, I assumed Piper, raised her hand. A high ponytail
on her head, she gave a show of swaying her hips in a short
skirt. She didn't read much like a "good girl," but the man
didn't seem too choosey tonight. He nodded and the girl who
intercepted us waved to Piper. Piper came over and once she
got inside the man's car, the pair drove away.

I saw this as nothing but a sign.

Lowering my head, I went to walk away.

"Hey!"

I kept going, but the girl touched my arm. I wiggled back,
but she raised her hands, indicating no threat. That didn't
mean she wasn't one.

She lowered her arms across her chest. "What did you
think you were doing, hon? You can't work privately here.
You're in territory. Wayne has this block."

I didn't have to explain myself. Removing myself from the
situation, I made a couple strides before she stepped in front
of me. I put space between us. "Sorry. I didn't know."

"Clearly," she said, and in the light, I could see blue
contacts behind her hot pink wig. They really stuck out since
her skin had such a dark hue. She crossed her arms. "You want

in? The guy was right, you do got that school girl thing going for you."

I pushed my bag up my arm. "No, thanks. It was a mistake. Again, I'm sorry."

Standing there, she watched me, nodding. After a moment, she made a few steps toward me in her strappy heels. She got close, real close, and tilted her head at me, her gaze sizing me up from head to toe.

What is she doing?

She lifted her head, apparently getting her fill, and when her eyes met mine, her pink hair swayed when she shook her head. "It really was a mistake, wasn't it? I guess I didn't see it at first, but you're really not working."

It was a mistake. One of too many. I stopped counting these days. When I didn't answer she appraised me. Gazing down my body, she stopped at my arms, then my legs exposed from my shorts. She smiled. "You dance though, right?" she asked.

My eyes widened, my mouth parted. "I did. How did you know?"

"Honey, no one has legs like that unless they're using them. And these arms," she said, gesturing toward them. My sleeves were short enough for them to be seen. "Perfect to handle yourself on a pole. You ever done exotic?" she asked, eyes lifting.

I swallowed. "Yes."

She raised her chin like she knew that's what I was going to say. She placed a hand on her curvy hip. "I'm guessing you just need some quick money, which is why you even considered that guy just now and if that's the case, I know where you can go. I dance at a place downtown. I can get you in. You do a good job and you could be walking away with a few Benjamin's. I can work it out with the owner. One night only."

One night only...

She made it sound so simple and it wasn't like I hadn't done this before. That's how I got by so long in New York, how I paid my rent when things got bad.

She went to walk away, not waiting for my response. But gazing back, she eyed me. She waited for me.

I shrugged my bag up my arm, following behind her. I could do this for just one night.

I could do this just one more time.

Thirteen

BRODY

SHE STRADDLED MY HIPS, all hands, breasts. It came to this like it always had. Chloe rolled her thick hips, her soft pillowy thighs pressing against my jeans. She lowered placing a warm mouth on my neck, kissing, and I let her, filling my hands with her ass to beckon her to do it harder and faster. Again, it always came to this... in the end. She moved, the flowery smell from her violet hair going with her as she made her way down my body. Her hands found their way under my shirt, my stomach, and then her lips touched down and replaced that of her hands.

I set my head back on the couch in her apartment, allowing her to go and fill a void. It was one she could probably never fill, but she knew that. She understood that, but she went anyway. She always did, her tongue pushing into my belly button. Her hands went higher, my shirt higher, and her mouth kissed up a straight line.

I grabbed her shoulders, bracing, and she laughed, not stopping as her fingers played to get my shirt higher. I braced her again and the hum from her laughter hit my abs.

"I want to see it," she said, fighting my hands to do just that.

Putting just enough force, I pulled her back, staring into her brown eyes. "It's not like I'm some weird oddity or something."

Her lips lifted, that red gloss she wore long gone. I had a feeling I could find it all over my neck and mouth. She pushed a hand into my hair, rubbing. "You're not. It just means you've been through stuff."

I had to laugh this time. "I don't even remember when it happened. It was a long time ago." And it had been. I'd gotten my scar when I was born.

Closing the space, she kissed me, her mouth so warm, so needed. "You're strong, Brody," she said, smiling. "You're a fighter. Even from the beginning."

Was I though? I didn't feel that fight these days, that strength. But Chloe didn't seem to care, her priorities in her lips on me. She travelled down, unstrapping my belt. Her hand ventured inside my jeans, cupping me over my boxers. Her other hand went for my chest again, my scar between my ribcage, but I grabbed her wrist.

She eyed me. "What's up?"

Honestly, I didn't know. I just knew I wasn't really feeling this. It didn't feel okay anymore. Reaching up, I squeezed her arm, rubbing. "Something just feels off."

She placed her hand behind my neck, frowning. "What exactly?"

Turning my head, I shook it. "This. Don't you just get... I don't know, over all this sometimes? I mean, isn't this lonely for you? Just this? I roll through town and... you know *this*?"

She knew exactly what I meant. This, us, and this friendship. We always found our way here for some reason and I didn't understand why.

She pressed her other hand to my neck. "No," she said,

answering my previous question. "Why would I be over this, *us*?"

I let out a breath, tapping a finger against her leg. "Because it isn't enough. It's so physical, vacant. Why is that enough for you?"

The words just came. They came and I had no idea why. Thinking about them, I wanted to take them back, apologize or something for saying them. It sounded rude I guess, as well as cold.

Chloe left my lap like I probably would have in her situation. She rubbed her hands down her face, and when she leaned back, she faced me. "You mean, why isn't this enough for you, right? That's what you're really asking."

Maybe, in a way, I was. I pushed my hand into my hair, my other on my stomach. The two of us sat in silence for bit, but what she said next had me turning my head.

"This is about her, isn't it? That girl you came to the bar with last week?"

I didn't say anything and she gave a dry laugh, shaking her head with it. Alex, my time with her, hadn't come into my head when I asked Chloe what I had. But the moment she brought Alex up, I couldn't find it in me to deny what she said.

Had it already been nearly a week since I'd last seen her? Since I last touched her...

I had a feeling the reality of that moved over my face. Chloe's eyes lifted, her body shifting while she rested a hand on her leg. "She's not good enough for you, Brody."

She didn't have a place to say what was right for me and what wasn't. She didn't even know me, not really anyway. Our friendship had blossomed in my short trips here and quickly went physical fast, unless she was with someone at the time. I looked at her. "Don't do that. You can't say that for me and you don't know her, so don't do that."

"And you know her?" she asked, raising and lifting her hand. "You bring her to the bar. She dances with *another* guy. You let her borrow your phone and she calls someone else 'baby' on the phone. God, Brody, and did you forget you caught her stealing from your wallet?"

I turned my head. "I never said that."

"But that's what she was doing. You know that's what she was about to do."

If she was, she probably felt she had to. She'd never... not without a reason.

Chloe pushed her hand through her hair. "You need to forget about that girl. She's fucking weak. And what the fuck would you do with a girl that's weak as shit?"

Alex wasn't weak. I only got a snapshot into her life, but that was enough to know she'd been around some folks that didn't treat her right and people who had to deal with that, the crap life threw at them, weren't weak. They were the strongest of any of us because they kept on despite the fact.

I buckled my pants. Standing, I rose to get the fuck out of here, but Chloe was in my face.

"She's *all* wrong for you. She barely put up a fight when I took her ass for all she had."

I had to have heard her wrong. Because she wouldn't go there. I thought her better than that.

But then she had the gall to look smug about it.

"Yeah, I robbed her," she said, nodding. "Little thing pulled a knife on me, but couldn't even hold her own for two seconds. I knocked it out of her hand and she didn't even fight me. She handed over all her cash like a weak little bitch."

I honed in on her, thinking she should thank God for not making her a guy. If she was, she wouldn't be standing here like a cocky little shit in front of me. "Give me what you took."

Her arms moved over her chest. "Sorry?"

She was testing my patience. "I said, give me the money you took from Alex. I won't ask you again."

She stared at me, hard, and though she looked like she'd do anything but comply, in the end, she did as I asked her.

Pulling down the front of her top, she stared right in my face. She did so boldly, unrelenting, and when she slid a wad of cash out of her shirt, I wanted to shake my head at both her and myself for not seeing her for her true colors. Or maybe I had, but had just been so lonely on the road I didn't care. I was paying for that mistake now.

She counted slowly, pulling bill after bill of twenties and even a couple hundreds. God, she took everything from Alex. Everything. She gave me the entire stack and the last thing I cared about was the formality of saying goodbye. I left and she followed me out of her apartment complex and to my truck. My truck. That should have told me what a mess everything was. I wasn't even on the clock and I came out to see Chloe. I could fuckin' kick myself a new hide.

I sat behind the wheel and Chloe stood outside, her arms crossed, until I powered the window down. I shrugged my shoulders, shaking my head. I didn't know what else there was left to say here, but then I realized I did have one thing.

"Was it all bullshit?" I asked, jaw clenched. "About Alex? When you said she was talking to someone else on the phone, calling whoever *baby* and shit? Did you just make that up?"

It hurt to say. The baby thing and damn, if I couldn't get that out of my voice.

And finally Chloe's guard went down a bit, her arms lowering as she stared at me. "No, and I do wish I was. I wasn't lying, Brody. I really don't think she's good for you."

Again, what would she know about that? Hell, maybe I wasn't the one worthy of Alex. I had left her after all, no benefit of the doubt given. I didn't respond and Chloe placed her hands on her hips, sighing.

"You're really going to do this?" she said, moving in. "To me? I thought we had some good times."

We had and I wouldn't deny that. But I fooled myself into thinking we had some kind of friendship beyond the physical, when all I really had was a girl wanting to relieve nothing but an itch and cause some drama along the way. I put my truck into gear, not looking at her.

"You see me roll through town," I said to her. "Just look away."

I peeled down the block. There was nothing else really to do here.

Fourteen

BRODY

IT TOOK me too few hours to make it back home, cutting more time off the drive than I should have at my speed and during that time, I thought. I thought about Alex and how I'd give anything just to know she was okay. I didn't know where to begin to find her, where to go, or even if I could. Almost a week had passed since I dropped her off and Alex was resourceful. She already showed her success with hitchhiking. Hell, I'd been one of the ones to pick her up, and what little I managed to sneak into her bag would only help her with that goal. I wouldn't put it past her to be long gone by now, out of town, and if she managed that, she had to have left hurt. She left hurt and alone without anyone in her corner. And damn, if she hadn't. I let Chloe manipulate the both of us. I knew Alex wouldn't steal from me, not unless she felt she had no other option. Chloe put her in a place to consider that.

God, where are you?

I watched the roads through the city like I'd find her, just waiting for me with that smile of hers and those eyes. I should have believed in her. She should have at least had me.

How fast it took me to get back to the city hit me and I

was forced to stop for gas just crossing the city lines. Doing so, I realized my place wasn't far from here. A few miles really. I didn't live as far away from town as the rest of my family. When Pop decided to move from the trailer, my younger brother wouldn't let him have it any other way with his new wealth, I moved back in, offering to take it off his hands. The rent couldn't be beat, outdoing my old apartment by a landslide, so I figured why not. It was a nice area and I grew up there. Pop moved closer to Gram and I took his old place despite protests and an offer for a new place myself from my brother. I stayed back while everyone else moved forward. I couldn't help but find that ironic, especially, with the way I chose to go as far as work.

The gas nozzle clicked, my tank full, and I pulled it out of my truck. My reflection could be seen in my window and I cringed, noticing Chloe's lip gloss on my cheek.

Disgusted, I replaced the gas nozzle, then pulled a towel from above the windshield cleaner. Scrubbing, I rubbed my skin nearly raw, not wanting anything more to do with the girl.

After tossing the towel, I replaced my gas cap. I got back into my truck to go, but when I did, I ended up just sitting there. I sat there with my hands crossed on the wheel. It was like Alex didn't even exist, she was in my life so briefly. I hadn't even managed to figure out her favorite color. Shit, her favorite food or what she liked to do on Saturday nights.

I didn't even know her last name.

Adjusting, I pulled out my phone. I tapped a bit and stopped immediately at the sight of me and her. She did exist. She did and I had proof here in my hands, her hand raised as I snapped a picture of her while we travelled in my truck. It had been on impulse at the time, capturing her, but now, I was glad I had as I still had something of her.

There had to be something I could do, a way to find her.

Racking my brain, something did come to me, but it could be grasping at straws. I had a couple buddies I could call in a favor with. They went into the police force after high school. Maybe someone had fit her profile or something over the last week. It wasn't much of a chance, but it was one.

I did a web search to find the non-emergency line, but my phone illuminated with a number I didn't recognize.

I answered. "Hello?" And damn, if there wasn't hope in my voice this was her on the other line. But it wouldn't be though. I never gave her my number. That fact still didn't keep my gut from jumping from anticipation.

Sitting there, I waited. I waited, but only silence remained on the other end.

"Hello?" I tried again. Met with more silence, I pulled my phone away, seeing the elapsed time. They didn't hang up, but they weren't speaking.

I don't have time for this.

My thumb hovered over the button to end the call, but then I heard a voice, a small voice. Lifting the phone, I placed it back to my ear. I didn't catch the voice, but the sniffing on the other end couldn't be denied.

"Hey, um," I paused, confused. "Is someone there? Alex? Is that you?"

The voice came immediately.

"Aunt Alex? Aunt Alex..." A gasp sounded in my ear. "My Aunt Alex. Is she there?"

He was a... child.

I slid the phone away, seeing the number. Scrolling around, this number displayed in yet another place: a sent call.

This was who she talked to?

"Aunt Alex?"

I brought the phone to my ear. It all made sense. It all finally made sense. I pushed my hand into my hair. "Uh, hi. Hello?" I didn't know what to say. This was her... nephew?

"Please. Please," he begged, the little kid. "Is she there?"

I let out a breath, wishing she was. "I'm sorry. She's not. This is Brody though. Her friend. I think she called you the other day on my phone."

And then one of the most horrible sounds radiated within my ears. It was something I hated, something that killed me any time my little niece would fall or hurt herself playing. It was the sound of agony. The sound of a child's pain.

"Where is she..." he said, the tears muffling his voice. He sniffed. "She promised she'd be here days ago, but then told me she couldn't the other day. I asked her why and she wouldn't tell me. Now, she hasn't called. She calls every night. Please. Where is she?"

Every night. She called every night. Her watch. Her watch went off two times when I was with her at the same time both nights and I couldn't deny the connection.

"She always calls..." he repeated. Crying so much, it was so hard to hear him at this point. "She always calls."

The words quite literally sent a sharp strike into my heart. If she didn't call something happened. If she didn't call something wasn't okay.

My breath went heavy, swallow. My head swam and I sat back, trying to fight the rush in my head.

Just stay cool. Just breathe.

With a few breaths, I got it back. The tears on the other end of the line continued, the agony, and I had a choice to make. I could tell this kid again his aunt wasn't here or I could give him a sense of security, one his aunt should have had the whole time.

"Hey," I said, preparing to sound nothing but confident in what I was about to tell him. "I did say she wasn't here, but that's only because I'm about to go pick her up."

His breath settled a bit, the tears subsiding, and when he spoke, I was grateful to hear some of that terror leave his voice.

"She... You're going to get her?"

I nodded like this kid could see. "Yep. She's waiting for me. She's waiting for me to come and get her, and when I do, she's gonna call you, buddy. You'll be the first person she calls. I'll make sure of it."

He whimpered, but this time, it didn't sound so sad. "Thanks."

I smiled. "No, problem."

"Can you tell her I made something at school for her today? She asked for a drawing with red color. I used extra crayon."

I feathered my hand through my hair and my lips couldn't help lifting. "Sure thing. Don't worry. I'll make sure she gets the message."

I got a few more thanks, a few more sniffs, and then he finally let me go. Starting my truck, I didn't hesitate behind the wheel. I took off as I had someone's aunt to pick up.

She was waiting for me.

I started with my buddies in the force, calling in that favor, and truth be told, they said Alex fit the physical description of many girls they encountered on their day to day. Especially, if she wore her wig and outfit I met her in. We had some rough neighborhoods and that description wasn't uncommon for girls on the streets. Still, they said they'd keep an active look out. I thanked them, grateful, but they were wrong about one thing. They were wrong about Alex being so similar to girls that maybe looked and dressed like her. Alex... she was different and that was the point.

I travelled long, rolling through the neighborhoods in the areas closest to where I dropped her off, and my first stop was the train station. The guys told me not to get my hopes up too much with that tactic. Too many days had passed since I left her and the odds of her staying in the area were slim. I had to try though. I had to hope. I even went inside the station and got no leads. No one who worked there recalled seeing her. No one.

"Why don't you try calling the local shelters?" Chad, one of my buddies suggested. "She might be staying there or had in the past. We'll give them a head's up you'll be calling so they don't give you any issues."

He gave me a list he brought up in his cruiser. Parking, I went down it call after all. The city didn't have many shelters, but a healthy few. On the fourth try, I'd been prepared to say this led to another dead end. The lady on the phone told me no and everything, but then she said wait. She said wait and my heart stopped.

My heart hoped.

"You said she could have short hair?" she asked me. "Cute, like Halle Berry?"

And damn, if Alex didn't give even her a run for her money with her beauty. I swallowed. "Yeah. That's what her hair looks like under the wig." I honestly, barely mentioned that to the other three places. I figured she'd be trying to hide behind her wig. She had so long with me until she trusted me.

"And her name again?" the woman asked.

"Alex. I don't know her last name."

Why hadn't I bothered to get that? I bet it was a good one, too. One that fit her like...

"Vaughn? Alex Vaughn. Female. She also put down Alexa when she signed in. Does that sound familiar?"

This woman didn't know it, but she curbed a feeling that hadn't let up since the night I let Alex go, since the night I lost her.

"Uh, yeah," I said, pushing my hand over my mouth. I couldn't believe it. She found her. I mean, it was a possibility this couldn't be her. But I... I just had a feeling. "She goes by Alexa, too."

"I think this is her. She had a wig fitting your early description in her bag. We have to check residents' belongings before we allow them to stay here. Safety precaution, you know? They also have to register and she did without complaint. A very nice girl, she seemed."

My face fell at the words. She said *seemed*, as in past tense.

She continued. "Unfortunately, I was forced to deny her access to the facility a few nights ago."

"How many nights?" I asked, getting a pen to write this all down. Anything would help.

"I'd say about three?" *She could still be here in town.* "She stayed with us one night, but came in late the second. We have a strict curfew here. I'm very sorry."

What she said was all right. She and the shelter she worked for provided safety for Alex for at least a night and I couldn't be mad at that. I lowered my pen. "Do you possibly know where she might have been headed? Did she mention anything or..."

She sighed and I didn't continue. "I'm sorry. We just get so many people here. It's hard to keep track."

But she did have something. A concrete place Alex had been within the last seventy-two hours. I could drive through the area and ask around. I sat back. "Hey, uh, it's okay. You definitely gave me something. This will help."

"I hope you find her. I truly do."

I went to hang up, but then I heard her voice in the receiver so I quickly pulled it back. "I'm sorry. What was that?"

"I just mentioned that she fits the profile."

I frowned, setting my arm on the wheel. "For what exactly, ma'am?"

"A few blocks from here, there's a heavy presence. Prostitution."

She said the words and the world spun, collided. She wouldn't, would she?

But she nearly had before.

"That's why men, pimps, set up shop nearby our facility. They recruit runaways. We're constantly sending the police that way, but it's hard for them to control."

Well, I knew the police, too. I got them on the phone after I hung up with the woman at the shelter. I explained my situation to my guys on the force, where Alex could currently be and what they might have to deal with because of it. They headed that way, telling me to wait before I did the same. Because if I did and I saw her... if someone had taken advantage of how vulnerable she was...

"We're here, Brody," Chad said in my ear. It was a good thing he called. I maybe had a minute left before I did something myself. "It's a real problem area," he continued. "And of course, they all scattered when we got here, but we managed to talk to a couple girls."

My breath was with one of my old friends. My last breath.

"Your girl is working on ninth," he said. "At *Tunnel Vision*."

Tunnel Vision... and then it all settled in. It hit hard. Alex was dancing, but not the type I'd seen at the park that day.

She was stripping.

I'd been to *Tunnel Vision* a few times, bachelor parties and whatever. And I guess if I was being real, a lonely night or two. The difference was I never knew someone dancing there. It made me sick knowing I'd gone in the past now for entertainment.

"You want us to come down?" Chad asked on the phone. "For back up?"

I wanted to do this myself, find her, and make her safe again. She should have always been safe and would be as long as she wanted that. I wouldn't leave her again as long as she needed that from me. Chad and my other friend, Brian, said I could head over as long as I didn't plan on making any trouble. Those folks ran an honest business and they didn't want me in there tearing it up and causing problems—Chad's words not mine. I had no plans to make any trouble and they'd have no problems with me.

As long as they didn't stand in my way.

Keeping my promise, I left my gun in my truck under the seat. I really didn't want any trouble. I just wanted Alex.

I wanted her so bad.

Neon lights greeted my way, *Tunnel Vision's* marquee letting me know I was at the right place. I'd come here before but it wasn't like the bouncers knew my name or something. I waited at the door and paid my cover like anyone else, then went inside.

Smoke and sweat lined the air, burned my eyes a bit and clouded my lungs. The ambience of places like this was always the same. I didn't let myself think about what else was wrapped up in that scent, that sweat, and made my way through the club. Girls in itty-bitty tops and guys downing the shots off the trays they held, blocked my way. I made it through them, declining drinks and girls offering their services with them. One grabbed my arm, hoping to get some money out of me in one of the private rooms in the back. I politely declined and kept moving. I scanned, searched, but I didn't see a girl with nut brown eyes and a sparkle in them. Alex was tall, too, and that would set her apart, but nothing.

"You seem like you're looking for someone, big guy."

A girl in a hot pink wig got my attention, putting her hand on my shoulder. "Can I help you with that?"

I really didn't have time for this, but I didn't want to put her off. I needed to know where Alex was and didn't want to get myself kicked out before I could.

I went to talk this one down as well when a name I wasn't prepared to hear again met my ears. But then it all made sense. She said she was her alter ego.

I understood why when I turned around and watched her dance. Alex swayed her hips, but she wasn't Alex here. She was *Valentine.* The announcer himself had called her in.

She walked around a pole in thick, silver heels. The heels matched what were only flower-shaped pasties on her nipples, her breasts covered in nothing but a fishnet top that pulled down to her thighs and her silver thong left nothing to the imagination below. Her leg around the pole, she flipped, spinning on it. She'd definitely done this before.

It was hard to watch, but not because I was disgusted. Her pupils dilated, she looked so empty, nothing behind her eyes with a twisted smile on her lips. She stumbled when she got off the pole and I knew she had something in her. I didn't know if it was drugs or alcohol.

I couldn't move for some reason. I found it hard to put into action what my next move should be. But then she saw me. She saw me right there in front. Her moves went full stop and with the way she looked at me, fear and hope behind her eyes all at the same time, I didn't stay put for long.

Everything blurred as I approached the stage, grabbed her, and took her in my arms. I faintly heard the girl who spoke behind me, the one with the pink hair. She yelled at me, fists slamming into my arm, but she sounded quiet, far away. I couldn't really hear clearly. I couldn't see anything but Alex, Alex pretty much naked and broken in my arms.

She pressed her face into my chest, rubbing, sighing, and everything was okay. Everything wasn't so bad anymore.

The fists in my arm became more prominent and somehow the girl in pink got through to me.

"Let her go, you fucker!" she shrieked, pulling on my shirt. She yelled, frantic for help. I assumed from the bouncers. She shook me again, trying to get Alex out of my arms. "You put her down and get out of here, you sick fuck!"

But I wouldn't put her down. She was going with me, even if I had to fight my way out of here with her. I felt bad for the promise I made to my friends. I didn't think I could keep that promise. From my peripheral, two large men in black came my way. They were fighting their way through the crowd that had gathered around Alex, me, and the girl in pink.

She tugged at Alex's arm this time, maybe thinking she could get more ground that way until her friends in black got to us. Alex lifted her head at the tug, but she didn't look at her. She looked at me. She looked at me and smiled.

"Brody..." she whispered, so faint. Then she said it again, "Brody."

And the girl let go of her, stepping back. She stepped back when Alex said my name and I was the one that smiled that time. It had only been a few days and I forgot what it felt like to hear my name on her lips, what it felt like to see her smile.

I brushed a finger to her cheek, wanting nothing but to take her away.

"Hey, darlin'," I said to her and she lifted her head.

That smile came back, her eyes closed. A warm sound hummed from her throat and she opened them. "I like when you call me that. I love it."

Her words squeezed my insides with the emotion in them.

"I'm sorry, but I'm going to have to ask you to put the girl down and leave."

I became aware of our audience again. The two bouncers

and now a little guy between them. He was the one who spoke. Dressed in a nice shirt and tie, I assumed he was the owner. The girl in pink stood between them and me. This could go bad very quickly. But I wouldn't be leaving without a fight, without Alex.

I adjusted her, but didn't put her down. "I have no problem leaving, but I'm not doing that without her. I know her and she's coming with me."

This guy laughed, shaking his head. "Put her down or we'll *make* you put her down."

I didn't budge and I knew what would happen next. I could only hope *they* were prepared. I knew how to handle myself when it came to a fight. It wouldn't be my first time being out numbered and my track record was pretty damn good. The guys in black rushed me but the girl in pink held back the charge. Raising her hand, she stopped them, then put the other on Alex's arm. She shook her. "Hey, baby girl. Is this your friend? The one you told me about?"

My eyes widened that she mentioned me, but then again, I never really let her go either. Alex simply grinned and when she pointed at me, her finger wobbly, the fact something was in her system became all too apparent.

"It's Brody," she said, proving she knew me once more, and the girl in pink smiled.

She squeezed Alex's arm. "And do you want to go with him? Brody?"

It only took her a second.

"Please," she said, burying her face into my chest, warming it in so many ways. "Please."

The girl in pink raised her hand, to the bouncers, to the owner, and in response, the owner lifted and lowered his hands. "What the fuck ever. She wasn't pulling her weight anyway. Take her, but you," he paused, pointing at the girl in pink. "You need to get back to work."

I didn't waste my chance. I headed out the way I came, but this time I had Alex. This time, I wasn't letting go. I got outside with her, but it wasn't until I made it to my truck, I noticed we had another companion. The girl in the pink wig flanked us and watched as I got Alex in the passenger seat of my truck. I had a blanket behind my seat and I pulled it out, covering her. I had a feeling she wouldn't want me to see her this way. I made sure she was wrapped up real good before I turned to the girl in pink. She had Alex's sparkly bag. She handed it to me and I took it.

"She's been staying with me," she said, "the last few days."

I nodded. I turned to Alex, the smile and lethargic state she was in not sitting well with me.

"What did she take?" I asked the girl in the wig. After putting Alex's bag in the back and making sure she was secure, I closed the door.

The girl crossed her arms. "I gave her some ecstasy. She said she'd danced before, but she wasn't getting into it like she should, which was pissing off my boss. I told her it would help so she took it at the beginning of her shift. She's starting to come down."

God, what I wouldn't give to go back. I never would have left her at the train station. I'd stranded her. The girl in the wig pulled something out of the pocket of her skirt, a wad of cash. She handed it out to me, tipping her chin toward my truck. "For her. Boss won't pay her now that she's left, but this is what she earned."

I felt weird about accepting this on her behalf, but I did as the girl in the wig seemed insistent about it, shaking it at me. I held it up. "Won't you need this?"

She waved me off. "I'll earn it back. She needs it. She wouldn't say what for, but I know she does."

I think she was right about that and I had a feeling it had something to do with the little guy I spoke to on the phone earlier. I thanked the girl for all her help and she smiled at me.

"Keep a better eye on her this time," she said, backing away.

She wouldn't have to worry about that and Alex wouldn't either.

ALEXA

A SHOT of pain radiated behind my eyes, blasting me awake. I rose and put my hands on my head, hoping to dull it but to no avail. After a moment or two, I opened my eyes to a dark room. Streetlights from outside glowed through the window and the bed I sat in became evident. I lifted the sheet covering me, seeing I was in an oversized shirt...with nothing but my underwear on underneath.

The world tilted then, the pain behind my eyes and the reality of my current situation slamming into me. I was in someone's bed. I was in someone's bed with barely any clothing on and no clear memory of how I got here or even where *here* was. Last I remembered, I had been at the club. It was supposed to have been my last night there, my earnings what I felt finally enough to give me and my family a good shot. We'd have some to live on. But now, someone had taken me...

My stomach twisted, curling in an intense knot. I retched then, covering my mouth, and clawed my way to the edge of the bed. I sought a trashcan, anything I could throw up in. I didn't see one, but then one was placed in front of me when someone rushed into the room. They sat beside me, a big, warm body and I gripped the can, the person who held it barely catching the vomit in time. A healthy amount of stomach bile and whatever food I had in my gut lined the bottom.

The influx of it all hurt, it burned, but I couldn't stop myself. The nausea only aided it and after a while, I couldn't even see the can through my tears. That's when the hand came, gently guiding me as I leaned forward to vomit more. The hand then rubbed me, warming my back in soothing circles. The motion didn't stop, the gesture, and finally, I was able to look up.

The fear left immediately.

Brody smiled, his perfect, pink lips curved up in the corner. Sleep pants covered tree trunk thighs, the rest of him bare as he hovered over me, warming my back.

I lurched again, part of it embarrassment and the other part because I was actually sick, so sick. Sitting there, he stayed with me. He took care of me.

I rose up, wiping off my mouth. Holding my stomach, I craned over the can he held, preparing for the next. The nausea I had was sharp and I didn't know if I could hold back. Managing to do so, I pressed my hand to my brow. "I don't..." I said breathy from the sensation. "I don't feel good."

His lip turned down, his hand lowering from my back.

"One of the side effects," he said, and though I knew he was right, my body never reacted this way before. I'd taken molly a couple times in the past at parties.

But I never mixed it with alcohol like I'd done tonight.

I feel so stupid.

Filling the can again, I shook above it, holding it, and Brody's hand returned to my back. I liked his hand there and I liked his body beside me. I liked how his muscles pierced his skin as he leaned over me and how he made me feel so small yet protected all at the same time.

He caught me staring and leaned back, not so close. I caught sight of his chest and a line there revealed itself. The skin was indented, white. Clearly an old scar, it separated the right side of his chest from the left, right over his heart.

He stood. "Sorry," he said, and I watched as he went to the set of drawers against the wall and retrieved a shirt from the inside. He drew it down his body, covering himself, and then returned, looking apologetic. He rested his hands in his lap. "I don't want to make you uncomfortable or anything." He pointed behind to the open door. "I was just sleeping on the couch and heard you. Sorry."

He didn't have to apologize, but I did wonder what happened to him, how he got such a large scar on his chest. He didn't say and he didn't have time. A wave of nausea hit and I gagged. Brody aimed the can I held in the direction of my mouth. I fought it though, the sensation, and ended up pulling away and keeping it in for now.

"Where am I?" I asked sniffing. My nose was running from all the vomiting. He handed me a tissue, then pressed a cold washcloth he seemed to get out of nowhere to my face.

He dabbed my brow, then my neck. "My place. Still in El Paso."

I found it hard to speak, Brody comforting me so delicately with the towel. I looked around, seeing the subtle living arrangements of the man. He had just what he needed, nothing more, nothing less, and his bed was big, warm.

I faced him. "How did you find me?"

He drew the towel away and poured some water on it from a pitcher located on an end table near the bed. He returned it to my face. His lips lifted into smile. "It was a... something. I had some help though. I called in a favor with some of my buddies. They're on the police force."

The night rushed back to me, broken and banging against my skull. Brody pulling me off the stage. Brody taking me and saving me from myself. How much had he *seen* of me on stage, as Valentine? How much had he...

I stared down, seeing the shirt I wore. Another shirt had fit so loosely on me before. It had been his.

"Did I..." I asked, swallowing. It wasn't the sickness this time. It was a lump, thick in my throat. "Did I *dress* myself?"

He didn't look at me, simply tended to my face as he nodded. "Mmhmm. You showered by yourself, too. I just guided your way."

Honestly, I expected nothing less from him. How ironic that the one person I didn't mind closeness with, an intimacy with, was the one person who wouldn't go there?

He took the towel back, setting it on his lap. "How do you feel?"

Thinking about my ailments, I took inventory, the piercing throb behind my head ever prominent. "My head hurts. And the nausea." I moved the can and realized my limbs felt heavy as well. I also had no idea if I felt exhausted because of all the vomiting or the ecstasy... the alcohol. I'd never gotten this sick before but a combination of what I had in my system made sense. It was the only way I could dance though. I couldn't get out of my head on stage. I kept thinking about deep blue eyes and what they'd think if they saw me.

I sighed, rubbing my own. I fought the ache behind them and so much more.

Brody lifted his hand, moving my way again, but then he stopped, hesitant. Eventually, he went on and when he did, returned it to my back. He rubbed like he had before, massaged, and I felt like liquid, the gesture helping in so many ways.

"You should rest," he said. "You have to be exhausted. I'm

sure the drugs kept you dancing all night despite what energy you actually had."

Yeah, it had. That was the point I guess.

"It's just after four," he continued. "Go ahead and try to get some more sleep…"

The words had me moving and he followed me with his gaze. With shaking limbs, I clawed my way to the end of the bed and nearly fell to the floor when I got to the edge. I was so weak, but I didn't care. Brody grabbed my shoulders, preventing the fall. "Alex—"

"It's Aiden!" I screamed, struggling to work my way out of his hands. "I have to call him. I always call him and I didn't call!"

It was the drugs. The drugs fucked with me and made me forget. I had to call him. He'd be so worried. I managed to get out of Brody's grasp and off the bed, but as soon as I did, I fell to my knees. I had no energy, but I didn't stop trying, pushing myself up, and Brody got me the rest of the way. He lifted me, getting me to my feet, and I only stopped struggling when he placed warm hands to my cheeks and stared into my eyes.

I was so tired I couldn't even keep the eye contact.

Sagging, I leaned my head against his chest and he brought his arms around me, saying something that couldn't be true. "He's okay," he kept saying. "He's fine. I talked to him."

I looked up, not thinking I heard him right. I couldn't have. He didn't know about Aiden. I never told him. I never got a chance to. But then he nodded, smiling as he pushed my short hair out of my eyes.

"Yeah," he confirmed. "I talked to him. Twice actually. He called me on my phone looking for you late last night. But once I got you, I knew you wouldn't be able to talk to him until you rested some of this off. I called him back. I covered. He's okay. I promise."

But how? No, he wouldn't be, and Brody, he couldn't

possibly understand. He didn't know why Aiden couldn't sleep.

I pulled back, shaking my head. "No. He gets nightmares, Brody. He won't—"

His hand kept my head from shaking. His other joined my cheek and he lowered to my level. "He's fine, Alex. I read him a story. He went right to sleep."

I blinked and his gentle laughter sounded. He pushed a thumb behind him. "I read him one of my niece's books. My brother's kid. I keep 'em for her when she comes over."

What he said had me at a loss. It wasn't possible. *He* wasn't possible. But he was standing here and he was taking care of all people—me.

He smiled at me. "I was only a temp, though. You gotta call him right away tomorrow. He made a drawing for you at school and wants to tell you about it himself. He sounded excited about it."

I nodded, not knowing what else to say. As it turned out, I didn't have to say anything at all.

Taking my hand, Brody brought me back to the bed and sat me down. He left and came back with two bottles of water. He set both by the bed. "These will keep you hydrated. You should drink when you can."

I nodded again and sat back to the baseboard, his baseboard. He went to the curtains and closed whatever light had been allowed in the room. It helped with my head. His outline went toward the door. He looked to leave, opening it and letting a little light in from the hallway, but him doing so made that thick ball gather in my throat again. And I didn't think it was because I was sick.

"Can you stay?" I found myself asking, begging. "It's just... I feel disoriented and I don't know if I can sleep..."

He didn't let me finish. He simply went to his closet, his figure pulling something out of it. A bundle ended up in his hands and when he placed it on the floor, laying it out, I assumed he'd take his position right there and sleep on the floor nearby.

The room went silent after he settled in, quiet. Pulling back the covers, I got back underneath them, settling in myself, and moments later, I heard his voice again.

"Let me know if you need anything," he said. "I'm not leaving. I'll be here."

I did need something, and as it turned out, he never left me.

Sixteen

BRODY

She rested the next twenty-four hours or so. She couldn't really do much else, she was so exhausted. I kept her hydrated, kept her comfortable, and by midday, she was able to eat some lighter stuff I had around my trailer and nothing that would upset her stomach too much. So weak, she hadn't even been able to leave the bedroom that day, but that hadn't been all bad. It hadn't because she was here, because she was safe, and the around-the-clock care didn't matter.

It didn't bother me at all.

I added an extra blanket while she slept. Something else she took up was chills around late afternoon.

She snuggled in. "I need to call Aiden," she whispered, drifting off. "I can't fall asleep."

I smiled. Taking a seat on the edge of the bed, I reached over to get the blanket completely around her. "Sleep. I'll wake you before your watch goes off."

I couldn't deny the smile on her lips, but then it faded, sleep taking her away from me.

Shifting, I went to move, but her head fell, leaning against my side. My arm was still in midair, ready to go and leave her to her peace, but I found myself settling in. I told myself that I moved a leg up to the bed not to wake her, then the other for the same reason. I sat there for a moment, my stomach doing crazy things and I confirmed the lie to myself.

Her arm slid around my waist then, absentmindedly, and this felt like it was going too far. She wasn't awake and me being here like this was pushing things. I went to move.

"Thank you," she said, sighing as she brushed her head against my side. "For waking me later. For everything."

I placed a hand on her arm, rubbing away those chills. I guess I wouldn't be moving right away after all.

Mr. Michaels, my boss, sighed on the other end of the line. I gathered I'd get this response after my request. And truth be told, the man was a douche and I expected nothing less than his annoyance at my legal right to use my vacation time.

"The whole thing?" he asked, sighing again. "You want to use your entire leave?"

Honestly, I'd use more if I could for this, for her. I think I knew what I was going to do the moment after I woke her last night and gave her my phone for her call. But hearing the soft words outside the door only solidified my decision today. I couldn't help hearing, the walls of my childhood home were so thin. I heard an aunt on the phone with her nephew, reassuring him that she'd be with him in days. But that wasn't all I heard, no. I also heard a strong woman in that room, one who'd do just about anything to keep that promise to that little boy. I knew she would because I'd seen firsthand what she was willing to do to get to him.

I rubbed my hand down my mouth, taking a seat at the kitchen table. Pop never could get us all in here to eat at the same time. He'd always give up and we'd eat in the living room around the TV.

"Yeah. I'll need the full ten days," I told Mr. Michaels now. It was decided. This trip was something I had to do.

"Fine, Brody. But you only get ten days. You take anymore and you know what happens."

Yeah, I did. I wouldn't have a job anymore.

I stressed to my boss that I understood and then gratefully let the man go. I headed back to my bedroom, but when I got there it was empty one sleeping girl. I scanned the trailer and it didn't take me long to find Alex. My pops' old place was pretty nice and spacious despite the trailer set up, but still, it wasn't that large.

She stood in the hallway, staring up at the wall ahead of her. Lifting her arm, the sleeve of the t-shirt I loaned her fell back to her shoulder, the length unable to conceal her shape, her smooth, brown legs as they were so long underneath it.

Leaning against the wall, I watched her, though a slight darkness under her eyes, she looked so much better this morning and I was so grateful. I'd never tell her, but she gave me a scare through the rough of it. I'd been around people who'd taken ecstasy before as I used to party a lot in my late teens and early twenties, but never had I seen such a harsh reaction. Yeah, this girl was definitely a fighter to be standing here so put together in front of me. No doubt about that. My gaze so focused on her, I didn't realize what I caught her doing. She touched the frame of a photograph, one from when I was a kid.

I joined her and got the warmest glance when she looked up at me.

"Your family?" she asked, turning to stare up at the photo of my brothers and me. The picture was an old one, too, Hayden standing behind my eight-year-old self with his hand on my shoulder, young himself at eleven. By my feet sat Griffin, on his knees in a set of blue coverall shorts. He hated the shit out of this picture. The kicker was Colton, barely one, in my arms. It was one of the rare moments when he wasn't screaming his head off at the lady behind the camera. I remembered so much that day. Maybe because it was just a nice memory or something, all of us being together and all that.

"Yeah, that's us," I said, folding my arms over my chest with a smile. "Nothing but a bunch of little trouble makers for my pop."

The photo of him took her attention next, a candid as he didn't like posed photos. He played basketball with Hayden, Griff, and me. We were in our teens and preteens and Colton played with his own ball off to the side of our neighborhood court with Gram. The man really set us up to be lovers of the game. Aunt Robin took this photo, I believed.

"You all look so happy," Alex said, reaching out toward that photo now. "So perfect."

She caught us at a good time, a time when Pop finally could root us in one place after seeking work for so many years. He'd worked for *Carter's* almost two years in that photo. It had been a time we all could breathe easy, the sadness of Mom in the days behind us instead of lingering over us. No, we didn't get over losing her. We never would, but we did move past it, and we'd done it together.

I drew in behind Alex, closer to the photo yes, but also closer to her.

Her head dipped before looking up at me. She pivoted, and then she was in front of me, a finger brush away.

"You look better," I told her. She looked more than that. So much more.

Her lips lifted, a slight pink hue to the fullness. She pushed a hand into her hair. "I didn't do it alone."

I had helped her get there, but *she* had the true fight in her. I wanted to touch her, just pull her in like I did at the night club a couple nights ago. But then, I remembered how I found her, and how that evening definitely hadn't seemed like her first time exotic dancing.

What wasn't she telling me? About herself? About Aiden and her need to get to him? The answers I might not like, but if she'd share them with me, I'd be more than willing to lend an ear or hand if she needed the help. Reaching out, I gave her that hand, but I had a feeling it was more for me than her.

She watched coming closer and her hand joined mine, right on the top, and gave my stomach that funny feeling once again.

"You want to go get some food?" I asked her, thinking she might want to get outside for a bit. "If your stomach's up for it, that is?"

Her gaze lingered on the simple hold we had on each other. Her thumb brushed the back of my hand and my lips lifted when she nodded.

I took Alex to one of those cafes in downtown El Paso, the ones where the drink glasses were all a different style and the menu had hard to pronounce entrees. Broken down, the words usually translated to soups and sandwiches, which I figured would do right by Alex's stomach. I knew about the place because my younger brothers wanted to go there one time, college boys or what have you. I figured it'd be a nice place for Alex to go to as well. It was colorful and nice on the eyes.

I opened the door for her with a chime and allowed her to go in before me. Eleven o'clock on a weekday, not many folks were dining just yet. Alex passed me, taking her seat at a booth, and I took mine across from her. She wore these shorts she got from her bag, a tank top, and tennis shoes. They must have been something she got while she'd been gone, and... she took my gaze like something crazy. She looked so simple, so perfect.

She caught me staring and her menu went in front of her

eyes. Like she was shy or something. The waitress penned down our order moments later. Alex got soup and a salad while I chose a sandwich. We finally had time alone and I reached into my pocket, taking out what I owed her. I pushed the wad of cash her way and she picked it up, sighing.

She chewed her lip. "Brody, I can't take anything more from you. Money especially. It just doesn't feel right."

She got it all wrong and that made sense. I placed my hands on the table. "It's actually yours," I said, pointing at the stack. "Your friend at the club, the one in the pink wig? She said it was, uh, your earnings. She wanted me to give it to you."

Her fingers toyed with the bills and her expression changed, sad instead of happy like I thought she'd be at getting what was hers. Setting it on the table, she did a quick feather through with her fingers and shook her head.

"What's up?" I asked her.

She faced me. "It's too much. I never earned this much the other nights."

She caught on quickly and I knew I had to explain.

Tapping my fists on the table, I sat back. "It's not just from the club."

Her eyes narrowed. "I don't understand."

"It's from Chloe," I said, coming right out with it. There wasn't a point in beating around the bush here. "What she took from you. She told me everything."

I watched her hard, trying to get into her headspace. But like many times before, Alex proved to be an extra careful concealer, of everything, her emotions and all.

She put her hand to her mouth. "I don't know what to say."

The thing is, I did. So much, really. I started with this. "You should have told me, Alex. You had me thinking..." I didn't want to finish. I couldn't stomach the words what she'd allowed me to believe about her, that she was even capable of stealing. "What she did to you was wrong and because of it, had you thinking you needed to..."

I could hear myself getting frustrated, with Chloe and with myself for getting all riled up because of her. I looked up and Alex's expression had me feeling so much worse, her eyes cringing.

"For what, Brody?" she asked, sitting back. "For thinking I had to what?"

I didn't understand the question as the answer I felt obvious. "For the other night. She pushed you into a corner for money."

Her arms folded over her chest. I had seen Alex closed off before. I found her that way, but even then wasn't like this. She shut down. She felt far away all of a sudden and I had no idea why.

She played with her water glass. "You think better of me than I am," she said, nodding with it. "I've done this before, Brody. Danced. So many times."

The words didn't surprise me. Though, she didn't look comfortable up there, she did know her way around the stage. I leaned in. "Anything you've done is whatever you felt you needed to do to survive, Alex. To get by and I get that. I respect that."

She pressed her lips together, looking on the cusp of shedding tears I had only heard on the road before, never right in front of me. I reached across the table, for her hand, to touch her, but I didn't make it far. The waitress came back with our order, placing my sandwich and chips in front of me and her order in front of her. I thanked her and she left, but I just stared at my food, losing my appetite all of a sudden. Alex didn't reach for her order either and I was ninety percent sure that didn't have anything to do with her stomach. She was just so guarded and she didn't have to be. I'd never judge her, ever, and I had a strong feeling all *this*, everything weaved up inside her wasn't just about her, but a little boy a couple states away.

"You dancing..." I started, thinking about how to word what I had to say next. There was no easy way. "You dancing or anything else you've had to do for money is okay—"

"It's only dancing," she said, breathing. She played with her napkin. "It's only ever been dancing. What you saw me doing, what you *found* me doing when we met, I'd never done before. That's was the first time, Brody. I swear. I've also sold drugs, but that was back in New York when things when got really bad. With that guy at the diner, I had nothing and he offered and I needed it. I needed it so bad for us—"

Her own words, she silenced. She didn't finish, but I had a feeling I knew where she was going. Kind of like I'd had a feeling about her. I had a feeling she had never tried to sell herself before that night. What she said only confirmed it. But what was going on? What all was she keeping in about her and...

Folding my hands, I rested them on the table. "How did your call go?" I dared to ask her, thinking this was exactly where I needed to go with the conversation. "Last night with your nephew?"

This hit a trigger like I knew it would. It hit because it was something personal. I'd heard some of what she and her nephew exchanged faintly through the door, but nothing of note. I just knew Aiden wanted her to come home so bad, urgently, and with what she was willing to do in order to make that happen, red flags were definitely set off with me.

Alex only shook her head in response, but that made me want to push more as she didn't look any closer to holding her tears back. In fact, they looked on the cusp of spilling over at any moment.

"Is he okay?" I asked, going there. "Aiden. Is he all right?"

Her arms folded over her chest and she whispered, "I don't know."

The words absolutely chilled me. I swallowed. "Why? Is he hurt? Is he in danger? Alex…"

I lost her again when she looked away, but she couldn't escape this time. No, I wouldn't let her. I grabbed her hand, holding it and keeping her here with me.

I squeezed. "I want to help you, but I can't do that if I don't know what I'm dealing with."

Her bottom lip slid into her mouth. She nibbled on it. "I can't ask that of you. Your help? I can't take another thing, Brody. Not another damn thing."

"You didn't ask," I told her, urging the statement. "You didn't, so if something's wrong I need you to tell me. I need you to let me help."

Her hand clenched in a tight fist on the table, so I slid over, taking that one, too. What I didn't expect was her to be holding something I hadn't seen in so long. She opened her hand and square in the middle, sat the mood ring I gave her on the road. She never got rid of it. She had it this whole time.

I placed my hand on top of it, holding hers underneath.

Please let me help you.

"There's a guy," she said, like she heard my silent plea. "There's a man."

It wasn't much but it was something. "Aiden's dad?"

She shook her head. "Aiden's dad is in jail. Has been since he was born. Real winners my sister chooses."

One thing the man did do was bring her nephew into this world and that could only be fate. I squeezed her hands and she continued.

"He was a guy who gave a good illusion. He was perfect." She paused, laughing a little. "My sister doesn't draw people like that. She never draws good people. She's such a mess."

"What happened?" I had a feeling I might not want the answer, but that didn't mean I didn't need it.

Her lips went tight. "He turned out to be a bad guy. A bad guy that did bad things and went to jail for them. But before that, he worked his way in. He got to her, my sister. He got her to trust him. He got *me* to trust him and think he was different. Growing up, my sister and I didn't have much. Our mom's serving time for drugs. Our dad, we have no idea where he is."

What she said wasn't easy to hear, not at all, and I hated we had as much in common as we did. We both grew up without a biological mother in our lives.

"And then, my sister had Aiden," she went on. "He was our only good thing. But even with him, he couldn't keep my sister and I from butting heads. We fought all the time, about the bills, her boyfriends. She had this one that spent all our rent money on drugs and she got high right alongside him. She even let him take the money set aside for Aiden's diapers one day, Brody," she paused, shaking her head. "The baby's diapers. I couldn't take it and she couldn't take the nagging from her *younger* sister. She kicked me out and I pretty much couch surfed through middle school."

She was so young to be on her own, just a baby herself.

"But then this guy came in," she said, folding her hands on the table. "He came in and made things different. My sister didn't get high anymore. She was responsible with her money. She even asked me to move back in just before high school. I would have too, but I got into a fine arts school on the coast for dancing. I was given a scholarship and boarding, doing things I thought were impossible, and my sister and this guy were so supportive. He even drove her and Aiden up to my recitals. He never missed one and looked happy to do it, to be there. He was just so nice. He was perfect until he wasn't."

Her voice cracked then, broke down, and choking, she got it back.

"I didn't see the bruises, Brody," she said, her eyes glassing. "I didn't see them. She always hid them when I saw her, and Aiden... he kept quiet for *years*."

My face blazed, and my hands in hers, I tried to keep them from shaking at this guy's cowardice. Because that's what a man was, a coward, to ever lay his hands on a woman.

"Did he hurt Aiden?" I asked, and I didn't know how I managed to voice the question. My right mind had left the moment she admitted what this fucker did. "Did he ever—"

"No." She sniffed. "Not him. I asked. He never laid hands on him, but did just as much damage. It would always happen the same time every night. He'd get off work, get home from the bar super late, and my baby..." She finally let it go then, her tears. "I thought Aiden just called to talk to me, Brody. But he called because he was in the closet as that man beat the shit out of my sister. And he still calls every night long after because of the nightmares."

I closed my eyes. The watch. Her watch. He needs a call the same time every night.

How fucked up...

"And he never told you?" I asked her. "Aiden, never told you what was going on?"

She shook her head. "I think he was just scared. He was just so small then. A little thing."

Letting out a breath, I relieved some anger no matter how little. "How did you find out?"

"My sister was good at hiding it, but she couldn't do it forever. I figured it out when she, Aiden, and I went to the beach. She admitted everything, but she wouldn't leave him. She wouldn't. She said she loved him and I told her if she didn't do it for herself, she had to do it for Aiden. She still didn't listen. She wouldn't tell. She stayed silent."

A single tear dropped from her cheek then and her hands were the ones that started shaking in mine this time.

"Alex?"

Her lashes blinked up. "She stayed silent, but I did something. I did something and he's in jail now for the bad things he did. At least, I thought he was."

I didn't understand, but she went on.

"After he started his sentence, my sister and I had a falling out. Any good relationship we'd developed after she got clean just wiped away as if it never happened. She blamed me for putting her boyfriend there. Pissed off, hurt, I went to New York and left California behind me. I thought I could make it out there. I danced so well in school. I really thought I could make it and knew it'd be the only shot I'd have at working out my problems with my sister. If I made something for myself, provided for her and Aiden both, I could pull them out of California and we could all just start over. We'd be a family and..."

Pushing our hands together, I rubbed hers. She didn't have to keep going with this and I hated to hear the pain in her voice. Eventually, I had to hear more.

"But it didn't work out that way," she whispered swallowing. "Days passed, *months* in which I couldn't find work. All the good leads I had going in fell through and no auditions led to anything worthwhile. I was stuck, couldn't pay my rent, and ended up dancing in nightclubs just to keep a roof over my head. But then those clubs turned into exotic ones and when I wasn't doing that, I was hustling and selling all kinds of things I'm not proud of. I almost came home so many times, my tail between my legs, but I chickened out every time. I guess it was my pride. But one day, I got a call from him, Aiden. A call that changed everything."

I was afraid to ask the extent. "What did he say?"

Her hand moved over her hair, lowering to her neck. "He

said he called. The guy. He called asking for my sister, Elena. They'd moved since he and Elena were together and a guy with a similar sounding voice called one day asking about my sister. Aiden wouldn't say anything to him, though. He was silent after the initial hello and ended up hanging up on him. He called me immediately after. Aiden thought he might be back. He thought he might be *out*."

I let out a breath, all this so much to take in. "But there could be a chance he's not back? He could have called your sister from the inside, and Alex, that might not even have been him on the phone. Aiden could have been mistaken."

She shook her and my gut did nothing but turn. "I looked him up. He was up for parole, and..."

He could get out and go for the family he believed sent him there.

"He's out, Brody," she said, nearly shaking. "It's all public record. He's out and I'm scared. What if he finds them? And when he does, what if he doesn't just go for Elena this time? What if he goes for Aiden?"

And she was going to take on all this alone, go to California into God only knew what. Alex, she was resourceful no doubt about that. But the odds were definitely stacked against her here.

I pushed my hand through my hair. "And you said, he hasn't come around yet?"

"Not that I know of. Aiden would have told me."

That was good, so good. But one other thing concerned me and that was her sister. She said her turning this guy in led to their falling out. What if she went all the way there and she was only met with resistance?

"What if your sister doesn't want the help?" I asked her, hating that I had to. But with what she told me, it was a possibility. "What if you get all the way there only for her to turn you away? What if she wants to be with this guy still?" It hurt to say because all women deserved more than that, but sometimes, they didn't realize that with the rest of the world.

"She won't," she said, way too quickly, and because she had, the words felt more wishful than certain.

I tapped my hands on the table. "How do you know, Alex?"

Her gaze left me then, out the window and to the late morning traffic. She blinked. "Because her life got so much better after they moved," she said. "And..." Her eyes fluttered away again and never returned this time. She chewed her lip. "She knows that and she told me if he ever came back, she'd do the right thing this time. She told me that. She told me that."

I wanted to question her, because with her story, that didn't seem to be the outcome that resulted from the falling out between she and her sister. I had no reason not to believe her, though. She hadn't given me one.

"So I'm going to go," she continued. "I'm going to go. I'm going to warn her and get her and Aiden out of there for a while. However long we need."

"No, you won't," I told her, my voice not faltering at all with the statement. "At least, not alone you aren't. I can't let you do that. Not by yourself."

"Brody—"

"Alex," I said. I wouldn't argue with her about this. This was a battle I refused to let up on. I squeezed her hands. "I'll take you. I'll get you there to Aiden and your sister. I worked the leave out with my job. It's done."

Her beautiful eyes settled on me, narrowed and hard in their gaze. She shook her head. "But why?" she asked, surprising me. "Why are you doing this? Why do you *keep* doing this? Helping me?"

The answer was something I felt was obvious, but I did her one better, bringing her hands together in mine. "Why don't you feel like you deserve it? The help?"

Her hand went underneath her eye again, then the other. She sniffed, looking away, and I kept on.

"Alex, I know I don't know you very well and because of that, this all might seem crazy. But the thing is, it doesn't to me. It doesn't at all and in fact, it makes nothing but sense."

Pausing, I lifted her hand. Inside, she still held that ring and I opened it, letting her see.

"*This* makes sense," I told her, lifting my gaze to her. I closed her hand in mine. "It just does and I... I want to help. Anyway I can and it doesn't have to be more than that. I want to help and I want you to let me."

I put it all out there, quite literally *everything*. I think I knew how I felt for a while now, about this girl that came to me in the night. Especially, after almost losing her.

"Let me help you," I urged; I stressed. "Let me do this with you."

She stared at my hands covering hers, the mood ring between us. I had no idea what color it was, but had a feeling if she looked at it, it would say everything she needed to know. I could feel it touching more of my hand than hers.

"Okay," she said, looking up at me. And then, a smile touched her lips, a smile I wanted so bad to lean over and cover with a kiss.

But I settled for my own: "Okay."

Seventeen

ALEXA

BRODY FELT confident he could get us to the coast in just under two days time. Not as fast as the train, but he said having a form of transportation on hand wouldn't be a bad thing. I trusted him, so I agreed.

I trusted him. I hadn't been able to do that for so long I wondered if I still knew how, but the minute Brody came around? It all felt natural. Being with him felt natural. Had that been what he meant at the cafe? About us making sense to him?

My gaze found him from the corner of my eye, his one hand on the wheel, and his other on mine, holding my hand like he'd done before. We just kind of fell into that when we got into his truck, naturally, and I didn't turn him away.

In fact, I welcomed it.

His hand in mine didn't feel like he wanted something from me. It felt like he was giving something, support, and I think that's exactly what it was. He knew I had a lot on my plate right now; Aiden and everything else. There was a barrier there, one he created, and that probably was best. My mind was so overwhelmed, I didn't know if I could give anything else and he understood that.

He always did the right thing.

I took what we had for what it was and we traveled for miles while we did, him telling his stories. I missed his stories so much. This was him trying to keep the mood light. In fact, he did most of the talking while I just listened and he even let me hold his phone in my lap just in case Aiden called. He really was great, so great. We stopped only two times in six hours, pulling over for the normal stuff, a rest stop or a restaurant to eat. We went another three before our next stop and the anxiousness shook my legs. We were about to hit state lines, something I'd been trying to do for so long. I felt like I'd been traveling months instead of weeks and Brody made that happen. I actually thought he'd push us through, drive through the night on our final leg, but he took an exit after our last rest stop. We'd only been driving an hour.

I looked over at him and got nothing but a smile and squeeze to my hand.

"What's going on?" I asked him, but I wasn't worried. Like I said, I trusted him. I believed in him.

He turned the wheel, steering down the exit ramp. "Giving you a break from your head."

I shook it then, not understanding.

His head tipped back with his laugh, the bill of his hat revealing his eyes. He glanced my way. "I've been watching you off and on all day, Alex. You need to get out of your head. You need to have some fun."

Fun? Still, I didn't understand. "Shouldn't we just push through? We're really making ground today."

"*Today* is now this evening. Did you notice?"

That sunset in the horizon showed me I hadn't. I really was stuck in my head.

The truck pushed back into traffic off the exit, the steady

stream of a small town instead of the fast pace of a highway. "I was going to pull us over for the night anyway in a couple miles and this 'fun,'" he paused, nodding with it, "will just be a side trip. I saw some signs on the road advertising it. If you're game, I'll take you."

I really didn't want to stop, but if he was going to stop anyway...

And then there was the way those blue eyes looked at me, drawing me in and everything.

His smile made me do the same, and so with that, I let him take me to "fun." And what did fun end up being? A small carnival in the middle nowhere. Lights flashed the air and electric music coordinated with it.

My jaw went slack at the bright set up. "Are you serious?" I hadn't been to one of these in so long.

His simply winked at me. "As a heart attack. It's time to let Valentine out tonight."

His reference to my stage name made me snort and after that, it turned into full-blown laugher. He came around to my side, holding out his hand.

I could only accept.

He tossed his hat in the back before we left, musing his hair all up and making it all sexy. And he was sexy. That couldn't be denied. Anybody could be that though, but not everyone could be Brody with his big heart.

Once we got to the gate, he paid my admission to my protest. I felt I had a running total with him already.

He pulled me in, lowering. "Relax, okay? Just have fun."

I'd sure try. After getting us a stack of tickets, we scoped out the area. This place was sure bustling for a tourist trap.

"Games, rides, or greasy food, darlin'?" he asked, staring down at me with a smile.

God, he could have anything he wanted from me, couldn't he? I decided on food because I thought that's what he might like. He was so big, I figured he'd always need it. I got chicken on a stick while he took advantage of the behemoth sized turkey legs the food truck had.

"Damn," he said, sizing it up. "I'm going to regret this later, but it's going to hurt so good."

I giggled, taking a bite of my chicken. I'd probably regret this just as much as him. We took our meat on a stroll when some taunting came at us from the right.

"Look at this chump," said a clown with white oil paint on his face. He sat in a dunk tank, screaming into his microphone. "Guy probably couldn't hit a parked car to win a stuffed animal for his girl."

Looking around, no one was behind Brody and me. Brody's finger went to his chest.

"Yeah, you sucka!" the clown went on, chuckling. "You get three tries for six tickets."

Brody eyed me, pushing his thumb behind him at the tank. "Highway robbery this guy."

He was definitely a character, but he called me Brody's girl, he couldn't be all that bad.

"C'mon, man! Things aren't getting any dryer over here. Don't be a wuss."

The clown proved to be very vocal, but Brody, the guy that he was, took it in good stride. Heading over to the booth, he paid for the tickets, accepting the balls for his shots. "Highway robbery," he said one last time, then, rearing back, he took his first shot. A sharp hit slammed the wall with the target, but landed just off to the right.

The clown cringed for Brody. "Ooo... Close but no cigar."

Brody pointed at him. "You're an asshole, my friend," he said, with a laugh. "But I got you."

The clown let out a roar. "Go for it. I'm willing to let you prove me wrong."

And so he attempted again, close, but the ball fell without

accomplishing its mission. The third shot failed just as the first two and the clown had a field day with that. I covered my mouth, trying not to laugh as Brody's run ended with defeat.

He took my hand in his, looking a little sour. "Come on. We're not giving this guy any more of our money."

"I want to try," I said, surprising him. His eyebrows flashed and I went off to the side, paying for a shot with three tickets. I prepared, looking for my angle, and when I pulled back, I let the ball fly. It hit the target with a thud and the clown slid off his seat into the water with a large splash. Sputtering, he came up with his red wig draping his face. He took it all in good stride though and the attendant who sold us our tickets for the shots aimed her arms at the prize wall. I picked my prize, then returned to a shocked Brody, his blue eyes wide like saucers.

I handed him the big, brown bear I chose. "A big bear for the big guy."

He laughed, shaking his head at me. Once he settled down, he nodded, taking the bear.

"Okay, so now that you made me look like a punk bitch, I need to redeem myself," he said, eyeing the games. My hand was back in his and he pulled me over to the game with basketballs and hoops. He had to get so many shots in so little time, that I worried for his pride. This would be tough.

He pulled back already short sleeves, revealing his biceps. "I'm gonna make quick work of this, darlin.' Just you watch now."

I wasn't confident but I humored him, so imagine my surprise when not only did he make the shots he needed in the few seconds he had, but he made *every* shot. One after the other, he sunk baskets like he was on the court instead of at a small carnival. Once he was done, he let me pick a prize and the bear I got ended up being bigger than the one I gave him.

"You're kidding." I blinked, shocked by what he told me

moments later. We were on the Ferris Wheel now. "Your brother is a professional basketball player?"

Brody merely gave that throaty chuckle, deep from his broad chest. He draped an arm behind the back of our car, the Ferris Wheel giving us both a wide view of the tiny carnival. Multi-colored lights glittered around us, lighting up the darkening sky. He looked my way. "The kid had to get it from somewhere."

I kicked his ankle across from me. His date for the evening was a big brown teddy, mine a tan colored one next to me. I giggled. "Modest much?"

He threw his head back, those blond strands flowing over his eyes when he came back. "My pop had us all playing at the rec center. It kept us all out of trouble and we made friends, too, so that was a bonus." He shrugged. "It was good times."

From his photos, his family seemed to have a lot of good times. What would that be like having so much and being so close? I loved my sister, but things sure had been hard for us; between us. Brody didn't go on and I noticed he never mentioned his mom in this equation of family. I also didn't see her in the family photo, only an older woman. I wondered if she was around. Not wanting to get too heavy, I left that alone. We were supposed to have a good time tonight and there was so much I didn't know about this guy. This kind guy that came to my rescue so many times.

He reached for my cotton candy and I gave him some. I loved sharing with him. "So why don't you play?" I asked.

A shoulder lifted as he shook his head. "I didn't have a passion for it. That's Griff's thing, the one who plays professionally. The baby of us is on that track, too. His name is Colton. I don't know. That's just not what I wanted to do."

I ate some of the blue fluff, letting it evaporate in my mouth. I went to ask him another question, but the candy hadn't fully dissolved yet. Brody noticed and his smile went in my direction. I covered my mouth with a laugh, wiping it right after. "Is truck driving your thing then?" I went on. "Traveling?"

"Nah, not really. It just pays the bills, you know?"

He had said that to me before, at the bar. I crossed my legs. "What do you want to do then?"

He sat back in the chair, his fingers dangling over the side-bars absentmindedly. He didn't answer the question right away and I didn't know why. Maybe he simply didn't know what he wanted to do yet. He was young, not much older than me.

His eyes narrowed, his gaze far away, but then he came back to me with that boyish grin of his.

"Would it be weird if I said anything I want?" he asked, and I shook my head. I think that's what we all wanted in the end. But it was an interesting response to the question. He stared off again. "Do you want to check that out before we leave?"

His added finger point took my attention below, down to a brightly colored building with abstract angles, a fun house. I was game if he was. We waited for the full rotation of our ride to conclude, then headed toward the house, my bear in my arms with Brody's under his. But getting closer my steps slowed, the lack of line evident. Usually that meant something if all the other rides were packed. We even had to wait ten minutes to get on the Ferris Wheel.

I touched Brody's arm and he stopped. "Should we do this? I mean, there's nobody here waiting. That usually means something, doesn't it?"

He set blue eyes on me. "This going to be too much for you or somethin,' Alex? This is a funhouse. I don't think anything in there will get you."

I scoffed, shaking my head. "Nothing's too much for me to handle."

His eyes crinkled in the corner at that, smiling with his lips. "I definitely know that." In the next moment, he slid my bear out from under my arm, then took his and mine both to the ticket guy. "Can you watch these for us, fella? We're going to take a round in the house."

The guy looked uninterested, but did take the bears, placing them behind his podium before taking our tickets. Brody's hand went out behind him, for mine, and I took it more than willingly.

He guided me inside through a striped hamster wheel, helping me keep my footing before we crossed it and went behind a dark curtain. All lights went off immediately and my heart did jump a bit.

"Don't lose me." I laughed, squeezing his hand.

He squeezed back. "Can't happen. Just stay close."

I did, putting my hand on a warm back. He stopped for a moment and my hand rested there. For just a moment though, just a moment. He went on and I got a glimpse of him. Strobe lights hit his big body and I shook my head at all the flashing.

"You all right back there, Alex?" he asked, pulling me forward.

"I'm glad I don't have epilepsy," I joked, tugging his hand.

"Right. Let's get out of this. We're moving. Watch your step."

A wooden step caused me to take one, leading up to five more. The stairs led to our first lit room, one all trippy with jagged angles. A set of house furniture was nailed to the top, giving the illusion we were in an upside down home.

I nudged his arm when I got beside him. "Aren't you glad you made me come in?" I joked, bumping him at how cheesy the set up was.

He rolled his eyes, but did take it in good stride. We went through a few more rooms, some really lame and some just trying too hard to entertain. We finally came to a house of mirrors, multiplying me ten times over, and I laughed at the abstract distortions. One made me look fifty feet tall and another a short, stubby thing. I put my hands out, placing them on the glass.

"This room is a little better," I said behind me. It was interesting seeing the different angles. I didn't hear a response though. I turned around and only saw myself in another mirror, then another when I took a step.

"Brody?" I called. I didn't remember losing his hand. I must have been distracted. I cupped my mouth. "Brody, where are you?"

Still nothing. I didn't know what to think. He was probably just trying to play a joke on me. I shook my head at the thought, placing my hands on my hips. "If you're trying to scare me, it's not going to work. I told you I can handle anything."

More silence and I couldn't get over how weak this attempt was to freak me out. He probably planned to jump out at any moment. I cupped my mouth again. "Brody, if you don't come out right now and quit playing around, I won't speak to you for the rest of this trip."

I had no plans to honor that of course. I just wanted him to come out, and to my surprise, he did right after the words left my lips. I thought he'd at least drag his joke out for a few more minutes, but he didn't. He came out, approaching me, and once he did, he didn't stop until he was in front of me. He got close—so close.

My breaths went shallow and I swallowed to get them right. "Why did you come out? I thought you'd carry this on for a minute or two."

His chest moved rapidly and I knew his breaths were short, too. He drew in even closer, blond lashes flicking down. "Because you asked me to," he said, and so direct, the statement couldn't be anything but true. He raised his hand and my gaze followed. His fingers went to my arm, cupping my shoulder before touching my neck. "You were just joking about that, right?" He gave a crooked smile. "About not talking to me."

I swallowed once more. "Correct."

His fingers didn't move another inch, but his body did. A warm chest touched mine and then a familiar mouth returned to my lips, one I only remembered in my dreams, it had been so long since I touched it, since he touched me. He kissed with vigor, hard and fast, and didn't pull back after a few moments like he had at the bar, no.

And I didn't pull back either.

An ache hit my throat as I wrapped my arms around his neck, my tongue whisked away in the heat he gave off. A rough groan touched the air, radiating deep from somewhere within the confines of his chest, and when it did, it casted off the mirrors within the wide room. It ricocheted like a constant boom and Brody, he held me, pinning me to the wall by my hips. My hands covered in lengthy blond wisps and the smell of the shampoo he used this morning made me muss it more.

Strong hands went to my thighs in response, his fingers hooking into the line of my jean shorts.

Touch me. Please touch me.

We went for it almost like he heard my silent plea. His large fingers unbuttoned the tiny fastener. I widened my legs, my sneakers squeaking on the tiles beneath us.

He dragged his mouth over my cheek, my zipper going down by his hand making me quiver. I grabbed the thickness of his arm and guided him, summoning him to touch me.

His hand went cautiously at first. Like he was scared I'd pull away or stop him, but I didn't. I *wouldn't*. I opened my legs wider and his fingers slid past the line of my panties. His other went to my hip. Bracing it, he lifted me and with only one hand, he held me against the wall.

I stared at him while he ventured, not letting go of his gaze as he brushed my mound, exploring, before pushing my sensitive lips apart.

My eyes closed as he played, his fingers finding a precise rhythm with my clit. His mouth found mine and he eased me up the wall by my bottom. A finger pushed its way inside me, then two. He crooked them and his thumb took its place, stroking me into ecstasy. He was greater than the euphoria of any drug. He always had been.

The mirrors bounced the sounds we made back to me, my cries and his groans. I listened to his voice, strained in his throat and his shallow breaths. I wanted to hear them as he made love to me all night.

I thrust my hips forward, trying to get him deeper. But he took care of that, his hand up my shirt, hot on my lower back. He brought me to him, never letting me get far, and I was surrounded by him in ways I was too scared to imagine before.

I pressed a hand to his cheek, sighing into his mouth as I drove my hips to meet his hand. His fingers pushed to the hilt, getting me off and fucking me so thoroughly.

"Come, Alexa," he beckoned, the word deep in my mouth as he kissed me. "Come so I can taste you."

My face found the crook of his neck, pushing into it, fighting the orgasm, but to no avail. My legs shook and my pussy easily gave into him. There was no fighting, not at all.

His thumb moved faster, dragging out the feeling. My juices coated his fingers, my walls pulsating around them, then very slowly, he lowered me to the ground, my sneakers touching the floor. His fingers left easy and then he did with them what he promised. He tasted one, pushing them both into his mouth. Closing his eyes, a warm sound hummed from his throat like he'd never had anything so satisfying. Once he was done, he guided me back to the mirror, zipping up my shorts. He got me together slowly, taking his time until some laughing sounded behind us, other people somewhere within the funhouse. Brody turned in that direction and when he came back, he did so with a wide smile.

I smiled, too.

He grabbed my hand, kissing the back before pulling me away with him, jellied-legs and all. When we came out, the attendant asked if we had a good time.

I couldn't even look at him with a straight face.

Eighteen

ALEXA

WE WENT into the motel room just after ten, the room dark but neither one of us changing that by turning on a light. Brody told me he'd booked two rooms, but we were only using one tonight.

Seeking hands pushed down on my thighs, bunching up the hem of my shorts. His mouth kissed a trail along my cheek, my neck, and then he sat on the bed, pulling me to him. He pressed his large hands to my thighs, squeezing before looking up at me.

"You want this?" he asked, his eyes searching for so many answers in mine. "We don't have to if you don't want this."

I closed the space between us. Blond tendrils covered my fingers when I pushed into them. I lowered my head, kissing deep into the locks and his hands braced me, holding me to him.

"Don't be so good," I whispered, kissing again, brushing my nose in the length. "Don't be so kind." Because he didn't need to be so gentle with me. I trusted him completely.

He lifted his head, summoning me to do the same. I

placed my hand on his cheek and he moved into it, sliding his mouth to my palm.

"I can't be any other way with you, Alex," he said, sighing warm heat over my fingers. "I won't be any other way."

Outlining his jaw with my thumbs, I made him look up at me, and when he did, I smiled. "That's why I want you to," I told him, meaning every word. "That's why I want you."

Those large hands allowed themselves to escape their barrier, *his* restraint when they pushed up my body. He gripped my shirt and I lifted my arms, letting him slid the tank off me. He dropped it to the floor, then skilled fingers unbuttoned my shorts for the second time tonight with a simple flick.

Moving my hips, I let him work them off me, his teeth going to the line of my panties. Using them, he revealed a tiny bit of flesh at my hip, nibbling as he pressed his lips to my skin and squeezed my thighs.

My head fell back and I held onto his shoulders, him going down at his own wonderfully slow pace. His soft mouth escaped breaths at the sensitive skin below my panty line and he cupped my mound while he kissed, played.

My legs quivered underneath me, Brody's shallow breaths turning me on even more below.

"You have such a beautiful body, Alexa. So perfect for my hands," he said, kissing up my thigh. "My mouth."

And he pressed that mouth right there, right between my legs, and sent a sharp tingle straight into my pussy lips, making them wetter. He sat me back as he rose like a mountain above me, a never-ending mountain that had my legs burning to be around him. I crawled back on the bed with my elbows and hands and he chased me, pulling his shirt over his head as he came.

I was met with a body I'd seen far too little of and never wanted to be away from again; muscles spacing off into individual sections, perfection in what they created as a whole. His abs disappeared into his jeans. His chest firm when I placed a hand on it. Sliding over my thumb, I touched that white line, the one that separated the right hemisphere of his chest from the left.

He watched me closely. He touched my hand, bringing it to his mouth and I knew, for now, that was something we'd leave at the door. He had a past just as much as I had, but like he did with me, I'd give him time. I'd give him whatever he needed.

He pushed his jeans down revealing black boxer briefs. He caught me smiling at those, him smiling as well, but then the expression disappeared. It went away when he pushed his face in between my thighs.

Upon pulling my panties down, the sound of his deep breaths drummed within the room. His nose got his fill and his mouth had its way. I threaded my hands in his hair, his tongue dancing its way between my lips, taking long strokes before flicking. He went lower, making a suction with his mouth. I reached down, playing with my bud.

His groan couldn't be denied and I assumed it was at what I was doing. His hand joined me, his other finally reaching up to touch my breast. He squeezed, his hand so big on the lace, so big.

"You're heaven," he said, sighing, but he was wrong about that. He was wrong because he was heaven. He came above me, lips wet and swollen. He used those lips to kiss me, his massive body covering me, surrounding me.

I couldn't stop shaking, but it wasn't because I was scared. I'd never felt something so emotional and all he was doing was kissing me, his lips pressing at the corner of my mouth so sweetly. The feeling overwhelmed me; the euphoria of it.

Reaching down, I pushed boxers down tree trunk thighs

and over a round bottom. I squeezed his ass then. I couldn't help it and he laughed into my neck, the sound like magic.

"You like that?" he asked, smiling. Reaching underneath me, he got a handful of mine. "I guess we both do."

I moaned, pressing my face into his chest, holding him tight. His fingers drew my bra straps down and a large mouth swallowed me whole, suckling my breast.

I tended to the other and his hand joined me. The disorientation came on then, the two of us pleasuring me at the same time. I got lost in the sounds he made and how much he seemed to get pleasure just out of hearing mine. I'd been with more men than I wished I had in the past, but that? Him? Was an absolute first for me.

A foil wrapper made it into his hand from the jeans he tossed. He reared back to his haunches, exposing himself as he rolled it on. A weaker girl might be intimidated by what he held so modestly in his hands, pulling that second skin on all the way to the base of a ready shaft, but I couldn't hide from that. I wanted it so much. I wanted him so much.

He covered me again and had the audacity to be so sweet, asking once more if I was sure.

I kissed him, easing my legs apart and let him fill me, let him reach me in a way I'd never been reached by anyone before him. He used those thighs to drive that force into me, holding the back of my neck while he guided himself in and out in steady repetition. He had so much power behind him, but he was always so gentle. He said he couldn't be any other way with me.

A hand slid down my back, turning me over, and I gripped the sheets as his heat blanketed me, his length sliding inside me from behind. Moans left my lips at every thrust, every forceful pound, his thighs hitting mine while he gasped my name.

I closed my eyes, trying not to get lost in it all, but in the back of my mind I knew the feat was hopeless. This was Brody and though, I hadn't known him long, I couldn't remember not being lost within him.

I didn't remember what it felt like not to be completely in love with him.

Brody

She had one of her beautiful brown legs curled over my hip, playing with my hair as I brushed my fingers down her arm. For the first time in *months,* things felt right. About my life... about everything and she did that. She let me have that in her.

I brought her to me, close, kissing her hair in the dark room. I only had moonlight through the window to see her, but I didn't need much more than that to see what I had.

"What's your name, Brody?" she whispered, burying her face in my neck and moving down to kiss my chest. "Your last name. What it is?"

That's something I only recently found out about her as well. How funny we didn't know such tiny details about each other, but I'd never felt closer to another person in my life.

I laughed, drawing in the natural honeyed scent of her hair. "Chandler. My name is Brody Chandler."

"Hmm," she said, sighing. "It suits you."

That made me smile and I kissed her hair again.

"Mine's Vaughn," came her voice out of the darkness, her fingers curling along my chest. "Alexa Vaughn."

I didn't tell her I knew. I wanted her to share that with me, share this moment with me. I threaded my fingers with hers. "Yours suits you, too," I told her. "It's beautiful like you."

She hid her face, going all bashful.

"Want to hear something crazy?" she asked, and I smiled once more.

"Always."

I expected to hear her voice right away, but it didn't come. I didn't mind though, lingering in the moment of just being with her. That was enough, but she ended up saying something after all, something that had my heart pounding crazy, something I had no idea how to anticipate.

"I think I'm in love with you," she whispered, so soft within my embrace. But I heard her. She couldn't hide from me.

I tipped her chin, adjusting to see her, and the fear behind her eyes was evident. I'd seen Alex scared before. It had been an image burned into my mind and one I wanted nothing but to remove. The situation in which we met had been a terrible one and though, this was a different moment, another type of fear had found its way to her brown eyes.

Her gaze drifted then, taking it away from me, the fear. "And I know how this must sound," she went on, for some reason thinking she had to explain and go on. "I do, Brody, but I... But I can't help..."

I brushed my thumb over her mouth forcing her lips to close, to stop explaining something that didn't need to be explained. She didn't need to go there because I understood. I understood completely.

Using my fingers, I raised her chin in the direction of my mouth, kissing it before finding her lips.

"No 'but,' Alex," I told her, lowering her to her back. I braced her shoulder, angling my mouth to find hers again. "No 'but.'"

I pulled her underneath me, settling in. She pushed her hands up my chest, to my neck, and into my hair, my painfully hard shaft coming to rest against her thigh. I took its width in my hands, putting a condom on before spreading her legs. I filled her, that warm glove pulling me in and pulsating around me.

"Brody..."

I covered her mouth, getting drunk off the sweetness of her lips and bracing the mattress behind her, I drove into her.

Three words left my lips and I said them again to drive them home.

"I love you, Alexa." I tasted her tongue, going deep. "But there's no 'but' for me. There never was."

Her lids folded, her eyes closed tight, and when she opened them, a glisten wrapped around the starlight there.

She pressed her palms to my face. "You do?"

Even still, she was questioning me this. I pressed a kiss to her forehead, moving to her ear. "I'm stupid in love with you."

Moving my hips, I beckoned her to do the same. Her hand slid to my ass and I let go of all restraint, rocking her back into the bed, squeezing her breasts until her legs quivered beneath me.

I joined her in the release, only leaving her body once we both had to breathe. I didn't relax for long, though. Moving, I brushed kisses down her chest, her tummy, and lower. I told her I loved her again as I made her come with my mouth. I'd tell her forever if I could.

Nineteen

ALEXA

With a hop, I snatched his cap off his head, making a beeline for his truck. Heavy footfalls stomped the rocks behind me and soon my sneakers were lifted from the ground.

Brody spun me around in his arms, blowing hot air onto my neck, and making me drop his hat I was laughing so hard.

"Ah!" I screamed, the heat turning into kisses. "Stop! Stop! Stop!"

He only growled, nibbling now. "You asked for it, Alex. You can't just go taking a guy's hat off his head when he least expects it."

His accent flowed with every word and I loved the hell out of it. Large hands made it to my ass, hiking me up his chest. I was forced to wrap my legs around his big body, not that I minded it.

Walking, he pressed me up against the door of his truck, taking the humor away and making me breathless. So caught up, I didn't think about where we were until I opened my eyes, noticing an audience in the motel's parking lot. The middle-aged white woman had her lips turned up through the front window of her truck and I patted Brody's chest to stop.

He sat me down, eyeing me curiously before following my gaze in that direction. Rolling his eyes, he said nothing but, "Let her watch," before taking my chin and directing my mouth to his again.

He kissed the reservations away, kissed me stupid like his love for me, and by the time we finished, we no longer had an audience, the truck long gone.

Bending down, Brody picked up his hat. He looked to put it on, but then placed it on my head, bending the bill with his fingers.

"Keep a watch on it for me?" he asked, and I nodded pushing my arms around his neck. His hands went to my hips and he lowered his forehead to mine. "Ready to go? Just a few more hours."

The strong sense of certainty I had now, showed me I didn't really have it before. I'd been ready to go to California because I had to be for Aiden, for my sister. But that didn't mean I really had been prepared for what I knew I potentially had to deal with mere miles away. My sister and I... we had a past and though, I felt confident, certain, I could handle her, I had no idea what lied ahead of me. I had been wishful though. I had to be and having Brody beside me only gave me confidence.

She's going to listen to reason. I'm sure of it. She has to.

Brody let any anxiety I had of what was to come fade away, pulling me to him as he opened his truck door. He guided me inside, that Brody grin on his full, pink lips, and that certainty made its way upon me again. It wrapped me up in its tightness, a security I not only appreciated, but gratefully had succumbed to. Things would be okay. He made things okay in more ways than one.

Brody's hand made it in mine only moments after he started the truck. A humming engine took me back on the road, but that handhold was the real thing that brought me there.

Biting my lip, I propped my feet up on the dashboard. Brody had air conditioning, but I chose to let the windows bring that cool air in. It was such a beautiful day, but maybe my new lease on life had something to do with that, too.

"Do you need to stop for anything before we hit state lines?" he asked after a few miles. "We can stop at the store."

We did have a continental breakfast at the motel, bagels and what not. But now that I thought about it...

I grinned turning to him. "Let's stop. I want to get some stuff for Aiden. He likes those oatmeal cream sandwiches. And maybe we could find a cute toy or something for him? He likes Legos."

I couldn't keep those away from him when he was younger and he loved the set I sent for him on his last birthday; his ninth.

Blue eyes warmed on me. "That sounds like a good idea. Let's get some fixin's for sandwiches, too. That way we won't have to stop for a while."

That Texan accent would continue to drive me wild well into my days and I secretly wished they would be well in. Thinking we'd need a list, I asked him if he had any paper as I pulled a pen out of my bag.

A turn of the wheel and he merged into the fast lane, some slow moving traffic ahead. He glanced my way while he navigated. "There might be some napkins in the glove compartment for you to write on."

That worked for me just fine and I popped the compartment open, rooting for the napkins I saw shoved in the back corner behind road maps and thick manufacture manuals. Brody noticed my struggle, doing a double take. Suddenly, his eyes widened and he raised his hand. "Alex, wait—"

An orange pill bottle fell out onto my lap, but it wasn't the only thing that rolled down the door of the compartment. Two other bottles followed, both with white pills inside and another white lid shoved in the back told me there were at least four. There were four orange medicine bottles of something and the unknown of that something had the hairs of my arm standing on end.

I picked one up, the name on the label long and foreign to me and Brody, he was too silent beside me. I lifted it, shaking the pills inside.

"What is..." But I didn't want to finish. I'd seen people with meds of this caliber before, *stashes* like this before. I used to sell them the stash.

Brody's gaze found the bottle, then mine. He shook his head. "Alex—"

"Are you a drug addict?" I couldn't breathe. My throat squeezed and a slap couldn't have sent Brody back more by what I said.

He blinked. "What? No, that's not... I mean, I'm not. No."

The way he fumbled on that quite literally made me sick to my stomach, the bile burning its way up my throat. He reached for me and I drew back, not wanting that at all.

He cringed. "Alex, that's not it."

And in what way could I take his word as law? I barely knew him. I barely knew him and I was in love with him. The realizations made my stomach turn even more. I leaned my head out the window, attempting to pull in some air and the grassy plains getting closer caused me to look up. We were also slowing down and the fact Brody was pulling us over became evident.

He put the truck in park and unbuckled his seatbelt. The open environment and a ready accessible door let me know I had an opportunity to run, but the constant ache in my heart made me stay.

I really do love him.

He turned to me, resting a large arm on the wheel and the mashup of emotions on his face told me he had so many words before he even said one. He gazed out the windshield to traffic. "I should have said something, but I'm not a drug addict. Though, that? I'd still have power there, I guess. I could fix that."

What did he mean?

He lifted his head, tipping his chin in the direction of the open glove compartment. "Check the labels. They're all prescription. They got my name on them and everything if you don't believe me."

The reassurance I thought I wanted, I suddenly didn't need. The feeling replaced rapidly from the anxiety of what he could have been to the fear of what he actually was.

"What..." My heart sped, rapid. "Are you sick? Are you..."

My gaze slid down then, to the t-shirt lining a broad chest that once kept me warm, kept me safe all night. It also covered a line, a white one he had yet to tell me about just like his meds.

"Does it have to do with that?" I asked and his gaze went there, landing on the same area that concerned me the most.

His hand went there, touching lightly before lifting his head. "Yes."

I swallowed before my next question. It was the only way I could ask him.

"Are you dying?"

And the words came out with a thick tone to which his eyes followed with a sadness.

Reaching out, he placed a hand to the side of my neck and I could breathe again with the slight shake of his head. "No, I'm not dying, so I don't want you to think that. But yes, I do have to take medications for my heart."

A sharp hit rattled within my own chest, the feeling he was

downplaying something. Because, if he had to take medications, *that* many medications for an organ that kept someone's entire body functioning, something serious had to be going on with him. It may not be death, but that didn't mean everything was all right.

I couldn't speak and another hand touched the other side of my neck. His eyes scanned mine. "Ask me anything," he said, brushing a finger along my jaw. "Ask me anything and I'll tell you."

He gave me the floor, so I started with this: "What's wrong with your heart?"

He chewed the inside of this cheek a bit, but then he spoke. "When I was a kid, barely one, I had to have a surgery. It was extensive, an open-heart surgery for a congenital birth defect. It was successful, though, and everything turned out okay."

"So you..." I paused trying to figure out how to go next. "So you take all these pills as maintenance?" I asked eyeing them, but shaking my head. He said the surgery was successful.

He went on. "No. After the surgery, I had a normal childhood. All that," he broke off, staring at the bottles, too. "All that's a recent development."

And so the breaths became hard again. "What is going on, Brody? Why do you have to take all that stuff?"

A hand left my cheek. It left to pick up one of the bottles. "Last year, I didn't drive a truck. I worked with my dad and brother at a large construction company. I did manual labor, heavy, and that's what I thought it was at first. Just all the hard work, you know?"

I swallowed as he turned the bottle.

He lowered it. "With all that, a guy normally gets fatigued, tired, and because I did sometimes, I ignored it for almost a month; the signs. I ignored the shortness of breath and how hard things seemed to get all the sudden. I just didn't take it at face value. I had worked all my life in hard labor like that and things always came easy to me. Funny enough, I thought I just had a cold or the flu or something. I thought it was something I could lick so I kept working. I kept pushing myself."

Shifting, I brought my legs up on the seat and underneath me. I didn't like what I was hearing, but I made myself listen. I had to.

He breathed. "My heart condition made me susceptible to all kinds of things as an adult, something I didn't know until well, I did. I found out the day when things got tight," he said, putting his hand on his chest. "They got tight right here. I'd been at work at the time and I... I collapsed. I collapsed right there in the break room."

I slid my hand over my mouth.

Oh my God.

He nodded like he knew my thoughts. "I'd been by myself and like an idiot, I tried to get back up and keep working. Thank God for my pop. He saw how I looked when I got out of the break room, must have caught on to how fucked up I looked, because he made me go home. I tried to, but barely made it to my truck. I ended up driving myself to the ER instead."

Chewing my lip, I decided to push him for the rest. "What did they tell you?"

I lost his eyes to road, his arm over the wheel. "A bunch of shit I didn't want to know," he said. "My heart doesn't work like it should. It's an issue with the valves and the cocktail," he said, tossing the bottle over with the rest. "Keeps them doing what they're supposed to be doing and regulates my blood pressure among other things. The doctor said I wouldn't need surgery. Just a lifestyle change, which I guess meant leaving the only job I've ever known how to do. My body couldn't handle the stress anymore."

The way he said that last bit hit me hard and something he'd said to me before slammed into me harder.

"Would it be weird if I said anything I want?" he'd mentioned to me at the carnival, and now, it all made sense. It all was achingly clear. Brody was being bound by something he couldn't control and that didn't sit well with him. It wouldn't with anyone.

We sat in silence on the shoulder of that highway, other cars zooming by. But I just sat there, thinking, and the longer I did, the longer I found it hard to just sit. Brody couldn't do anything harsh with his body and though I didn't know the extent, I knew the situation in which we met couldn't have helped. He fought for me that day and that's when I realized something.

He could have died for me that day.

Brody

She was quiet, so quiet.

I slid a hand over her shoulder, squeezing. "Alex?" I questioned, trying to get into her head space.

This was a lot to take in, the mental wraparound of it I was still working my way to process through to this day. But she didn't have to worry about me. Physically, I had this thing down. I had been keeping up on my meds and hadn't run into any problems yet. Still, I could imagine she had some concerns. She looked up at me and I didn't see that though, her worry. Instead, narrowed brown eyes stared back at me and full lips went tight into a hard frown.

She put her hand to her brow, pushing her fingers into her short hair. "So you had to leave your job because your body couldn't handle it, right? It was too much on your heart?"

Hearing the words so bluntly made it beat harder. She put it all out there, vocalizing something I, myself, found to be a hard feat. I nodded. "Yeah, but you don't need to worry. This is something I've had to deal with for quite a few months now and I'm to the point where I've got it managed. I keep up on my medications and—"

"But you still went in," she bit out, nostrils flaring. "You still broke down the door of that bathroom at that diner and... And..."

Her hands went up to her hair, elbows on her raised knees up on the seat. "You could have died," she sniffed, turning to me, and the water glassing her eyes was evident. "All it would have taken was the wrong hit. Him sending a blow into your chest or you—your heart could have given out in that fight and *still* you saved me. You saved me..."

Her small body went breathy, her chest rising and falling, and I pushed a hand to her cheek, forcing those glassy eyes to look up at me. I leaned in cradling her face between my hands.

"I was fine that day, Alexa. Nothing happened."

"But it could have!" she shot back. "It could have been the opposite of fine. It could have left you dead, but you did it anyway."

Her body shook, tremors under my hands and I brushed her cheeks with my thumbs, shaking my head. "I wasn't thinking about me," I told her, because I wasn't. How could I? It was her. She was the only thing on my mind.

"But you should have," she said blinking her tears way. "You should have thought about that. If something happened... If I never got to know you..."

She closed her eyes, leaning her forehead against mine and forcing my cap off her head. It fell to the truck floor, but she paid it no mind, pushing her tiny fingers into my hair.

"If I never got to be with you..."

I pulled her into my lap after she said that, holding her

close to me; my heart. That space between my neck and shoulder dampened with her tears and I placed a hand on her hair. "Don't cry. Don't cry, it kills me."

"I can't help it," she said, sniffing as she lifted her head. "You know it could have turned out differently."

I did know that, but I also knew another thing. I ended up getting this job because of my heart condition and I ended up finding her because of this job.

That could only be fate.

But from the way she reacted, these series of events didn't affect her the same way. She was scared. She was scared for me.

"Alex—"

"I want you to let me go at this alone," she said, surprising me when she rose up and she reached out, touching my face so gently like she could break me. "I need you to drop me off. I need to go the rest of the way by myself. What if my sister's ex turns up? I can't, Brody. He could be a loose cannon and I can't put you in any kind of situation where you'd get hurt."

I took her chin. "We already had this discussion, Alex. You already know I'm going. I'm with you on this and nothing's changed on that."

"But that was before," she breathed, sniffing. "I can't let anything happen to you. I won't let him have power over anyone else like..."

The words left when her eyes closed.

They left when I kissed her lips.

Bracing her cheek, I put everything into it. I wasn't going anywhere. I wasn't leaving her. I already had to make sacrifices because of my condition and I refused to let her be one of them.

Her lips fell from mine but not really. Bruised, they hovered over my mouth, her gaze that way, too.

"He's hurt so many," she whispered touching my lips.

"He's already broken my family once. I won't let him break us, too."

I brought my arms around her waist. "We don't know he's back and if he is, he won't have the power. You said yourself your sister will make the right choice this time. He has nothing to hold power over."

Her gaze escaped then, fleeting, and I made her look at me when I slid my fingers along a strand of her hair. "Don't worry, Alexa. We're in this together."

Her hand moved up to cover mine. Her eyes closed and when she opened them, she closed the space, brushing our noses. "You don't fight. If we see him, we leave. You don't fight anymore for me. Promise me."

It was a promise I didn't feel at all good about giving. The unknown met us in California, but I could promise her one thing. If he made an appearance, we'd come up with a new plan, a safe plan for all parties.

"We'll figure it out if we see him," I told her. "But I promise no fighting. I won't fight."

"And if something changes," she said, slipping both hands over my heart, "here, you tell me. If your condition at all takes a turn, you'll tell me."

She didn't know it, but she was the only one that knew. I had told her more than I told anyone. I told her more than even my family.

I smiled, dampening my lips before leaving a kiss on hers. I didn't tell her she was the first to know. I wanted to show her instead.

Her arms moved around my neck, her mouth opening with her kiss. "Can I do anything?" she asked pulling back slightly. "Anything to help? Maybe if you tell me what you take and what day and time, I can organize them. And do you watch your eating? I can help with that. With dancing, I had to do that all the time."

Smiling, I brushed her nose. "I could stand to eat better."

Her lips moved up in the corner in response. "Okay, we'll do that. Aiden also has a special diet. He's diabetic. We'll all do it together."

Her words reached me in a place I didn't expect. I'd been battling this alone since I found out. I had to, I felt like, for the sake of my family. They'd already been through a lot, so much in the last year with my pop's own health scare and they didn't need another burden to deal with. With that, I decided to take on the load myself. It had been so hard to deal with alone.

So damn hard.

I brought her closer to me, encasing her frame completely in my arms. "Where have you been?"

She hugged my neck, burying her face there. "Trying to find you."

I captured her lips under mine, her breath, and parting her mouth, I let her know something. She wouldn't *not* have a way of finding me again. I'd be here whenever she needed me and I had a feeling I had the same thing from her. And she showed me that, easing those thighs apart over my lap.

She smiled, smelling like water lilies while she slid fingers down my biceps, moving her mouth to kiss my neck. My cock pierced my jeans, shooting up to seek that heat above it, but her hand made a fine replacement. She rubbed over me, undoing her shorts, and I laughed, easing her back a bit.

I touched her neck. "I don't want to get you arrested." We were still on the shoulder of traffic after all.

She simply replaced my hand with hers, sliding her zipper down and pushing my hand inside over her mound. Her lips hovered over my mouth. "You're worth getting arrested over."

I'd never let that happen, though. And I think it was the same for her. We had to get on the road, but these moments we took if only for a few seconds before we did.

A phone chirped in the air and we were denied that.

Alex sat up with it, pulling my phone out of her back pocket. I'd been letting her hold onto it just in case. She frowned while looking at the front and when she crawled back over to her seat, I leaned in, watching to see what was up.

"Aiden?" she automatically said. No, hello. Not one. Her hand gripped the phone. "Aiden, what's going on? Are you there? Why did you call? Talk to me."

Pulling the phone away, she stared at it. "He's not saying anything, but it's one of his numbers. He used my sister's landline."

I took the phone, pressing it to my ear. I didn't hear him at all, but I did hear something, rustling. I put the phone on speaker, but held it out.

That's when we heard a scream.

Alex ripped the phone away, horror on her face. "Aiden? Aiden, baby what's going on?"

But it wasn't Aiden. The scream was female and it's constant shrilling tone sent the hairs on my arm standing on end, as well as a sharp turn in my stomach. Alex screamed into the phone, but I could barely hear it over the one coming from my cell. She kept on, crying for Aiden to respond, but he wouldn't. Eventually the screaming stopped, a break. Alex opened her mouth again to speak, but I stopped her raising my hand.

"Maybe he can't talk," I told her. "Maybe he can hear us but he can't speak out loud." It was the only reason I could formulate that he would call and not respond. He wanted us to hear something. He wanted his aunt to hear something and that something was making a woman scream.

Alex pulled the phone toward her mouth, her hand shaking. "Aiden, baby, if you can hear me," she said looking up at me. "I'm coming. We're coming."

Twenty

ALEXA

BRODY GOT us to California in half the amount of time it probably should have taken and it was a miracle we weren't pulled over. Brody went well over the speed limit and nearly into triple digits; the clock on us, the clock on me. I recognized the voice too well through the phone. It was one that used to giggle alongside me, playing tag when we were children.

Brody made me call the cops after I heard Elena's voice. He had to because I could barely keep the phone in my hands I was shaking so hard. So he dialed for me, taking the call before I was able to take it myself and respond with vacant answers, the shock unable to recede. They called me back right before we hit city limits, telling me what I didn't want to hear.

"No one was there," they'd said, making me think I was crazy. "Perhaps, you were mistaken."

But Aiden, he'd called from the house phone. No, I wasn't mistaken and made the cops check twice just to be sure. By the grace of God, they had, staggering their arrival to Elena's home an hour later, but again they told me the same thing. The apartment was empty. They'd checked through the windows. The apartment wasn't in disarray and no one answered the door. They circled the complex, but again ended up with nothing. They told me Elena might have left and I should keep calling to check, so I did. But that didn't ebb the feeling, the feeling Elena and Aiden didn't leave. It was a feeling they were still there.

Brody's hand squeezed mine and I looked up at him.

It will be okay, his blue eyes read to me, and they'd done that since the call, provided that reassurance so much stronger than words.

I'd take them even if it wasn't true.

Elena didn't live on the coast, her tiny spot rooted in the outskirts between occasionally planted palms trees within the concrete jungle of affordable housing. She had an apartment on third floor of a small complex, blue and white with brown shutters. From the outside, everything looked so normal, undisturbed like the cops said.

"They could still be in there," I told Brody now, and he nodded, unbuckling his seatbelt.

He put his hand on the door. "I'm going to go check. Just make sure everything is okay, and then you can—"

"No!" I grabbed him, bracing his arm. "You can't. What if he's in there? What if..."

"Okay. Okay," he said, bringing me into his chest, his hands, his body calming me down. His warm breath went down the strands of my hair, his fingers threading through. "What do you want to do then?"

One thing was for certain, I didn't want him to go inside. I didn't want him, his heart, to take the risk, but if my sister was in there... If *he* left her for dead after doing something to her...

I swallowed, asking Brody to circle the block instead. He asked me what we were looking for, but only I knew. I looked for any signs of him, a body, a car. He used to drive this old white Corolla, as the lot was empty of any vehicle at all, I had no idea if not spotting it was a good thing or a bad thing.

"We can just take a look," Brody whispered to me. We'd long since stopped, back in the parking lot. "Just let me take a look, Alexa."

Holding my arms, a shudder broke through me. That's the last thing I wanted. That's the last damn thing. His hand came to settle on my shoulder.

"I'll come right back if I hear anything," he assured me. "Anything at all."

Brown eyes flashed before me, young ones that always looked for me and ears that always listened though miles away from him. If Aiden was in there, I needed to know.

So sick, I nodded and not a moment later, a door clicked open, Brody's truck door ajar.

I can't let him do this.

I was out of the truck before I could think, but Brody, he was bigger. He was faster. He got me in his arms, bracing mine.

"No," was all he said. "No."

But he couldn't stop me. He'd have to restrain me to do so and that's something Brody Chandler would never do.

"If we're just coming back," I told him. "Then I'm going, too."

He stared at me, long and hard, and for just a moment, I believed he might actually try to hold me back. Instead, he kissed my forehead, telling me to wait a second while he closed the truck door, the open vehicle still dinging in the air. Standing there, I let him, choosing to stare up at the apartment while I waited. For some reason, I believed doing that would tell me something. Brody took a minute and I turned, watching him straightening his shirt over his jeans while he made strides back to me. His arm came around my waist and then we went.

We took the stairs with caution, Brody's arm around me the whole way. We got to the third level, to my sister's door, and everything really did look on the up and up. That's when Brody's arm left me, his hand poising to knock, but I waved him not to.

Allowing myself to breathe, I pulled my sparkly bag around my front and took out the key designated for emergencies. I had it made from the one she forced me to give back after our falling out. I went to put it in the lock, but Brody touched my hand.

"We shouldn't," he said, but I felt like I had to.

"We leave if we hear something," I told him, trying to keep the shake out of my voice. But I was scared, scared of so many things.

His long fingers looped in mine. He kissed the back of my hand. "You let me go first."

God...

Taking my key, he pushed it in himself, so quiet despite being so big. He slipped inside, the crack in the door giving me my own vantage point after he did. The living room clear, even the TV was off. She always had the TV on and music. She often played it while she cooked.

Brody told me to let him go, but I couldn't help letting my fingers push the door open wider and eventually, I stepped in, too. He'd gone somewhere, Brody, into another room and I somehow lost him.

My heartbeat whispering his name with my steps. He didn't answer and I felt like vomiting.

"Brody," I shuddered out. "Brody, where are you?"

Nothing.

My eyes blinking, coating, I forced bravery in my steps. I didn't hear him, but was trying to be so quiet because that had been the original plan.

I maneuvered around furniture, items of Elena's history and mine. She got everything when I left. I couldn't take anything with me and memories surfaced at an old blanket on the window. Mom had made that in the rare times when she had been sober. She used to read us stories underneath it, but now? Elena was using it as a window cover, something to block out the sun.

Closing my eyes, my steps took me away from that. I traveled wayward and I didn't know where I was going, but then I came across a room, one with plastic stars on the ceiling and army men on the bed.

Aiden's room was empty, vacant like the rest of the apartment I'd seen, and that would have made sense. But one thing in the room made the vacancy more than confusing.

I picked up the action figure, life-sized with boxing gloves on, and the room tilted. I sank to the bed with it, feeling it as if it were still warm.

"Alex?" came my name followed by a deep breath. "Thank God."

I looked up to see Brody coming to me, his hand on my arm before dropping to his knees. "I asked you to wait," he said, his voice terse, frustrated. "You didn't see anything did you? The rest of the apartment is clear, but..."

The tears came in a wave I didn't expect and as I attempted to pull in breaths, I discovered quickly the feat wasn't easy. Hyperventilating, my shoulders shook and Brody's hands came down on them. He guided me forward, making me put my face between my knees and I cradled Aiden's doll. I cradled it so hard.

"Hey," he soothed, his hand moving circles over my back. "It's going to be okay. We'll find them."

But what if it was too late? What if we found them too late? I rose up with the doll, the tears flooding more as I put a hand over my mouth.

"He never goes anywhere without this," the words came out choked. "Brody, something bad happened."

His face looked pained, pained for me. He squeezed my

shoulder. "We will figure this out. We won't stop looking until we find—"

A noise made him pull me to him, noise coming directly ahead us.

The shuffle in the closet sounded again, but this time, I had to listen for it and when I did, a near-muted sniff hit the air.

I dropped the doll, rising up.

"Alex, wait." Brody's hand came into mine, but I let go. I had a feeling I needed to for a second.

I reached for the brass handle, but Brody got it first, shielding me with his big body. But he didn't need to. He didn't. I just had a feeling and that feeling proved to be something worth holding stake in at the sight of a little boy; a boy with coarse hair and brown skin. He lifted his head, it buried within the confines of his arms gripped around his legs. He did so cautiously and when he saw me behind watery brown eyes, the tear soaked cheeks pairing with them, my nine-year-old nephew lowered his knees. A large wet spot revealed damp pants and the puddle on the hardwood floor around him. His fear made my heart ache.

I tried to be strong. I did, but tears fell and I was unable to stop them. I fell to the floor and he met me halfway, shaking in my arms. I couldn't even ask him what happened, where *he* was, because I couldn't form coherent words. The only thing I could do was quiet him, soothingly rubbing his back and telling him things I wasn't sure of. I didn't know if everything would be okay, if he'd be okay.

I didn't know what he'd seen.

Steps sounded lightly, coming up on my side; Brody. His form blasted a fear in my nephew's eyes and he cowered, crawling into my lap like when he was younger.

I touched his cheek. "This is my friend Brody," I said,

giving Aiden my best reassuring smile. "I heard you guys have been talking."

His brown eyes gazed up to him and his arms loosen from around my neck.

Brody smiled at him then, waving slightly and my heart eased when Aiden lifted his hand and did the same. I squeezed his arm. "Brody's here to help," I paused, staring up at him, and he nodded, confirming with a smile.

It started slow, but Aiden managed to smile at him. "Thank you," he whispered, and Brody lowered his chin to him again.

With shaking legs, Aiden started to stand and I helped, telling him we needed to get him changed. Brody left the room without being told, letting us, and while I found some fresh underwear and pants, I went for a cautious question.

"Aiden, you called us," I started, slipping his arm into a new shirt, too. He'd sweated this one out. The portable phone still sat in the bottom of the closest, confirming the call, and Aiden breathed, gasping. His body shook again like he was cold.

"He hurt mom," he whispered, dipping his head. Tears filled his eyes once more. "He twisted her arm and told me to leave the room. I didn't want to, but Mama told me..."

"Where is she, sweetie?" I asked, chilled. I didn't know if I was strong enough to know, but awareness that my sister never left her son unattended made me.

A small hand came up to his eyes, wiping the tears away. He opened his mouth to say something, but he couldn't, shaking his hand.

I covered his head. "It's okay. It's okay. We'll figure it out." Pausing, I swallowed. Gazing around the room, I spotted his overnight bag. "Let's get you a bag. I think we should leave for a little bit."

Barely a second passed before Brody came into the room

after I called him. I was slipping the last of Aiden's clothes into his bag. Aiden had stopped crying at this point, but I was quite sure that took everything he had. I passed a glance over my shoulder, to Brody. "He doesn't know where his mom is."

"What do you want to do?" he asked me.

I grabbed Aiden's bag standing. "Get out of here. I don't want to run into him. We'll call the police when we get on the road."

The tears started again, dripping down to my nephew's fresh t-shirt. "They'll find Mama?"

The last thing I wanted to do was lie to Aiden or give him false hope, but at this point, I had to do anything to get some of that fear out of his eyes. I touched his cheek. "They'll handle everything. Don't worry."

Brody took Aiden's bag. I got my nephew's hand, heading toward the door of the apartment, but he jerked me back and I nearly lost it. I faced him. "Aiden—"

"Joe!" he called, tugging at my hand again. "I left him. We have to go get him."

I didn't want to spend another moment here, but anything I could do to make the transition leaving better for my nephew, I would do it. I turned to tell Brody we were going back. There was no way I was letting Aiden go by himself, but Brody was already leaving my side.

He set the bag down. "The action figure, right?"

God, why was he so perfect? I nodded, watching him leave behind us. Bringing Aiden close to me, I lowered. "He's going to get it. He'll be right back—"

Something spilled. Liquid hitting tiles. It came from the kitchen ahead and wet steps had every hair on my neck standing on end.

My legs froze. They froze in place and I couldn't make them move.

"Aunt Alex," Aiden whisper shouted, tugging at my hand.

Move. Move.

Gripping Aiden's hand, I pivoted, but the sight of something familiar caused me to stop. I stopped because I knew her. I knew that messy brown bun and the matching freckles that dusted that light complexion of her cheeks.

Elena had a mop in her hand when she came into the door frame. Sighing, she moved the mop over the floor, soaking up whatever she spilled, but she only did so with one arm. The other she nursed, cringing like she'd been hurt.

"Mama!" rang beside me, and she looked up. She sniffed up, rubbing her nose, but I saw no tears in her eyes, no. She hadn't been crying at all. It was a different sniff and she wiped her nose, squinting at him like at first she didn't know him. But then something clicked. It must have because that's when she dropped the mop.

"Aiden," she said, her eyes wide, and he tugged to be let go. He tugged, but I only let him get as far as the length of his arm. He stepped back and that's when my appearance suddenly became known to my sister. I knew because her eyes narrowed and my name left low sounding from her lips.

"Alex?"

My name came from behind me, Brody. His hands settled on my shoulders, but didn't tug me away. He only stood there, supporting, and my sister couldn't have looked more confused, shaking her head.

"What's all this?" she asked, and the question could almost come across as accusatory. Like *I'd* been the one to do something wrong by coming here.

I brought Aiden closer. "He called me," I responded simply back. I jutted my chin toward her arm. "What's all that? What's up with your arm?"

Her hand moved back to it hanging limply at her side. She squeezed it before sniffing again and I recognized the action this time along with the hazy look of her eyes. She was high, a way I'd seen her too many times to count.

My next question was laced with something too, anger. "Where is he?" I asked, because now what was going on became clear. He did this and he couldn't be far.

Her face clouded with her own anger. "Balcony," she said. "We had to. Someone called the cops."

The balcony.

Brody must have missed checking there and it was my sister's words that drove even more fear. Even now, she was standing by him. Even now after all this time and yet another injury. The difference now, I didn't have time for them. I had to act, quickly.

Brody's hand slid down into mine. "We need go, Alex." We were always so in sync.

Dipping down, I grabbed Aiden's bag. Standing, I went to turn, but Brody squeezed my arm. His eyes narrowed and he couldn't have looked more confused. He tipped his chin in my sister's direction. "What about...?" he said, glancing at Elena before back at me.

I didn't say a word. I didn't because I had nothing to say about Elena. There was nothing more because I recognized the same ignorance in her eyes, the same refusal to think about anyone but herself and I wouldn't fight with her. I had no energy for it this time.

Brody stood there during my silence, his head tilted. "She's not coming with us, is she?" he asked, and something flashed over his eyes after that. It was something that had me uneasy, something that flipped my stomach in a million ways over. No, Elena wasn't coming with us, and in my heart, I knew she wouldn't even before I stepped into this apartment.

"It's a reunion," came a voice and I fell back into Brody.

An arm came around my sister, pale and laced with thick scraggly hair. That dark hair matched the scruff on his chin and the messy mass he had hallowed over his head. Nathan looked like he'd stepped right out of prison yesterday, far from the man he was before he went in.

Far from the illusion.

He had about a decade on my sister's twenty-eight years. He had a maturity that should have sent off alarm bells for me from the jump, but I let him worm his way in. I let him because I think I needed something positive in my life, for my family, too, and he knew that. He *preyed* on that.

He preyed on me.

He got closer, tugging my sister toward him, and I drew into Brody. He glanced down at me, then passed a look over to Nathan. I felt a hand come down on me then, over my hip and pulling in. Brody left no space between us, and even tugged on Aiden's backpack a bit, closing any gaps left between any of us. That got Nathan's attention, boy did it. He grinned a bit, flicking something out of his teeth and onto the floor.

I cringed.

"I see you got yourself another," he said, smirking a bit. "Tell me, man. Did she get you with that little cunt, too?"

The very words caused Brody to shift behind me, as well as causing the thick bile to creep up my throat.

Nathan appraised me after that, hard, and I closed my eyes away, feeling every moment as if touched, caressed.

You can't let him get in your head. You can't. Not anymore.

I opened my eyes, fighting back. I wasn't that young girl anymore and he wouldn't make me feel that way again.

"Because let me tell you something," he continued, a weird twinkle in his eyes. "She ain't worth it."

If not for me and Aiden as a barrier I know Brody would have moved. I felt the impact behind me and I squeezed his hand. I squeezed and he stayed put. He told me he wouldn't fight and I held his hand so he wouldn't. He exchanged a glance with me and though, unheated, I could feel the questions there.

I looked away so he wouldn't seek them from me anymore, but couldn't escape Elena. She stared at me, so hard it hurt, and I knew she hadn't missed what Nathan said no matter how high. It had been the reason for so many issues between us.

It had been the reason neither one of us spoke to the other anymore.

Smiling like he knew he got to all of us, Nathan kissed the top of my sister's head, and the pull he did to do so, shoved her wounded arm into his side.

The pain made her entire body shudder.

My fingers dug into my side, doing all I could to keep from reaching out and grabbing her. I pleaded to her with my eyes. "Elena," I chewed on my lip. "Please. You don't have to stay. We can go."

"Go where?" The very notion made Nathan laugh, but it came out all phlegmy, raspy. He sniffed, and I assumed, he had his fair share of drugs, too. He wrapped his arms around Elena, possessive in their nature. He lifted his eyes to us. "Where's the fire?"

"Alexa?" It was Brody who spoke behind me, an urgency in his voice. His hand braced Aiden's bag, and the next step, I knew he'd be backing us out.

With slow steps, he started to, and maybe that's when Elena finally knew what was happening. Shimmying, she moved from within Nathan's grasp and I think he let go only because of sheer surprise. She fled toward us and a hope bubbled up inside me. She was coming. She was leaving him and coming with us, but the light inside snuffed so quickly. She started tugging on Aiden's bag, yelling things like, "You're not taking my baby," and "And he's not coming with you."

The struggle made Aiden cry, the tears falling down his

cheeks. He kept saying he wanted to go with me and he kept *screaming* for her to come with us. And me? I was caught up in the fray, one hand holding my nephew to me while the other tried to hold on to a piece of Elena, too. Despite myself, what she did to me and made me feel in the past, I couldn't let her go.

Nathan rolled his eyes. "Bitch," he snapped my way. "Just let the boy fuckin' go with his mama."

He made lazy steps my way, but stopped so abruptly it got all of our attention. His hands lifted then, backing away, and a look behind me told me why.

Brody.

He pulled something out I hadn't seen in so many days, but this time the gun didn't scare me. I knew it was there to protect me and my family.

Elena gasped, holding on to Aiden, but my nephew didn't direct any fear that way. I think because he understood the protection, too.

The gun was pointed at Nathan after all.

Understanding that, Nathan shook his head, his expression untelling. "Stay cool, my friend. It ain't gotta be this way."

Brody's eyes narrowed into slits. "I'm not your friend and you need to go in the kitchen."

Whatever friendly banter Nathan was trying to give him was replaced with anger. He took a step back and Brody matched it, going around us. He tilted his head back to me, but not his eyes. "Take them to the truck," he said, but I put my hand on his back.

"Not without you."

His eyes nearly closed at my words. Like they weren't what he wanted to hear. Like they frustrated him. He took more steps and Nathan must have known to keep backing up with each one. Together, we all ended up in the kitchen, stepping over a dark brown liquid on the floor. A bottle of whiskey and a tumbler sat the kitchen counter not far by and the thought crossed my mind that he sent my sister into the kitchen to get him a drink. I wouldn't put it past him.

Nathan backed out onto the open balcony. He kept his hands up the entire time, even while Brody slid the glass door closed and locked him in.

"It won't hold him for long," he said, but he didn't lower the gun. He held it there and I had a feeling if he pulled the trigger it would hit Nathan point blank between the eyes.

It was time to go now.

Moving, I tugged at Aiden. He unfroze easy, but Elena, not so much. She stared at Nathan, shaking her head, and I feared she'd stay here. She'd let him out and he would come after us. Her son started to move though and gratefully, whatever invisible tether Nathan had severed with the steps. Together, they turned their back on Nathan and he was left there, outside with his hands raised.

Brody and I were the last to leave and I didn't fail to notice what Nathan did before we left him. Lowering his arms, he lifted a single finger and pointed.

He pointed directly at Brody.

Twenty-One

BRODY

I TAPPED ON THE DOOR, my hand rested on it while I waited for it to open. A darkness hovered over the peephole and I didn't blame her for checking. She should check. She should always check, always.

The door opened quickly and sugar brown eyes cast their glow on me. She'd wrapped me up quickly, hadn't she? Even from the beginning. Even from that terrible day I found her.

Alex stared at me, her shirt loose at her shoulders and a towel wrapped around her head. Her soft lily scent filled the air even in the wide abyss of nighttime around me. She also looked worried, her mouth in a frown, and that's something else I didn't blame her for.

I pushed my hands into my jean pockets. "Can we talk?" I felt we had a lot to talk about, so many things.

She nodded, then turned widening the motel door of the room next to mine. A mother and child revealed, him at her feet while she braided his hair into thick, perfect rows.

Alex dropped her hand from the door, looking behind her. "I'm gonna talk to Brody for a second."

Aiden leaned out of his momma's hands and his worry

challenged Alex's when she opened the door. "Where will you go?"

She smiled at him. "Just outside the door. Right outside."

He sat back and all the while his momma didn't react, especially to Alex speaking. Her hands just continued to move, ignoring anything but what she was doing. Aiden's hand lifted, waving to me.

My eyes couldn't help crinkling at the kid. He was the one bright spot that managed to come out of this situation today. I lifted my own hand, waving him goodnight before Alex closed the door behind herself. She went to the railings of the second floor, laying her arms on them while I lounged back beside her.

"How are they?" I asked her. Though Aiden seemed all right he couldn't possibly be and as far as Alex's sister, she said nothing, absolutely nothing the entire drive here.

Which only amplified my questions for Alex even more.

Alex covered herself like she had so many times in my truck. If a guy didn't know her, one might mistake her for being cold, but I had been around her long enough to know it was something she did when she was uneasy, nervous. She breathed. "He's been quiet," she said. "But I plan on talking to him a little before he goes to sleep. I'm worried. He's been through so much."

And she was right about that. I'd only seen a snapshot today and couldn't imagine. He was a strong kid to even be functioning at all right now, hella strong.

"As far as my sister," she continued. "She's not talking to me."

That also remained consistent, which brought me to what I wanted to talk to her about tonight. I had to admit I put that off until now, late in the evening. I needed time to think. I needed time to formulate the right words without coming across the wrong way. But no matter how long I considered, no matter how long I took, I still couldn't come to terms with all that happened. Today, I saw a broken woman, one who had no intention of leaving her abuser. I didn't think she ever had the intention despite what her sister had told me mere days ago.

"You lied to me, Alex," I came right out with it. "You lied to me about your sister. You said there would be no way she'd stay with him. You said she'd do the right thing this time. I mean," I paused for a moment, feeling my pulse tick and with it, my heart racing.

Calm down. Breathe.

I opened my eyes. "I feel like we pretty much took her against her will. She only came because we had Aiden."

"I know." The word came out whispered, light, and I knew, *she knew* exactly what she did. She knew exactly what would happen today.

"You knew," I repeated, but not with a question. It had been a statement just as well as she was standing in front of me. I shook my head. "And you thought you'd take him? Just walk away and she'd let you?"

Her eyes closed over the lids, her lips tight. "I don't know. I... I hoped to get her to come with us."

She hoped. She *hoped*. I swallowed. "And what of the lie? Why lie to me?" Because that's what hurt the most. For some reason she felt she had to.

Turning, those first few tears fell from her eyes and it pained me that I was such a big reason they were there. "It didn't sound like you'd let me go," she whispered, head down. "If I didn't."

She was damn right about that and she now confirmed what I believed that day at the cafe. She was going to go in there and get them. She was going to go in without a plan into a scenario that could have ended so badly.

I knew because I had to have a gun just to get us out of it.

Honestly, I didn't know what frustrated me more, her complete disregard for the danger of the situation or her lack of concern for herself.

I pushed my hand into my hair, forcing myself to be here and out of the anger of my head. But despite myself, it was so goddamn hard to see through the haze.

If I'd lost her today...

"Things could have turned out so much differently, Alex."

"I know," she said, and pushing off the banister, she swallowed. "But it didn't and I have Aiden. I have him safe and I have Elena."

But for how long? She physically had her sister, but mentally, I wasn't so sure. I gestured toward the room. "You can't keep her here, Alex. And that guy?"

Thoughts of things he'd said sent me to a dark place again, a haze surrounding me I couldn't easily come out of like I had before.

"Did she get you with that little cunt, too?"

I wanted to *annihilate* him after he said that, the only thing keeping me from doing so was my promise to the woman I loved. And I did love her. I loved her so damn much, but she was keeping things from me, keeping things from me even still.

"Why did that *guy* say what he did about you? About..." My heart raced, the pounding drumming through my head, but I couldn't stop it this time. I couldn't calm it.

A pent up breath shuddered through me. "Why did he say that stuff about you? About you and him?"

Because she couldn't have. She couldn't have possibly been with... with him. But then, she shrank before me, her eyes doing everything but looking into mine and my hand found her shoulder, my other tipping her chin to look at me.

"What happened?" I asked, making myself. So many things needed answers. So many things didn't make sense, but

I needed to know and she needed to be the one to tell me. I didn't push Alex. I refused in the past as I didn't want to pressure her. I always let her come to me, but here, now this was important. This was something I needed from her, but when she stepped back I knew I wouldn't get it and when she shook her head, it scared me I never would.

Her hands went to her lips and only a few words fell from them.

"I'm sorry," she said, her head continuing to shake. "I'm sorry, but I..." Tears filled her mouth, tiny streams down her cheeks. They went on forever and flowed freely.

"I can't," she finished, and I had no idea what to say to that. I had no idea what to *do* with that or how to even feel. Because after all this time and after everything had been said and done...

She still didn't trust me.

She removed the towel and her hand pushed through her hair, so beautiful in even the simplest way. That's why I'd fallen for her. That's why I loved her.

Pushing my hands into my pockets, I straightened up. I forced myself to sober up.

"What do you need then?" I asked her. "What do you need from me?" The cold I never meant to surface, but damn if I couldn't fight that in my voice. The tone had been the only way to mask other things, hurt amongst them. Pushing it down, I tipped my chin toward the motel room. "What do you need for them? I'll help you with wherever you want to go or whatever you want to do."

She had my heart this woman. She had my soul and that's why her eyes squeezed so tight, pained and tortured me more. I wanted to default immediately, grab her, and make her safe, but she was making it so hard, because every time we moved forward, she'd find a way to revert back. She kept finding ways to push me away.

Her fingers came under her eyes, wiping away the tears. She sniffed. "You don't have to," she said, going into her own default. She stepped back. "With the money I have, I'll get us to where we need to go. Someplace safe."

I rubbed the back of my head, my frustrations and everything else I couldn't smooth out or remove. But even with them, I couldn't ignore what she'd said. I couldn't ignore what she wanted and what I, too, felt she needed. That went beyond any frustrations I had. I needed her safe more than anything I could possibly ever need, and so I offered, hoping and praying she'd take it.

"If you're willing," I told her, looking up at her. "And if your sister is, too, as I think she needs to decide on her own, I know a place. We can head there tomorrow and it's safe."

In fact, it was more than safe, so much more.

Twenty-Two

ALEXA

WHY DOES he still want to help me?

He wouldn't if he knew the truth.

I stood there that night, listening to him, and once he was done. Once he *told* me where he wanted to take me and my family, I protested immediately. He wanted to protect us, protect me, under the shelter of his *own* family's roof, his grandmother's in particular.

"You'll be safe there," he said. "You, Aiden, and your sister."

Why is he still doing this...? Why?

The question of his willingness to help loomed again as I stared into his eyes that night, the ones that looked at me in such a different way than even twenty-four hours ago. I lost something familiar in them. I lost that love that used to shine so bright in only minutes. That seemed to make sense, though. He'd given it to me so quickly, his heart.

The night saw me tossing and turning, anxiety and guilt storming over me in their chilling waves. I had taken Brody up on his offer. I allowed myself to give into my own fear. My nephew, he needed something positive. He needed something safe, and if Brody felt his family's place was that, I couldn't turn a blind eye to it.

No matter how much I didn't deserve that or him.

The next morning, I told Aiden the plan, and though he seemed hesitant, quiet like he had been the night before, he agreed. He agreed as long as I'd be there.

"Of course, baby," I told him, kissing his hair. "Now go wash up."

He did, sliding off the queen bed the three of us shared last night. He ended up being Switzerland between my sister and I, neural between the two worlds.

He hung on the door of the bathroom. "Brody will be there too, right?" he asked, his voice light. "And his gun?"

I hated that he thought we'd need it, but he was nine. He wasn't dumb.

"Brody will be there and don't worry about the other thing. Go wash up."

Nodding, he headed away to do what he'd been told, gathering Joe along the way. The front door opened shortly after that, sending my heart into overdrive. The appearance of my sister marked no danger to me, but her coming in didn't make my heart settle any less. She stepped into the room, turning back to flick a lit cigarette out the door. A cloud of smoke left her lips and filled the room.

"I'm assuming you heard the plan?" I asked her, sliding Aiden's clothes into his bag. The window had been open after all. That's the only way Aiden let her go out to smoke. He needed a visual of both of us at all times. We more than abided.

Elena strode past me, ignoring me as she got her own bag off the floor. Her purse had been the only thing she managed to take with her in the shuffle and that's probably because it had been right by the door. I wouldn't mention it to her, but I checked it last night after she went to sleep. I had to make sure she had no means of contact and no way to contact *him.*

Elena raised her bag and cringed before she even got to full height. She must have forgotten about the sharp reminder of the man who'd done it to her. She didn't say a word when she nursed it and I assumed I'd be ignored, but then she spoke and I almost wished she'd chosen the route of silence.

"Mmmhmm," she said, sniffing. She was doing that a lot, sniffing. She pushed the back of hand over her face, the oval ring she wore hitting her nose. Taking a chair, she shoved her box of cigarettes inside her purse, fumbling around it.

"I'm assuming you're still trying to turn my son against me?" The words stung. They hurt as if shot through my chest. I didn't turn Aiden against her. I didn't have to. She did a good job of that all by herself.

I settled my arms over Aiden's bag. "He hurt you, Elena," and she knew who. I didn't have to say. "Your arm? You didn't do that to yourself."

She kept digging in her purse. "And what?" she asked, shooting me a look. "You thought you needed to play hero? No one asked you to do that. No one *ever* asks you to do that."

I only let her keep going because the bathroom door closed us off from her son's ears, but I didn't need to sit there and take it.

Getting up, I gathered the rest of Aiden's things scattered around the floor. Silence settled across the room, but it wasn't long before it was broken again.

"I'm not going with you," Elena said, her voice clipped, sharp behind me. "And you're not taking my son."

Huffing, I righted. "The alternative is me calling the police. Nathan *twisted* your arm in front of him, Elena. I'm sure the authorities would love to hear that."

She shook her head, lengthy brown strands moving over eyes so familiar to me. Eyes just like mine. We had the same eyes given to us by our mom. She sneered, narrowing them. "You're so good at that, aren't you? Telling on folks?"

I wouldn't let her do this. I got up to clean the room and she followed me.

"Is this for attention?" she asked, jabbing me more with her words. "You coming in here being super woman with your caveman next door?"

She couldn't prod me. I continued to move, but that didn't stop her from trying.

"You think that makes you better, too, don't you?" she went on. "You flashing around that tank with his little accent and saving us riffraff from ourselves?"

I didn't know why I chose to answer, but I did, turning. "Of course not. You know it's not like that, Elena. I don't think that."

"Oh, but you do," she snipped, tossing her bag on the chair. "You *always* do. If it wasn't for you... If it wasn't for you..."

Her voice got caught up at the end, the truth of her emotions cutting past that hard exterior. They said how she truly felt, how she'd *always* felt about me, and that told me nothing changed. I wondered if it ever would.

Sickened by how she felt and so much more, I stepped back from her. I didn't want to be near her. "You're still doing this. You're *still* blaming me for everything he did when the only party to blame is him."

She looked away, but I continued. I made myself.

"You know your son has nightmares?" I went on, highlighting yet another element of the man she brought into his life. "Nightmares from watching his mama being hurt?"

The evidence of them I saw only last night. I got to hold him through them, though. I got to hold him and he slept. "And now you bring the very source of his terror back into his life. It's selfish, Elena. Selfish."

"Nathan only did what he did yesterday because of you," she said, shooting a finger at me. "He's angry, Alex. He's angry because of you."

I shook my head at her. "So now what?" I asked her, raising and dropping my hands. "He's angry and will always be, so where does that leave *you*, Elena? Where does it leave Aiden? Does he just sit back? Sit back, watch, and *learn*, from that?"

Her jaw moved a bit, her nostrils flaring. "My business is my business and Nathan isn't a violent man."

"Only when he drinks, right?" I said, sarcasm in my voice. "Well, he wasn't drunk that day in the car, Elena. He wasn't drunk when he—"

"Stop!" she raised her hand and I knew I lost her. I always did when we got to that point.

Giving up, I picked up Aiden's bag. "I'm taking Aiden away. I'm taking him someplace safe and you can come if you want to, but no one is making you."

She didn't say a word when I went to the bathroom door and stopping, I put my hand on it. "But if you do come? The drugs stay here."

Because I knew she had them. I searched her bag just last night.

I went to turn the knob of the bathroom and heard her voice. It made me close my eyes.

"Always so good," she muttered. "Always so perfect with her perfect life and little boyfriend."

If only she knew the truth, because if she did, maybe she wouldn't have been so cruel. My life wasn't perfect and I didn't have a boyfriend either. I had a feeling I gave him up just last night. I gave him up for her.

Twenty-Three

BRODY

THE WELCOME PARTY came in the form of my gram. Standing tall, her little hands on her hips, she stood on the porch in her cowboy boots and Stetson hat as if three whole feet taller than her short stature. She made the world go round, this woman. She kept my family's world going around.

Which was why it was so hard to come here today.

She lifted her hand, waving in the direction of my truck coming up her graveled path, and I greeted her back through the window, knowing the rest of the passengers might be too scared or too uneasy to do the same.

Like I knew, the small family remained silent, their hands in their laps. They'd barely spoken the entire drive, not even at the rest stops. I hoped this trip would help with that in some way and allow them to let their minds go a bit after everything that came about yesterday. My gram's place had a way of aiding in escape and the company? It definitely didn't hurt either.

She had sunshine on her face, my gram. Only going as far as the steps, she let us come the rest of the way. She always knew how to handle things.

I had warned her of course of what was to come. I had to for the obvious and though, she didn't care like I knew she wouldn't, that didn't mean me coming to her in this way didn't concern her. I'd been doing that a lot lately—concerning everybody.

Coming up the steps, I squeezed her as if nothing was wrong.

"Hey, Gram."

Her smile shined, her hand coming down on my back. "Sweet darlin'."

She always could revert me back, back to the time when she'd been the one taller than me. I drew back, turning toward the folks I knew lingered at the bottom of the steps. That's where they stopped after we all got out.

I went back down to them and instinctually went to grab the back of Alex's elbow to guide her, to help her, but before the moment of contact, my hand held its station. I simply hovered, letting her know it was okay to come forward.

I tried to ignore what flashed across her face, how the action made her sad looking, made her frown.

"Gram, this is Alex. Alexa," I said, introducing the her. "And, Alex, this is my Grandma Rose."

Though, she had her big hat on, I could still make out Gram's gray eyes. They lingered warmly over Alex, but I didn't miss their pass over me. Gram held her hand out. "Nice, to meet you, Alexa."

Alex smiled a little, so meek, her hand went out rather slowly, shaking it. "Thanks for letting us stay here," she said, gesturing to her small family. Her sister stood on the bottom step, and in between them, Aiden held both their hands on the middle stair, an action figure's head poking out the back of his book bag.

"My sister and nephew thank you, too," she went on.

My gram couldn't have looked more pleased, her hands

rested in front of her apron. She gazed around a bit, giving Aiden one of her warmest smiles. "My pleasure."

Aiden had been through a lot, yesterday what I was sure was only a snapshot I'd seen of his life, so when the smile went unreturned, I wasn't surprised. His head dipped a bit instead, stepping behind Alex, but Gram didn't take any offense. That wasn't her nature.

"I'm sure y'all are tired," she went on instead, not missing a beat. "I've cleaned up some rooms for you on the second floor."

"Oh, we only need one." Alex was the one to speak on behalf of her family again. "We wouldn't want to inconvenience you. One will be fine. We don't need a lot of space."

Gram didn't argue, though, she did look a little sad.

That got my heart a bit, too.

Gram stepped aside, holding her arms out to let them all know it was okay, her home was okay, and though Alex passed, taking Aiden and Elena with her, I knew it would take some time for them all to believe that. The last to get one of Gram's friendly smiles was Alexa's sister, Elena, but like her son, I knew that one wouldn't be returned—though for a different reason. Even if Alex was alone with, her I had a feeling she wouldn't smile.

They all went in the house and Gram called, "First room at the top of stairs."

They found the stairwell quickly as it was right within view of the door and didn't hesitate going up. I was sure because that meant seclusion soon, security. I didn't want to bother them, so I stayed with Gram, thanking her.

I had explained some things on the phone last night. I told her I had a friend and that friend and her family needed some help. I went into the details of the day after that, about California and the riffraff left behind, and she all but shamed me for even asking and not just coming.

"We'll only be a few days," I told her now.

"They can stay as long as they'd like, Brody," Gram responded, and I knew that's exactly how it'd be with her. She told me something similar last night, but this situation I never intended on being permanent. I had a place of my own. In fact, the only way I was okay with the temporary arrangement was because Gram would be alone these next few days anyway, my Aunt Robin away at a trade show, and me coming with Alex and her family meant she'd have some company. I didn't like her being in a big house by herself so the arrangement worked out for both parties.

I acknowledged what she said with a nod, though, I had no intention of taking her up on the offer. We really just needed the few days, some time away. I went to go inside, but she touched my arm, sliding it down to my wrist and squeezing.

"She's real pretty, Brody," she said, surprising me, and then she smiled a little, but I noticed it was also sad.

"If she's your reason," she went on. "Your reason for being gone? That's okay," she said. "Just know that's okay."

She was the one to leave me standing there then and the cowardice shook me to my very bones.

Because I let her walk away thinking just that.

Twenty-Four

ALEXA

SOMETHING VIOLENT, sharp, hit me from my front and I thrashed, cowering. Holding myself tight, I formed a little ball. By being small, I hoped to be able to evade it, but no, that only made it worse. Me attempting to protect myself only made him come for me faster.

He ripped at my arms, hitting me with a grimace on his lips, and I'd never forget it. That's what made the bile first rise.

He hit again, catching my cheek this time.

"No!" I cried. I cried so hard. "No, leave me alone."

"Alex!"

I twisted. I turned.

"Aunt Alex!"

My eyes shot open, darkness of the night surrounding me in the wide bed. Beside me, my nephew bended and bowed wildly, calling both my name and his mama's, and she was there, too, Elena. Her eyes wide at me, she swallowed. She swallowed so hard with her hand hovering over my arm. Had she been the one to wake me up?

Aiden corkscrewed again and I let my thoughts hang where they were. I went to wake him up from his nightmare, but a hand came down on me. I think it had been the same one to bring me out of my own nightmare.

"I got it," Elena snipped, shaking him.

Her son gasped out of his sleep, still calling my name, still calling Elena's. He got a visual on both of us, though, and he calmed down, and though I wanted to hold him, Elena got to him first. She brought her to him, letting him cry on her while she whispered soothing words.

"Joe? Where's Joe?" he called, crying into her neck.

My head still spinning, I patted the bed in the dark room. I found the action figure on the end, but again Elena was there. She stole it from under my outstretched hand and fell back, tucking it underneath Aiden's arm.

I could do nothing but let her.

Lying back, I did what I could from my side. I rubbed my nephew's back, comforting close, and I didn't relax until he finally calmed down from his dream. His mama helped him there, yes, but something told me if I hadn't been so adamant she wouldn't have bothered.

She only seemed to care when I did.

With the dream, I never thought I'd be able to make it back into slumber. I would be too lost in my head and stuck in the madness of it. But something happened throughout the night and something changed as I felt the morning sun cast its glow on my cheek in the early morning. I awoke to a calm heart, as well as the smell of warm biscuits weaving their way through my lungs.

I gripped the blanket around me, pulling it close, and when I rose up, lying back against the headboard, I saw Brody through a window.

Raising an ax, he drove it clear through a small stump of

wood, but after he did, he rested for a moment. He rested, putting his foot up on the broken pieces, and his long fingers wiped at his brow. That rest didn't sit well with me, nor what he was doing, at all. He was pushing himself, pushing himself unnecessarily for some reason.

Stepping down from the stump, he raised that ax again and I willed him not to. I begged. I pleaded even from so far away. Opening my mouth, I almost called to him, but like he knew, he stopped.

He stopped.

His eyes lifted then. They lifted my way, and when they did, he lowered that ax entirely.

I shook my head at him, as if saying don't do this, and he didn't. He listened. The ax he rested against the fence outside and the lumber he cut, the two small pieces, he picked up and headed back toward the house with them.

I could breathe again.

"Aunt Alex?"

My nephew lay under the blankets, shrugging out of them. He sat up and I brought my arms around him, hugging him good morning. He smiled then, making my heart warm.

"You sleep okay?" I asked him, and he nodded, yawning.

His mouth closed, looking sleepy, but also awake in that just woke up daze. He placed his hands in his lap. "Is that bacon, you think?" he asked. He whispered the words like the very sound of them would make the smell fade. I smelled it, too.

I rubbed his arm. "I think so. You hungry?"

He seemed unsure how to respond to that, but that was Aiden, though. He never asked for anything. He always just took what he was given. I was sure because of years of so many limited options. He held his doll, Joe, wrapping his arms around him.

I tilted my head. "It's okay if you are. Hungry?"

That got a nod then and I ran my fingers over his braids.

"Do you wanna go check it out?" I asked. I prodded knowing he'd need it.

He looked at his mama still sleeping. Sometime during the night, Elena had turned on her belly, her arm over the side of the bed. He looked at me. "You think that would be okay?" Maybe it was my fault that he felt he had to ask. We'd taken dinner up here last night and I hadn't fought Brody's grandma when she knocked on our door and offered that option instead of us coming down.

I tapped his leg. "Come on. We'll go down and see what that bacon's about."

He smiled a little, but frowned a little too in Elena's direction. I told him I'd wake her while he got washed up. This room even had a connected bathroom. We investigated last night.

He slid off the bed, taking Joe with him and gazed down at my sister. It took a bit of confidence to reach over and wake her up, especially after last night, but I tried to when I touched her arm. That touch turned into a shake though, and that one-hand shake turned into two.

"Elena," I said to her. "Elena, wake up."

A noise left her mouth. She turned on her back and her hand flew in the air as if to slap me away. But something told me she had no idea she'd even tried to do that. Her hand landed on the pillow and when it did, the ring she wore opened. Something white fell out of it, powder, and I knew exactly what it was.

I didn't even think when I grabbed her hand, sliding the ring off. She didn't even move. I went immediately to the window and poured all the power out into the air, fire in my cheeks. Sometime in the night she'd managed to get high and she did it despite the fact her son needed her all night.

Why did she keep doing this to herself? To Aiden?

To me?

Once I knew the ring was clear, I returned it to its owner, not even bothering to be gentle. She'd be out all day. I'd seen this too many times before. What I did do was leave the ring open with her arm in a random angle on the bed. She'd think she spilled it all by herself that way. She had a healthy amount of residue on her pillow, but I wouldn't put it past her to believe she snorted it all last night. She'd done worse.

Aiden came out of the bathroom moments later and when he asked about his mom, I had to do something I hated. I had to lie to him.

Brody

I didn't want her to see me that way, but knew it was a possibility when Gram asked me to go get firewood this morning. She always asked me to do it. She always asked me because that had always been my chore even from the time when I'd been a kid. I had always been the biggest, the strongest.

How times had changed.

Today, had been a bad day and, though, I knew I had those sometimes, they had been few and far between. My medications made sure of that. So when I woke up this morning, feeling all kinds of spent, I understood immediately that it was stress.

I placed the firewood into the hearth, one by one, the method allowing me to use the least bit of effort. The fireplace going was a given since Gram had guests. She liked it crackling in the morning for when people woke up and I didn't fight her. I loved the smell. That combined with her home cooking, I couldn't help be drawn into it. Skillet hash browns, sawmill gravy, and buttermilk biscuits surrounded me. They surrounded me with home.

Stress, so much stress. Calm down.

Forcing the thoughts, I went into the kitchen and the sight of a girl and her nephew took me by surprise. They hadn't been in there only moments prior when I walked from the back porch with the firewood, but now they sat eating those biscuits and gravy, and the girl? She was damn beautiful.

I wanted to wrap my arms around Alex immediately. It had been too long. Too much time had passed since... I touched her.

I chose the opposite seat across from her though, the one near the stove and near my gram. Gram turned around as I made my way, hugging me and thanking me for the firewood. I kissed her cheek before sitting down and telling the folks across from me, "Mornin.'"

They both said "good morning," though, shy about it. Especially, Alex. I'd say that had been her nature, but she hadn't been that way in so long with me.

"Did y'all, uh," I asked her picking up the coffee press pot. "Did you both sleep okay?" I offered her coffee first, but she waved her hand allowing me to go for my own.

"Yeah, it was great," she said. She turned to my gram. "And thanks so much for letting us stay for a little while. We really appreciate it."

Gram's hands stopped over her skillet. Tilting her head, she picked it up and came over. "Of course, darlin.' Of course," she said, scooping some eggs onto Aiden's plate. She smiled at him. "It's not a problem."

Alex lowered, placing her hand on her nephew's head. "Tell her thank you."

"Thank you," he whispered, but something told me he had a voice in him. He just wasn't ready to use it quite yet. His arms moved around his toy and I couldn't help smiling. He really didn't go anywhere without him.

I sat the pot down after pouring a full cup, noting an absence from the party. "Your sister okay?" I asked, and Alex's eyes flashed like she just became aware.

She went small. "Uh, huh. She's just feeling a little under the weather."

"Oh, no." Gram lowered her skillet. "I'll bring her up some tea and something light. That'll help."

Alex's hands shot up in front of herself. "No need. I think she just needs to sleep. Sleep it off. I plan to check on her later."

Those brown eyes averted after that, from me, from everyone, and something told me it wasn't so simple.

I breathed, trying not to let that bother me. I wanted to know more, but the fact of the matter was Alex had shut me out again. She shut me out and I didn't know how to deal with that. I didn't know how *not* to help her, care about her. Gram came around with the bacon and when she got to Aiden's plate, Alex said just a piece or two before taking some herself.

"He's diabetic," she said, and when Gram came over to my plate, Alex watched me. She watched me not decline. I took several pieces and hoped she wouldn't call attention to that. She didn't. Though, she did frown.

"Brody, darlin'?" my gram said, placing that bacon plate in the middle for all. "Do you think while you're here you can help me with something?"

"Sure," I told her. "What do you need?" We both knew she didn't have to ask, but that was Gram's way.

She held the back of an empty chair. "Some feed came in yesterday. It's in the shed and needs to be taken to the barn. I'd normally have one of the hands get it..."

"Not a problem," I told her, not thinking much over it.

Gram smiled. "It'll need to go in the barn for the milking cow. It's only a few fifty pound bags. You'll get it done in no time."

Now that did get Alex stirring a little, especially when I told Gram once again no problem. That's because it wasn't a problem. I didn't do work like this all the time so it wasn't a big deal, but Alex? She didn't let it go that easily. In fact, she sat forward and my heart raced as my first fear came before me. She didn't know my gram was in the dark about my heart condition.

She didn't know she was the only one I told.

"Brody, I think you shouldn't," she started, but her mouth shut when I said something once again.

"No big deal, Gram," I told her, and turned my head after that. I had to. That look that washed over Alex's face, her clearly being dismissed, I couldn't face. It hurt me. My saving grace came in the form of her nephew, taking the conversation in a different direction.

"You guys have cows?" he asked, sitting up. "Real cows?"

Gram put her hand on the back of his chair. "We do, darlin', as well as chickens and a few goats."

"And don't forget the horses, Gram," I finished for her with a smile.

That sent Aiden in a legitimate frenzy. He wasn't shy about turning to Alex and asking if he could see them. He wanted to see everything and Gram suggested he come out when I did to move the feed. We could venture around her land and then end there. Aiden begged again, needing his aunt's approval first, but she turned to me, making eye contact like she needed mine.

"We'll go out after breakfast," I told her, and hoped what happened at the table stayed there.

Twenty-Five

ALEXA

HE WAS MORE upset with me than I thought; mad. A chill came from Brody I never felt before, and now, it seemed like he wasn't even taking care of himself. I feared a connection, a connection to me and his health, but I couldn't even ask him about it. He blocked me out. He drew away from me.

Kinda like I'd done to him.

Holding Aiden's hand, I was forced to ignore what happened at the table and Brody made that easy. He didn't address any of that. He just focused on taking me and my nephew around the ranch and that's when some of the tension abated. His attention went to the land and this beautiful place of wide hills and rocky peaks he called home. And he was at home here. He was *comfortable* among family. He showed us around with his grandma and didn't go far from her side. When he wasn't with her, he was with Aiden. He showed him everything, pointing out all the animals and even the plants, giving their backgrounds. Like our own little nature guide in this arid land of hills and valley. It was so different from anywhere I'd been and I had travelled all over the country, a wanderer. But Brody, he wasn't a wanderer. This was his place. He belonged here and I got that more and more as we walked.

Later in the day, Aiden squealed from under Dolly, an old dairy cow. He'd been given the chance to milk her with permission from Brody's grandma and the milk squirting out of the pail at him, had taken him by surprise. That squeal had only been marked by a laugh, though, a *laugh* and I watched in fascination at the possibility, the magic of it. A shot of milk hit the pail once more, but Brody was there in a flash to help my nephew get the old cow under control, nothing but a smile on his face as he did. Squatting down, he got beside Aiden in his faded jeans. They were all dirtied up and ripped, like he'd put some work into them before coming here. He also had his messy blond hair under a large hat. His grandma gave us all one for the sun today after we'd broke shortly for lunch.

"Like this, bud. You can't let Dolly get one on you," Brody said, squeezing the cow udder. The milk came out in a steady stream and Aiden watched closely, studying. Eventually, Brody scooted aside and let Aiden take things away again. He did it this time perfectly and Brody stood, his hands on his hips as he watched his young protégé with a smile.

I stepped forward and Brody's blue eyes flickered up, catching me like a stunned gazelle. Just as quickly, his gaze left and something turned in me, something deep, something that hurt. He stood, pointing behind him.

"Gram, I'm going to go ahead and get those bags. The feed?" he said.

And so my stomach flipped again. I didn't want him to do this, to push himself for no reason. I was sure his grandma would understand letting him take it easy.

Why doesn't he just ask?

Brody's eyes connected with mine, staring a hole right through me, and my thoughts of before surfaced. I questioned if he was doing this all, going overboard, because of me, but I couldn't protest even if it were true. I didn't feel it was appropriate.

Instead, I let him go. He disappeared around a corner in the back of the barn and I chose to go to my nephew, popping a squat beside him on a turned-over crate. He was where my focus should be.

Him and Elena were the choice I made.

I sat there, rubbing his back, and Brody's Grandma Rose brushed the brown cow above him, unable to stop her grin as she watched Aiden master her cow. She lowered the brush. "We'll have milk for weeks at this rate, darlin.' Keep up the good work."

And my nephew, in all his cow-milking glory, showed his teeth with pride. He'd done that so many times today. We'd been all over the ranch and Rose had allowed Aiden to do some chores. Not only did he do them, but *loved* doing them. Perhaps, he was feeling a sense of comfort here, too, a love for this place, too, and I was so glad.

Wheels squeaked behind me, and Brody came out with a wheel barrow.

Thank God, he's at least using that.

He left the barn without a word through the front door. I tried not to let that bother me. Laying the brush down, Rose bent. She exchanged the pail Aiden managed to fill half way. "We'll have this tonight," she said, raising it. "I plan on making fried chicken. We'll use it in the mashed potatoes."

I didn't know what excited Aiden more. The fact that we'd be having what I knew to be such a great meal from our hostess or that we'd be consuming the fruits of his hard work.

"Can I help?" he asked her. "With dinner?"

Who was this little boy and where was my nephew? Chores were something I could never get him to do back when I lived with him and my sister, but now the very thought couldn't keep the smile off his face.

I hugged him, so grateful. I owed yet another thing to Brody, another debt.

Rose patted Dolly. "Of course, sweet pea. I'm getting started on it real soon. Maybe in about an hour?"

"Yeah!"

"So, that's just in time then," I said, bringing him close. "For you to go lay down and take it easy for a bit." We'd been running since early this morning, stopping only to have a quick lunch, so he had to be tired.

He frowned, concentrating on his task under the cow. "I don't need to rest, Aunt Alex. I'm fine." But even as he said it, his eyes drooped. Like the very thought made him realize how tired he was.

I nudged his leg. "Just a quick one. You've been all over the place today."

It didn't look like he wanted to, but he let go of Dolly, standing when I did. Bending down, he picked up Joe. He'd had a front row seat while Aiden milked. Holding the toy under his arm, he faced Rose. "Ms. Rose, can we use all the other stuff we got today for dinner?"

By "stuff," he referred to all the magic of her garden. He picked all kinds of things today. All kinds of delicious-looking things.

Ms. Rose herself placed her hands on her hips. "Now, I can't see why not. You have to be careful offering to help me with all this, though, youngin'. I might end up offering you a job as one of my hands."

The proposal couldn't have gone over better with him. Aiden looked on the verge of bursting, but my little ranch hand needed a nap first before doing any more heavy labor. I smoothed my hand over his head before taking his palm. "Come on, you little crazy. You can help after you've slept."

He nodded his head of braided locks, that sleep suddenly moving over his face and hazing his eyes. I supposed this all was catching up with him after all. We started to walk away when a body stopped directly in front us.

Elena.

She looked half awake, barely there, and I didn't miss the anger, the tension wrinkling her brow.

Does she know? Does she know I threw away her stash?

"Elena," I said, trying to play it off. "Is everything, okay? Are you feeling better?"

Her eyebrows narrowed and honestly, I thought this was it. The bomb was about to drop and she was going to do this right now. She was going to do it in front of her son and Brody's wonderful grandma. Instead, she grabbed Aiden's hand. "Where are you going with my kid?"

"They were going inside to rest," came from my side. Rose. Her hands in her apron, the warmest expression lit her face and it reminded me so much of another. It reminded me because it put me at ease. She smiled. "Do y'all want me to lead you back to the house?"

Elena's jaw moved a bit and maybe because she couldn't find a place for her anger in front of his kind woman. With Ms. Rose's sunshine emanating, it was so hard. Eventually, Elena shook her head, telling her, "That's okay," before looking at me. "And I'll do it. I'll take him in."

I let out a breath. "Elena..."

But she was already walking away, taking Aiden with her. He turned, gazing at me over his shoulder, but I waved him on, letting him know it was okay.

Joe went up to his chin and that had been the first time all day he had to have him so close. Eventually, he let his mama tug him forward and the two headed in the general direction of the house.

"You know, I had a sister, too." It was Rose. It was Grandma Rose again. "An older one, once upon a time."

"Yeah?" I questioned, watching mine walk away. It felt like so far away.

Rose nodded. "We fought all the time. Like cats and dogs, but things changed. They changed when I made myself known."

I had no time to let my thoughts even wonder over that with her. Her grandson came in, big and all encompassing. Wheelbarrow full, Brody pushed those heavy bags and if he hadn't told me about his heart, I never would have questioned any lack of strength. That's because he didn't lack any. He never would.

Rose touched my arm. "I'll make sure they get back to the house okay," she said, patting my shoulder before going over to Brody. She directed him exactly where to wheel them, but told him not to worry about putting them away. She had people coming in to do that later to feed the cow and the other animals. After that, she left and that left her grandson and me out of sorts. We were out of sorts because we were alone again.

Ten or so feet maybe stood between us, ten short, yet excruciatingly long feet. I felt them in so many ways.

His large hands went into his jean pockets, his brown boot digging into the dirt. "I uh, passed Aiden on the way back. Aiden and your sister."

My own hands went into the back of my jean shorts. "Yeah. They went in for a nap. She took him."

He nodded with that. "She didn't look sick. Is she better?"

Better? No, she wasn't better. I wasn't sure she'd ever be. As I couldn't answer him honestly, I simply shrugged and we stood there with silence, so much silence. The two of us in there so long, I thought Brody might simply walk away. *We'd* walk away from each other and everything else. What I didn't expect was him to come closer. I didn't expect him to come to me.

I felt him everywhere, though, he didn't touch me. His

body cast a shadow, a warm envelope that hovered all around me. His fingers went up and I lost my breath, the callused pads choosing to touch my sleeve. He played with the material between his fingertips, not saying a single word until, well, he did.

"Wanna take a walk?" he asked, and I... I said yes.

The walk turned out to be one of forever, his grandma's beautiful property surrounding us as we strode through the abyss of it. We passed ranch hands manning the land. Others took care of the small animals grazing and Brody knew them all, lifting a hand in greeting to everyone. They all seemed happy to be here. I couldn't blame them because *here* was wonderful.

I pushed my hands in my back pockets, kicking a stray rock ahead. "Your grandma is nice," I told him. They were the first words I said really and I chose them well. They made him smile.

Brody's head went back with it. "Yeah, she is."

"What did, uh," I started, placing a boot in front of the other. "What did you tell her about us? About where we came from and why?" That's something I hadn't asked him, but judging by the nonchalant way she handled us being here, he had to have told her something lighter than...

"The truth," he said, suddenly surprising me. In fact, he said it so simply and without reprieve that I envied him. I envied his ability to tell the truth. Maybe if I had, things would have been different. *We* would have been different. His hands settled atop a wooden fence we approached, his gaze searching the wide field it incased.

"I tell them..." he started, but his eyes went narrow. They softened, creasing tight in the corners like he caught the high sun in them. The tip of his hat tipped down, the hem lined in a thin layer of sweat. He lifted it, catching a few beads with the back to his hand. "I tell them everything," he ended up finishing his sentence with. He swallowed, lips tight. "My family. I tell them everything."

My arm wrapped around the fence post, I studied him. I eyed his stature, slumped, and his eyes lost. This so wasn't like Brody. It wasn't like him at all. The appearance of a gentle beast brought me out of my thoughts, as well as ignited some light back into Brody's blue eyes. The horse pushed its face into Brody's hands when he lifted them, nudging him for attention. He gave in right away, his thick fingers moving in light strokes between two large nut brown eyes. The caress, the care of it, reminded me of the ways in which he, too, brought me to surrender. He touched me in ways so delicately. He made me feel. He made me *want* to feel.

"You ever ridden?" he asked, helping me escape the conclaves of me mind.

I shook my head, my arm falling down the post. "Not unless the ponies at the zoo count," I said, laughing a little, and that made magic happen. He laughed, too.

Stepping with he or she, Brody brought the horse my way, a tip of his hat gesturing me to touch her. Reaching out, I was surprised by the silky feeling. I mean, the skin looked soft, but a fine velvet my hand didn't expect. I very much liked it and turned out the horse did, too, running its face along my hand.

Brody fell back to the post, letting the two of us have our moment. His fingers tapping against his chest, he seemed to consider something while we did. "You wouldn't want to...?" he paused, his jaw working a little. He tipped back his hat. "You wouldn't want to ride her, would you? I can show you how if you want."

My fingers slid from the horse, not really expecting that. Things had been so weird and awkward between us, but now he was wanting to spend time with me again. Maybe it was fleeting but he did. Chewing my lip, I went to tell him I wanted to, but thought about something as I faced the direction of the house. I faced the weight of my obligations.

"It's getting kind of late is all," I told him. The words hurt to even think about, but felt far worse said. I wanted nothing more than to spend time with him, ride with him. I pulled my hat off. "It's just, it's Aiden. I probably shouldn't be away too long. I need to be there when he gets up. And also... I think he'd want to ride, too. I know he would." The horses were one thing he'd been super excited to see, but we hadn't made it this far out today. If he were here now, he'd definitely want to ride with us.

Brody's smile faded a little, which consequently made part of me sear inside. Gazing away, he looked like he'd let it go, but then he turned my way. "Maybe just a few minutes then," he said, making me blink, and also blowing me away for the second time in short minutes. He shrugged a little. "A short ride won't take long. We won't go far and I'd be happy to take him out tomorrow. Weather is always good for it here. I don't mind. I love riding."

He should have given up after I declined. Everything pointed toward that route, but he didn't.

And I loved him for it.

I never imagined myself to be much of a country gal and heck, no way a horse rider. But once I got up there, up on Delilah as Brody called her, I noticed immediately the air was different. The *world* was different and I got to enjoy it with him.

Brody trotted beside me, a cautious hand ready and waiting to help at any given moment. He'd been doing that the whole ride since the crash course he gave me. "You got her all right?" he asked, passing a look over to me.

With gentle steps, I did. I totally did. I nodded and that

hand of his went back; Brody directing us. We went downhill a bit, a dirt trail that took us into another land, another land where the world opened up. There were no buildings, just mountainous land.

And it was amazing.

Canyons of a golden brown contrasted the green and yellow blades of short grass under our horse's hooves. We bobbed with every step, the world a bottle of trapped sunshine in the oasis we'd somehow found ourselves in.

"Something, isn't it?" They were the first words he said in many steps, many gallops. Brody seemed so at home here and seeing all this, I understood why. His eyes narrowed with the bright reflection of the lowering sun. He pulled down his hat, protecting his eyes and took us into it, those brown hilltops soaring with waves of sunshine.

I allowed myself to breathe it in. I took it all in. How cool would it be to live here? To be a *part* of this every day from the time of waking up to closing your eyes. I'd lived a lot of places, but nothing and nowhere was like this.

We stationed out there for a while, just sitting atop our horses, their warm bodies rising and falling gently underneath. Eventually, Brody summoned Charlie, his own riding horse, and my heart did a bit of a drop. We had ridden for a little bit and I assumed it was time to end the ride. It was time to head back to the house. Brody maneuvered Charlie, and though he did turn, we didn't head back. He simply redirected us to the side, to a tree in particular. Brody ended up dismounting there, motioning me to do the same after he tied up Charlie to a thick branch.

Frozen, I realized I didn't know how to do that—get down, and that must have read all over my face.

A smile pushed into the corner of his full lips. Taking off his hat, he placed it between two thick branches, then came over, holding out his hands to me. I took them without thought, bringing my leg around, and Brody did the rest. Before I knew it, I was in his arms, the back of my jeans sliding down velvet and my front sliding down him.

I brought my arms around his neck for security, but they stayed long after my shoes hit the ground. His heart beat so hard when I got there, thumping clear through both his shirt and mine. The muscle inside my chest matched the rapid beat and I followed them both, each responding to the other as if dancing.

My hands slid down his collar, this moment reminding me of one not so long ago. It was the first moment I silently begged him to kiss me at the bar. My lips pleaded for it now and my heart bled for it. It bled because I knew deep down he wouldn't. There was still too much between us. There was too much that wouldn't let go of us.

My fingers slid from his shirt when he created the distance I assumed matched what had formed between us over the last couple days. Reaching around me, he grabbed Delilah and I stepped back out of his way. He tied both horses to the tree and I waited patiently, trying not to let what happened play out all over my face.

You did this to yourself. It's your fault.

His sweet smell brought him back to me and out of the thicket of thoughts in my head. In his hand, he had a blanket and as Charlie had saddlebags, that's probably where it came from. Brody snapped it out and it fluttered like a calm wave to the ground. His hand splayed out toward the blanket, inviting me to it, and he took his seat only after I chose mine, the right side.

Sliding my hat off, I tucked my foot under my knee, marveling at the new vantage point. "This place," I said, studying the amber hills. "It's magic."

Leaning forward, Brody's arms wrested atop his large legs. He didn't say anything, but a sudden smile moving across his face made me call attention to it. I couldn't help it I guess.

"What?" I asked him, feeling shy all the sudden. "Is that dumb?"

Some of those lengthy blond tendrils moved across his brow with the breeze. He shook his head. "No," he said, facing me. His boots secured into the blanket when he raised his knees higher. "It's just funny you said that."

"Why?"

His smile went full then. "Because that's probably why he took us here," he said, gazing toward the land again. "My pop. He brought me and my brothers here once when we were kids. This exact spot." His finger pushed out toward the area. "I guess it just makes sense with what you said."

I wanted to ask him more. I wanted to ask him how so, but something told me not to.

I crossed my legs, going silent, and that's when he spoke. That's also when the smile left his lips.

"He told us about momma here," he said. Sitting back, he watched the sky. "An evening similar to this when the sun was setting."

His mom. That had been one person he'd never mentioned to me before. He talked about his brothers every so often and his dad of course. His grandma was even in his pictures at home, but no mom. No mom. He squinted with the sun. "She liked to make her disappearances, my momma. We wouldn't see her for weeks at a time."

He picked up a blade of grass, tossing it before resting his legs on his knees again. He shrugged. "Here's where Pop told us she wouldn't be... she wouldn't be here anymore. She left for good and wouldn't be coming back this time."

His voice didn't hold any pain like I expected it would from his admission. Perhaps the wounds were no longer fresh.

Perhaps he was at peace, but regardless, I didn't miss the power in his words.

And the fact that he was sharing them with me.

"He said we'd be okay, though," Brody went on. He faced me then, and when he did, he smiled once more. "And in the end, we ended up being so. That's why I said what I did about you saying this place being magic." He eyes scanned the sky. "I guess there is a little bit of it out here. A lot really."

Those blue eyes found mine, those sparkling ones. I nodded in confirmation of his statement, acknowledging it, but that's where it ended for me. I had to end it there. I couldn't believe in magic, because every time I let myself... Every time I tried...

I closed my eyes, falling into myself, my head. I couldn't break free of it this time. I couldn't recover from the loss because I was still grieving. I once believed the gift of Brody had been magic, but he, too, I managed to lose.

His finger came to my cheek and that's when I realized I was crying. He turned me, a hand on my knee, and couldn't have looked more confused as to why I'd broken down right here before him. I didn't blame him. That was something I was also trying to discover, trying to fight. I averted my eyes like that would help, but then that finger tipped my chin and I couldn't hide. He never let me hide.

"Alex?" he asked.

I looked away again, sniffing. "I know what you need from me. I know you want me to be open with you, honest." I gazed away, the tears moving down my cheeks. "And you deserve that, Brody. You deserve that."

The words looked like it pained him to hear, his eyes creasing. His hand came up to touch my face. "Alexa..."

I looked down. I couldn't do it. I wasn't strong enough and his eyes didn't make it easier, the concern crumpled within them.

He raised my chin by my cheeks, leaning in. "You listen to me. You don't have to tell me anything you don't want to. I've been a jerk, Alex. I've been..." His jaw moved, his blond lashes shifting over his eyes. He gazed up. "I've been dumb. I don't want you saying anything you're not ready to. I'll wait, Alexa. I'll wait as long as you want me to."

But that's the thing.

He shouldn't have to.

~

Brody

"I'm the bad thing," she whispered. Her voice was so quiet, so aching. "I was the bad thing he did."

I stared at her, not knowing what to make of that statement. Bad thing? How was she ever? She was never.

She opened her mouth again, gasping for breath with no words and I wanted her to stop. Whatever she was trying to tell me... it hurt her. It was causing pain to line her face, her cheeks.

I touched one and a tear rolled down them. A piece of me broke inside when it did. This was my fault. I made her feel like she had to talk to me. I admit I had been frustrated. Alex had been closing herself off since I met her and I guess my breaking point made me freeze her out. *This* wasn't what I wanted, though, her crying and forcing herself to talk to me. I wanted her to open her heart to me, but not until she was ready.

"Alex, don't," I urged. I had made a mistake. I knew that now. Moving my hands to her shoulders, I leaned my forehead against hers. "You don't have to do this. Don't feel like you have to."

"I'm just…" she whispered, shaking. "I'm scared you won't want to be with me anymore."

My eyes closed tight. I brought her into my arms and she felt so small. She always felt so small; that first day so vulnerable. I kissed her forehead. "Nothing you could tell me could ever make me not want to be with you." And I meant it. I meant every goddamn word, but that didn't stop her. It didn't stop her from shaking her head.

"You'll see me differently." She sniffed, pulling away. "And then I'll be alone. That's why my sister won't talk to me. That's why I'm alone."

I grabbed her arms. "Alex—"

"It was *me*, Brody. I'm why Nathan got locked up. *I'm* why he served time. *Me.*"

My brain grasped to make sense of any and all things she was saying. It all was a thicket of words, jumbled, but then, I took a step back from my head. I listened. I took them in.

"I'm the bad thing… I was the bad thing he did."

My jaw locked, my body frozen. Her words bolted me, shattered me.

But they broke her more.

Her head down, the tears fell from her eyes and I held her quivering body, bringing her into me. Her fingers tangled in my shirt, the water from her eyes dampening it and all the while I held her, trying, *fighting*, to stay right here. I fought from doing something else, because if what I feared were true… if I understood correctly what she was telling me, there was no reason I should be standing here right now.

There's no reason *he* shouldn't be dead right now.

"It happened when I was sixteen," she whispered. I shook. She went on. "And Elena…" She breathed. She cried. "She didn't believe me at first."

I closed my eyes, holding her tighter. I had to. I had to in order to keep myself sane. How could her sister not believe her? How could she...

"But I had proof," she continued. "I went to the hospital and... and..."

"Stop," I told her. I *urged* her, but not because I couldn't take it. I didn't want her to take it, to relive it like she clearly was in her mind. "You don't have to. You don't."

"But then she said I asked for it." I could barely hear her now. Tears, so many tears. She sniffed them back. "She said I did with my clothes and the way I dressed. She said I led him on. She said I teased. She said..."

I couldn't help it after that.

I snapped.

Blinded to the rage, I could only hear Alex in the distance. She pleaded with me. She called *to* me and I answered with words I faintly remembered.

"Home." I told her when she asked where we were going. I had been untying the horses. "Why?" she asked then and I couldn't tell her. I didn't want her to stop me. Regardless, her questions continued, her concern, and even though I chose not to answer them, that didn't matter.

She figured it out.

She grabbed my arm. "You're *not* going to him. You're not going to do anything."

I came out of it for a moment; my head. I didn't know how I managed, but I did, and I caged her face with my hands. I had to make her understand.

"He needs to pay," I told her. "Something needs to be done."

Her lip quivered. "Something like how? He served his time, Brody. He went to jail."

He went to jail, yes, but that didn't mean he paid for the crime he committed. I grabbed the reins of Delilah and Charlie. "We're going back to Gram's. Then you're going to stay there until I come back."

"And then I'll lose you, too!" she cried, falling back from me. "I'll lose you, too, like I lost everyone and everything to him. I lost my sister because of him. She froze me out, kept Aiden away, and now, I'll lose you, too, to him. I've lost everything to him, Brody. I've lost myself."

She said she lost...

Herself.

She walked away and I let her, the reins falling from my fingers. She didn't go far, to the tree I drew the horses from, but while she did, I stood with my thoughts. She thought she lost herself to him, Nathan, and now that she had, so many things were clear.

I saw that in her eyes, her thoughts of loss. Alex and her worth, she didn't connect sometimes. She didn't see what I'd always seen and she let people take advantage of her because of it. I saw it with that guy at the bar. I saw it with Chloe and even well before that. I met her in attempts to sell herself and I found her later on selling herself on stage. She felt she needed the money, yes, but I wondered if another way had even crossed her mind. Like, she defaulted to those routes with no other thoughts of the alternative. It was almost like she didn't feel she deserved any better and in fact, I knew that's exactly how she felt. I knew because she couldn't answer me the day at the café when I asked her why she didn't feel like she'd deserved help.

It all made sense now.

I went over to her. Her back was turned, her arms folded over her chest, but she still passed a look over her shoulder at me. I got within range and her hands went out to me, pressing firmly on my chest. They went in to cover my heart.

"You're not going," she said.

I grabbed her hands, shaking my head. "I'm not."

A little breath left her mouth. Her eyes closed and something inside me went peaceful. I thought that could only happen after settling the score with Nathan. I suppose, in the end, I didn't have to have that. I wanted it desperately, adamantly, but I didn't have to have it. Something I did need? Her. I needed her. I needed *this*... with her.

She was enough.

"You're enough," I told her, letting those words fall from my lips and pulling my arms around her, I let my mouth touch her ear. "You're enough and he hasn't taken anything from you. You're here. Every wonderful piece of you is here, Alex. Your strength. Your bravery. You're here, Alex, and you're here with me."

The words caused more teary tracks to run down her pretty face. I didn't want to make her cry, but she needed to hear this. She needed to *believe* in this because it was true.

I kissed her after that and she let me. She let me touch her. She let me run kisses down her neck until I reached the soft flesh of her breasts past the collar of her shirt. I squeezed her hip.

"I can stop," I told her, tasting her. I doubted my control if I continued to her kiss her this way.

Her fingers curled down my biceps, making me fight my need for her body even more with the pain.

"Please don't," she breathed over my mouth, and I picked her up, her soft pillow thighs tucked around me. She pulled at my t-shirt from behind and relieved us both of it when I pressed her down to the blanket I had laid out. It got caught in my hair during the shuffle, making us both laugh a little, but I quieted her with a kiss, the only time I'd exchange her voice for anything else.

Her fingers went to her mouth when I unzipped her shorts, the material binding over the flare of her hips before I slid them down and off. She had such beautiful hips, thighs. I bent, tasting between them. Her smell, her essence, did something to me. It made me crazy. It made a lust flow over me I couldn't contain.

Her legs fell apart and she played with my hair, soft noises humming from her throat with the tremble of her thighs.

My fingers slid past her panties, my tongue doing the same. I chased her taste inside of them, my mouth finding her sweet spot and sucking. Her walls called for me, pulsating around my tongue. She wanted me inside her. She wanted me inside her so bad.

Her head fell back. "Brody..." she whispered. She ached. Her fingernails welted my shoulder with red tracks. I feasted more, dragging my tongue along one of her lips, finding her clit. I flicked the tiny bud, pushing two fingers inside her. Her body hummed more.

"Take me," she said, and I covered her mouth. I covered her body, ripping away her clothing until I felt the warmth of her body underneath mine. She was soft everywhere I was hard, her smell light to the edge of mine. I snapped her bra, finding a dark nipple with my mouth. I skidded it with my teeth.

"Alex..." I breathed, feeling her hands on my jeans. She opened them and cupped me, letting me drive into her hand. I wanted her badly, too. She squeezed, playing with my balls when she slid her hand inside my boxers.

I closed my eyes, my lips forgetting all functionality over her mouth. I groaned, pressed into her hand, and she chewed my lip, breathing soft kisses. Her hand touched my cheek and I opened my eyes. Crazy how she managed to be even more beautiful this close. I could see every bit of amber in her eyes, the light tones that turned into dark.

I kissed her eyelashes, pushing down my jeans and boxers. After I did, I surrounded her. She lay underneath me completely naked, all flushed cheeks and warm brown skin, and I thought myself so lucky. How lucky I was to have this. How lucky I was that she let me have this.

And I told her that. My words made her cry again. She cried so much, but it wasn't bad this time. It wasn't bad because I knew it was because she was happy.

I sheathed myself, pushing the condom wrapping into my jeans, and then I took her hips, tugging her to me. Holding myself, I watched as she accepted me, her body expanding and taking as much as she was given. I filled her and then I drove deep, her soft bottom bouncing on the blanket as I found a pace with her. I never forced myself. I never did with Alex. It was about watching and studying what *she* needed. I did that and I found what I needed, too. We were so in sync, she and I. We always had been.

I came to her when her lips trembled. My mouth covered hers and I rotated my hips, hers swiveling in response. She called my name, begging for depth, begging for *me*, and I gave it to her. I gave her everything I had to give and more.

"I love you," I told her, feeling those walls contract, and I throbbed, exploding inside her. Pumping my hips, I rode it out, letting her words drive me on. Her "I love yous" took me home. They completed every bit of me.

Twenty-Six

ALEXA

We made it back to the ranch house with the setting sun, just enough light to see our way. Brody held my hand after we returned the horses, both of us silent in our strides. That didn't seem to matter though. The silence was just as wonderful as talking. There was such thickness in the air between us, but none of it was tension. None of it was *secrets* and I didn't know how I had kept him out for so long. It felt so good just to be open with him, honest. Bringing my hand up, he kissed my ring, the mood ring he gave me. I never took it off, not since that time at the park.

Together, we stepped to go inside via the back porch, but Brody stopped, his gaze going over my shoulder. He drew back and I followed him down the steps. He didn't even notice me pull up beside him. He looked around the house at the drive-way. A large blue pickup was parked behind his. It was a little newer though and cleaner.

Taking off his hat, he grabbed my hand before I could make anything of it, and kissed me before any words could form. I would let him kiss me forever.

His hands settled on my hips. "I'll meet you inside, okay? No doubt Gram's got things going in there for dinner."

Crap. That meant Aiden had to be up from his nap by now. I didn't mean to stay out this long. Stepping up, I kissed him. "Okay, hurry. I'll be waiting."

His lips lifted into a wide smile. He kissed me again and patted my hip as I took a step up. He disappeared around the house and I went inside, smelling the food that Gram had started. I picked up my feet and found the little boy I was looking for. The thing was, he was different and this different was so, so good.

Standing over the table, he mashed a huge bowl of potatoes with a large handled masher and the joy he had while he did it, warmed my heart. His partner in crime, Joe, sat at a seat at the table, but the thing is, he wasn't within arm's reach. He sat in his own chair on the other side while my nephew independently cooked.

This place really is magic.

I came over to Aiden and both he and Rose slid me one of their large smiles. Rose sat down the chicken she just prepped for the batter, wiping her hand on her apron. "How was your walk with, Brody?" she asked, and when I shook my head, not understanding how she knew, she tilted hers. "I saw ya'll head west. I figured you were going for a walk."

"Yeah, how was it?" came Aiden's question, and my face warmed by being put on the spot by everyone.

The walk was good, but for obvious reasons, I stayed casual about it. I gripped the back of a chair, bumping Aiden's hip. "It was fine. How was your nap? I'm sorry I wasn't around."

He shrugged mashing more. "It was fine, Aunt Alex. No big deal."

No. Big. Deal. How I loved to hear those words. I gazed around, noticing the person who was supposed to make it no big deal was absent. She was supposed to put him down. I faced Aiden. "Where's your mama?"

"Sleep," he said, and his smile left a little. "I tried to get her up when Ms. Rose knocked. She was still tired though."

Tired. Tired. I shook my head. Ms. Rose herself looked at me, tipping her chin before going back to her chicken. I squeezed Aiden's shoulder. "I'm going to go check on her, then wash up for your and Ms. Rose's dinner."

That amazing glee spread out over his face. "You'll like it. We used the stuff I picked."

I moved a hand down his braids, telling him I would. I didn't make any attempts to be quiet as I went upstairs. It was evening and my sister should be up anyway. I went inside and to my surprise, she was awake. She was up and sitting on the windowsill staring out. The open door caused her to face me and she blew smoke into the room.

Smoking. Why wasn't I surprised?

"Nice to see you up," I told her, not bothering to hide my tone. I wasn't happy with her. I wasn't happy and was tired of trying to pretend *for* her.

Her hands went together over something. I assumed her pack of cigarettes. She tilted her head. "And where have you been?"

I didn't want to answer that question and I shouldn't have to. I stepped back. "I'm going to go shower. Your *son's* making us dinner. You might want to wash up for it, too, after I'm done." She slept all day. She probably should to get clean.

In more ways than one.

I left before she could say anything, tossing my hat to the bed before getting that shower started in the connected bathroom. Frazzled with my sister, I forgot my clothes so I went back out. That's when I noticed what was in her hands—a cellphone.

She didn't bother hiding it when I came in and the fact she

had one chilled me to the bone. Where had she been keeping that? On her? I checked everywhere else…

Silent, I watched her fingers hover over the buttons, a flip phone.

"I can't have anything, can I?" she asked, the question so serious. Her jaw clenched as she gazed up at me. "I saw you come back. I saw you were out with him. You have everything and I have nothing. I always have nothing."

Her hands continued to move over the buttons, shaking more than even her words had, and I stepped closer, my heart beating with dread.

"Elena, you…" I breathed. "What did you…?" I couldn't say it. I was too scared.

In the end, I made myself.

"Did you call him?" I asked, swallowing down the bile, the fear. "Did you tell him where we were?"

Every question had me ready to faint, the bad always seeming to follow the good in my life.

Please tell me you didn't.

Sniffing, she lowered the phone. It was one of her signature sniffs and I wondered if she had more drugs stashed away. She looked up. "And what would I have told him? Come get me. I'm out in the middle of fucking nowhere? The only thing I know is that we're somewhere in Texas."

And Brody had driven the back roads because of that. We'd done it more so in case of being followed, but Elena had definitely been in the back of my thoughts. Even still, she did see some things along the way. She saw landmarks and indicators.

Her ponytail swept over her shoulder when her head shook. "So you and your little boyfriend don't have to worry. I haven't told him where we are."

"But you have talked to him, right? You've been talking to him?"

She didn't say anything after that, but she didn't have to. *I* had a lot of things to say on the other hand and instead of holding my tongue, holding back, I chose to voice them.

"But why, Elena?" I asked her. The words gritted through my teeth. I had to in order to keep in my anger. It was anger I built up for a long time and it was animosity I had forever. My arms moved over my chest. "You don't need to be with him. He's no good for you. He hurts you. He hurt me—"

"Don't!" she shot, her finger aimed in my direction. "Don't you do that. Don't you spread your filth. Don't you spread your lies."

"But they're not and what's worse, you *know* they're not."

"You know what I know," she said, getting up. "I know what you do to guys. I told you. I *watched* you down there just now. That's what you do. You did it to Nathan and you're doing it to that guy now to get what you want."

I wouldn't do this with her. I refused.

"This isn't going to happen," I told her, lifting my hands. "I'm not doing this and I won't let you do this—not anymore." And the avoidance wasn't for her sake. It was for me.

My heart couldn't handle it.

Dropping my arms, I went to take my shower, but she followed me, grabbing my arm before I could make it to the bathroom. She whipped me around and it took all I had to stay calm.

"And you know what it is you do to guys?" she continued, her hands on her hips. "You *tease*. You flirt. You shake your shit around, so what else was Nathan supposed to think?"

"Even if that were true," I said, swallowing hard. "Did that give him justification to do what he did? Did that give him permission or reason to—"

"You're a whore!" she screamed, and it wasn't just me close to tears. They filled her eyes. They flew down her cheeks. She lifted a finger again. "You're a dirty little whore that takes everything, my son included. You always get everything you want, but you can't have him. You can't have Nathan and you won't sour him either. You won't take away the only thing I have. You won't do it anymore, Alexa. No more."

Her words had me trembling, shaking, and the disgust in them caused the tears to stream down my cheeks. She turned to walk away and I almost let her. I had so many times after she'd said things like this to me in the past, but this time I couldn't. This time I opened my mouth.

"He told me we were gonna surprise you."

She stopped at my voice, gazing over her shoulder.

"It was your birthday," I sniffed, breathing through the tears. "Remember that?"

Her lashes shifted, going down. Of course she remembered. Neither one of us forgot that day.

"He had balloons in the back of the car. A cake and everything. It had a see-through lid so I could see it." My smile went crooked through my tears. "I remembered it was beautiful and thinking you'd like the color."

Her lips parted after that, her lashes blinking.

"He knew I'd get in the car," I told her, feeling the very words. I could never forget that day no matter how I tried. "He knew. He drove all the way to my school and told me it would mean a lot to you if I came over for your birthday. I dropped everything. I didn't go to class that day and he knew I wouldn't. He knew I would do anything for you."

It was at this point she shook her head, her blinking incessant, but even then that couldn't stop the first tear. A second followed and a third would have but her hand moved over her eyes, stopping them. I let her stay there in silence for only moment. She needed to hear this. She finally did.

"You know I cried the whole time?" I confessed, the words muffled in a large ball in my throat. I wiped my eyes now, catching tears. "He only stopped after I threw up. Only after I covered his entire shirt. He said I disgusted him."

She cringed, the air from her lungs seeping out in staggered breaths from her chest. "Alex…" she whispered, her voice strained. "Alex, don't," she said. "Alex, stop," but I couldn't though.

I wouldn't.

"But he didn't," I told her, closing the distance between us. "He didn't stop after I screamed. After I begged. It took *that*, Elena. It took me choking on his smell, gagging on the feel of him touching me and violating me until it all became too much. Until I couldn't take it anymore and vomited all over him. That's what I had to do to make him stop, Elena! It came to that and only that."

Her whole body quivered, the tears running in a rapid stream down her face and she didn't wipe them away. There were so many she didn't bother and all the while she kept saying no. She kept saying stop, but my words still came. I wouldn't stop. Not this time. I was tired of her judgment and her blaming me for something beyond my control. The only blame rested with the sick bastard who took advantage of my love for my sister, of a trust I had for the man she brought into our lives and no more could she be allowed to mar me with a past I wouldn't have had to endure if not for her thoughtless decisions. I refused to carry the weight of it and someone not too long ago made me realize I never should have felt I had to. He loved me and he made me see that.

The words spewed from my lips, every one worse than the next and eventually, the reality of them became too much for my sister. She attempted to leave the room, a mess of salty trails down her face, but I grabbed her arm and made her look at me. Over her shoulder came something I didn't expect and that something burned more than any words she could have said to me.

Her hand fell free from my face and I let go of her, pressing my palm to the heat on my cheek. She stared at me, a shock rippling through such an exquisite face. And she was beautiful. She always had been no matter how high. No matter how out of it she ever was.

She covered her mouth, her hand still hovering in the air, but she couldn't take it back. She couldn't take a lot of things back. She lowered her hand. "Alex, I'm..."

I left the room, down the stairs, and to where I didn't know. I ended up outside, heading toward the side of the house to catch my breath and think. A water faucet connected to the side of the house and I turned it on, washing the tears from my eyes. Using my shirt, I dried myself off. That's when I heard his voice; Brody's and one other.

Inching, I gazed around toward the back of the house and that's where I caught sight of Brody. Arms crossed and lips tight, he lounged against wood pillars of the house and he had a guy in front of him, a guy that looked a lot like him but distorted. Not in a bad way, but just different. He was leaner and had long blond hair tied back in a ponytail.

And he looked just as tense as Brody.

Brody swung the guy a glance. "You still haven't told me why you're here, Hayden," he said, and the guy, Hayden, shrugged.

He leaned back on barrel behind him. "I could say the same about you, brother."

Brother. He must be the other one from the pictures. Brody said the one who played basketball lived in Miami and youngest at college.

Brody rubbed the back of his neck like he was over this, tired of whatever this was they were doing outside and Hayden didn't look too amused himself.

He sighed. "I spoke to Gram," he said, and that got Brody's attention again.

"Gram," he repeated. "About what?"

Hayden waved a hand out like Brody's answer was obvious. "She told me that you're here," he went on. "That you're *not* on the road doing what all of us thought you were doing. Working? That is why you're on the road, right? To work?"

Brody pushed off the wall. "Don't condescend me, Hay, and so what I'm here. She told you that and you decided to drive all the way out here? To what? Check up on me?"

Hayden shook his head. He put his hand on his chest. "I came here to get Sarah's school bag. She left it when she came to visit Gram last week. I called to tell her I was coming to get it and she told me about you when I called. And she also mentioned that you weren't alone."

"Jesus." The word left Brody's lips and I didn't know what to make of it. It didn't feel good though. Probably because I had no idea of the context.

Brody kicked a boot in front of the other, falling back to the wall, but like Elena, Hayden wouldn't let up. Older siblings tended to do that.

"So why don't you let me in on what you're really doing, Brody," Hayden went on. "Who is it you brought with you? Gram mentioned a girl and her family. I mean, are you even still driving the rig or are you just bullshitting around?"

Brody cut him a look. "I can't believe you just asked me that."

"I mean, can you blame me? You're here. You're *not* working like you said you were. You're not doing the very thing *you said* was the reason you didn't want to be a part of the family business."

The family business? He never mentioned that.

"So all I come up with is you not working has to do with this girl and her family. Are you seeing her? Are you guys..."

He didn't finish and Brody raised his head. "What do you want to ask, Hay? You came all the way here. Ask."

I hung on the next question, everything around me stopping, waiting.

Hayden leaned back. "Are you guys together?"

"We are." The words left his mouth so quickly, and when an "I love her" followed, my heart squeezed.

Closing my eyes, I fell back to the house, letting myself go back to that day, the one in which we met. That day had been so horrible at first, then so suddenly so great.

God, I love him so much, too.

Pushing off the house, I opened my eyes, forgetting that someone outside of us was present in the conversation. I didn't know Brody's brother and because I didn't, I had no idea if this news would sit well with him, but then the man with the ponytail lifted his lips. The smile widened and I wondered why I thought Brody's declaration would even be an issue. He was kin of Brody and that had to mean something.

"That's great, Brody," Hayden said in response, and holding the back of his neck, he blew out a little breath. Almost like he was relieved that was Brody's answer. Hayden tucked his arms over his chest. "That's really great. Why didn't you just say that? That you were seeing someone? You didn't have to be all tight-lipped about it."

Brody remained silent, his lashes flickering down, and Hayden put his hand on his shoulder, squeezing.

"If you guys just need your space," he paused, nodding. "If you need time with this being new, that's fine. Just tell us. We understand. Pop and the business... it will wait."

He mentioned the business again. What kind of business was it? And why had the very words made Brody's face tense, his eyes narrow in the corners?

Brody stood to full height and when he did, Hayden's hand fell from his shoulder.

Brody touched his own chest. "I'm not doing the business because I have other interests. I told you that."

A mash up of emotions ran across Hayden's face, confusion bringing his eyebrows together. He rubbed his hand over his mouth. "I know what you said, but that just doesn't make sense. It doesn't and I can't accept that."

"What about it doesn't make sense?"

"Brody—"

Brody's hands flew up. They laced behind the back of his neck, and he spun once before facing his brother. "I don't get why you just can't let this go, why *everyone* can't just let this go."

"Because it's not like you," Hayden blazed, his nostrils flaring. But it didn't seem like anger, more emotional. This conversation trigged emotion. His hand scrubbed down his face, and it landed in the air, pointing directly into Brody's chest. "It's not like you to completely disregard how this entire family feels to fulfill your own self interests. You *know* how much this business means to Pop, how much he wanted us *all* to be a part of this. You, me, Colton, and Griffin. He wanted us all in this together and because he does, you also know how it made him feel when you said no. You know it... You know it hurt him."

He lost Brody's gaze with that, his jaw working and the tension flooding his eyes. I considered what Hayden said and I realized something. I hadn't known Brody long, but I had learned so much about him. His family was his heart and if what Hayden said was true, he was right. Declining something as big as this, didn't seem like Brody. In fact, it wasn't like him at all.

Brody's hands went loose from his neck, his eyes shooting up to the sky.

"I can't," he said, his fingers pushing through his hair. Frustration and everything else lined his blue eyes and a breath made just as much emotion flood through his face as had his brother only moments prior. "I just can't," he finished, and the words reminded me of something, someone.

I'd said those same words to him.

But they didn't make Hayden back down. His hand raised, hovering over his brother's arm. "You can't? Why, Brody? You—"

"I can't apologize," he continued, stepping back from the hand. "I'm sorry, Hayden, but I can't feel bad for wanting to do something else with my life. I'm sorry."

He left him, going inside the house, and I wanted to follow. I wanted to, but I heard her voice.

"Do you have room for one more?" she said. *Elena* said, and a male voice followed, telling her, "Sure. Where are you going?"

An engine kicked up, then rocks and I ran. I ran toward the front of the house. I had always been fast. I even did track a year in school, but that didn't matter. I didn't make it. When I made it to the front of the house, bending over to catch my breath, I saw my sister pull away. She was sitting in the open bed of a truck, other ranch hands I recognized from my walk with Brody surrounding her. The last look she gave me was when I called her, but just as quickly...

She looked away.

Twenty-Seven

ELENA

Alex,

We should have never been this way, you and me. We should have been close. We should have been friends. We should have been sisters and we haven't been for a long time because of me. I let you take care of me and Aiden despite you being younger, and then had the nerve to be angry because you did. I pegged you as the problem in my life when really, that had been me the whole time. It's always been me. I know that now.

I'm sorry I hurt you, Alexa. I'm sorry I let someone into our lives and gave them the opportunity to hurt you. When Nathan hit me, I think I let him because I felt I deserved it. Maybe in the back of my mind I always knew the truth. I knew who the real victim was. I knew all along it was you.

What happened upstairs was another example of me failing you and I have failed you. I've failed my son, but most of all, I've failed myself. I want to be better, Alex. I need to be better for you and my son. I want you to know things with Nathan are over and your failures with me are done, too. I've decided to leave for a little while. I need to get better and the first step I think are the drugs. I'm going to seek out a program, something to help me with my addiction and when I get back, I hope to be what you need. I hope to be what my son needs. In order to do this, I need to ask for a favor I know I don't deserve from you. But the thing is, I'm going to ask anyway. I'm scared of the alternative if I don't. I'm scared of how I'll be if I don't. I need you to watch over Aiden until I get back. You'll take care of him just fine. I know you will. As far as what to tell him, say what you feel is best. I'll answer to whatever you say when I come back. I have no problem with that. I trust your judgment.

Please tell my son I love him and please know I love you.

- Elena

P.S. I've left my phone with this letter. Please keep it. I'll call. I promise.

Twenty-Eight

ALEXA

Four Months Later

SHE MISSED so many moments already, so many smiles lost. She was missing them now, Aiden's gentle grin. He'd done it all the whole way here in the back of the truck, a present as big as he was pressed firmly to his chest. Next to him was a book bag with the Batman symbol on the front, a familiar action figure's head sticking out the top. Normally, that bag held his books for school, but today, along with Joe, it had overnight clothes stuffed to the brim inside. I know because I packed them there myself. She'd miss this, too. Elena. She wouldn't see him off to his first overnight since he started his new school. She wouldn't see him grin and pass off that big present to that first friend who gave him a chance, Preston. She wouldn't see that and I wondered how many more moments she'd miss.

Reaching over, I found the steering wheel while the guy behind it leaned back, letting me tap it. Brody captured me with one of his smiles then and watched as the horn got the attention of a little boy.

I turned to see Aiden's reaction as well and the sound alerted him like I hoped it would, his smile widening. He didn't have a reason to smile, not with everything that had happened in such a short lifetime, but my nephew managed the impossible.

He waved at me and Brody, both he and Preston in front of Preston's parent's big house. They lived in the suburbs, he and his family.

I lifted my hand back of course and Brody did too, his fingers raising slightly from the wheel. Aiden waved so hard I thought he just might fly away. He'd soar away like my heart always had for him. Eventually, Preston's mom waved the boys in, her form in between the spaces of the bright yellow balloons she held for her son's birthday overnight. She gave us a send off, too, smiling behind large black frames before she closed the door. I stared at the wood of it for a while, not knowing what else to do.

"What if he has a nightmare?" I whispered.

Brody heard me. He always did.

His hand moved over mine in my lap. "Then he'll call," came his voice, soft and strong.

I turned, seeing his lips move up into that boyish Brody grin. I breathed. "What if he cries?" I asked him, because Aiden still had his days. These past few months had been hard. They would have been hard for anyone without their mama.

Brody's fingers moved, looping and creating a web with mine. He gazed above me to the door of Preston's house. "Then we'll be here."

His arm pushed behind my neck after that and then he started his truck. He took us away and I settled into what he said while at the same time resting under his arm. He said "we," but what I valued in that the most was I knew he meant every ounce of the word.

After dropping Aiden off, we pulled up to Brody's trailer. Brody had opened his space up to Aiden and me for the past few months and though, I didn't intend on this arrangement being permanent—we would eventually need to establish something of our own as to not overstay our welcome— Brody's kindness had definitely been that to us lately, a stable home.

Brody parked the truck in the driveway connected to his trailer, his long arm draped over my shoulder. Turning, he brushed a kiss to the crown of my head and I closed my eyes, letting myself fall away in this tiny space with him. He was so big. He was so warm. He all-consumed like a comfy, Brody blanket and I was enjoying every minute I got underneath him. Today, marked his arrival home after being gone for almost two weeks, the road and his rig taking him away from both me, Aiden, and the trailer. Tonight, though?

Tonight, he was all mine.

I forced myself out of my daze, getting started on that. The seatbelt unbuckled quickly and I turned, unfastening his. We'd have our own party tonight, our own sleepover right here at home.

Shrugging back, Brody laughed, letting me get the belt off him. He placed his wrist on the wheel. "Eager for something, darlin'?"

God, he still drove me crazy with that *word*. He'd always drive me crazy in the best possible way. I slid out of the truck and he followed my lead. After pulling out his overnight bag he used on the road from the backseat of the truck, he slammed the door, then raced me to his front stoop. Upon reaching it, his staircase became the spot for a mass of giggles and grabbing. Brody's hands took no prisoners, nor did they ask for permission. They never needed it as they explored and played over the curves of my body. He kissed me, his arm looped around my back, and somehow despite the Brody wave, I had been able to unlock his door one-handed with the key he gave me.

My keys hit the entry way and his bag followed when he reached around me and let us inside. His large brown boot kicked the door shut and he spun me, pulling my body flush against his. We crashed together like two perfect waves, his own burning with heat and I thought I just might fall into it. I'd fall into him and hoped to God to never be let go.

He backed me up, ripping up the hem of my shirt and my butt smacked the door. A sharp and distinct *crunch* hit the air and a wave of dread sent my hand out. Without thinking, I pushed Brody away, sliding from underneath him. The closest light was a lamp. It sat on the table near Brody's upholstered couch. I turned it on, huffing as I reached back into my pocket.

My sister's phone lay squarely in my hand and I turned it, inspecting.

Oh, God no. Please God, no.

My hands shook so bad I didn't notice the crack at first. I'd been moving the phone around too much, but it was there. The back where the battery covered it split right down the plastic. Turning it around, I flipped the phone opened and dialed, listening.

A ring saved my life. A ring saved my world.

Brody's landline went off right near the lamp and I shut the phone, the tone silencing.

That's when his hand came down on my shoulder.

Brody's lips found my hairline, kissing softly before moving down to my cheek. His large arms folded around my waist.

"It's okay," he said, kissing my neck, then my shoulder

bone. "It's okay. No harm done and I'm sorry. I should have been more careful."

He did nothing wrong. I was the one who had the responsibility. This phone was my only link to her, so if I broke it...

She really wouldn't come back.

Eyes closed, I stood there for a moment, breathing, *trying* to breathe and Brody, he didn't rush me. He soothed me. His gentle voice bled softly into my ear, saying all kinds of things I needed to hear. He kept saying it would be okay. He kept saying she would call, but she'd been gone so long, my sister becoming more of a memory now than real and I felt terrible. Because every day that passed, I was unsure if I wanted her to be any more than that to me—a memory.

But then I thought of Aiden and how much he needed her.

I lowered the phone, opening my eyes, and Brody's arms released their hold on me when I turned within them. I put my hand over his heart, feeling that strong thump, then brought myself to his neck by his shirt. I kissed him there, his neck. His sharp scent excited me and a rumble within his chest turned me on.

I kissed his collar. "I don't want to talk about her," I said, and I didn't. I just wanted him. He'd been gone for too long. Two weeks too long.

He said no words of disagreement, walking with me as I backed up and led him to the couch. I placed the phone down gently on the coffee table in front of it and he didn't fight me when I touched his chest.

He fell back to sofa, his big body covering two of the three sections. He watched me, his arms going behind his back and I held his thighs, lowering myself to the floor. I took off his shoes, his socks next. Standing, I pushed my hands along the grooves of his jeans, my thumbs using the inseam as a guide to him. The blue in his irises flared, his lids heavy, and his lips parted. He licked them and grabbed my hips when I used my knees to settle on his lap.

He held me there, his t-shirt straining with every rapid inhale and exhale of his large chest.

I pulled my shirt off, my own chest moving, and his fingers padded up my sides. He brought me to him by my hips, placing one hard kiss between my breasts. He let go as I backed up and slid down his body. He could do nothing but watch me; sit back and watch as I opened his jeans. He could do nothing but let me please him.

A crinkle hit the air when I unzipped his jeans and the bulge in his pants twitched to be felt and tasted through his boxers. The very prospect made my mouth water and I didn't want to wait, but made myself go slow for him.

I moved my hand over the dark briefs, outlining his size. So much. I more than filled my hand and his came down on mine, squeezing with mine. A few staggered breaths left his full, pink lips and he let go when I pulled him free of his boxers.

He sprang out, erect in the air, and my nostrils filled with his distinct scent, sharp and male. Watching me, I pressed my lips to the head, using my tongue to flick the cap.

He groaned, his fingers digging into the sofa. He twitched and I moved my thumb over the dewy bead seeping out of his pulsing shaft. I used it, gripping the mass and drawing my hand up and down in a constraint rhythm. I couldn't take it anymore and took him whole in my mouth, my eyes watering at the sudden pressure hitting my throat. My mouth widened for his size and I sucked, playing with his balls.

His hand came down on the back of my head, his fingers moving down to cup my neck. He squeezed, pulling a breath through his teeth. His legs widening, he told me where to get him just right, his hand at the back of my neck guiding my pace.

I sucked harder and he lifted his hips. His knuckles went white over the couch cushions and I knew he was holding back. Cupping his balls, I played, bobbing over his girth. I went faster, urging him not to hold back. He didn't have to be gentle with me. I told him that.

He couldn't take it anymore.

He drove his hips, his dick like a rapid piston in my throat and I gagged, making myself go on. He tasted so good and I felt him swell, ready to fill my mouth.

He fell back into the couch, to pull out, but I followed him, determined to take him to the end. I gripped his thighs and hovered above him, giving him one last long draw.

Salty liquid filled my mouth, bursting, and I swallowed, feeling Brody's hands come down my back. His head fell back, his eyes closing, and I sucked him dry, taking all he could give me.

His length pulsed, throbbed as I released him. I wiped my mouth, Brody's eyes hazy below me. He looked completely sated, that flare of blue sex drunk. I stood, but he brought me back to him.

His hands on my hips, he pressed a kiss to my tummy, using his fingers to unzip my shorts. I told him he didn't have to as he touched his lips to my mound, using his fingers to slide my panties down my thighs. I was pleased by pleasing him and didn't need anything in return, but there was no telling Brody that. He always took care of me.

Even from the beginning.

"You work next Friday, right? That's your long day?" Brody's arm came around me, spearing a piece of breaded sesame chicken from the to-go carton resting in my blanketed lap. He surrounded me everywhere really; his naked legs, chest, and arms. We sat in a sea of blankets from his bed, eating the Chinese take out we had delivered by candlelight in his living room.

And we were completely spent from quite a few tumbles. He'd been gone for two weeks and it couldn't be helped.

Brody fed me the chicken and his lips lifted following my sound of enjoyment.

Chewing, I considered what he'd said, then shook my head when I realized the answer to his question. I swallowed. "No, actually. I would be but no. My hours are being cut."

He frowned, getting more chicken around me for himself this time. "What happened?"

"Nothing but the fact that it sucks working for a corporation." My job at the gym, I loved really. I got to teach contemporary and alternative dance as well as ballet to the youth members, but as I was new, my hours got cut first when the word came down from corporate. I shrugged. "The time just isn't there and there are too many employees." Which really sucked as I was trying to become more self-sufficient. Brody had done so much for Aiden and me since Elena left. What was a crippling setback emotionally ended up not being one geographically and that had only been because of him.

"I'll probably have to start looking for something else, you know?" I told him now. "To fill in the gap. But as far as Friday, no. I'm free."

His hand lowered, releasing the fork into the take out container. He replaced it with my arm, squeezing, and didn't speak for a moment. I touched his fingers and his blond lashes flickered up.

I tilted my head. "I'm going to be okay. I know I can find something else."

He shook his head, his lengthy blond waves flowing with it. "I'm not worried about that and really, you know you don't have to work. I make enough to cover the household expenses."

But just because he did, didn't mean he should. I wanted to carry my own weight, as well as not be a reminder to him, a constant one that he didn't have to do anything of these kind things for me or my nephew. I didn't want to be his burden. I also didn't fail to notice that his time on the road took him away even longer lately. He spent more hours than ever working and I had a feeling that had something to do with the new patrons living his home.

Though, he'd never tell me that.

His fingers brushed down my arm. "So you wouldn't want to go to my Gram's house Friday then, would you?" His shoulder lifted and lowered. "Since you have the time off, you might want to use it for yourself and that's okay. Gram's just having this dinner thing and invited us to go. You, me, and Aiden."

"Of course," I told him genuinely excited. Rose had been such a support system to us. The day Elena left, that's where Aiden and I stayed for a couple weeks when Brody ultimately had to go back to work the first time. She made everything easier for Aiden, yes, but especially for me. And like from Brody, nothing about the gesture came across as an obligation, but a genuine want to help; a genuine kindness.

Leaning into him, I thought about that, tilting my head to look up at that strong jaw. I kissed the edge of it. "And Aiden will be super excited, too," I told him, falling back. "Tell her we'd love to come."

His brow lifted. Like he was surprised about my excitement for some reason. "Okay. Yeah, I'll tell her."

Moving, he went for an egg roll, dipping it in sweet and sour sauce. He offered me a bite first and I chewed, realizing something.

"Don't you have to work Friday?" I asked him, swallowing

my bite. He kept his schedule on the fridge and I memorized it. I always knew when he'd be away and I felt it with every breath.

He wiped his mouth with a napkin. "Nope. I've had that weekend off for months." I stopped eating, curious, and he noticed when his lashes flickered up. Sitting up, he brushed his fingers with that same napkin before tossing it. "That's what the dinner is for, well, part of it."

I sat up now, listening, and he rested an arm over my knees, the other behind my neck.

"My family," he said, flicking the fluffy material across my kneecaps with his fingertips. "They got a business going. I guess you could call it a family business. It's opening that weekend and the dinner was my gram's idea. She wants everyone to get together before the ribbon cutting in the morning. My brothers are coming down and everything. Colt from college and Griffin and his wife Roxie from Miami. It's the first time we've all been together in a while and Gram's pretty excited about it. She and my Aunt Robin. You haven't met her yet. She was at a trade show when you and Aiden stayed, but she'll be there. She, as well as my older brother Hayden, and my pop of course. He's technically the main owner of the business. *Chandler & Sons* is what it's called."

With what he said, I should naturally be worried. He said his whole family would pretty much attend this dinner. His *entire* immediate family I would be sharing an eating space with and though, a lot of pressure came with that, I found my concerns for that evening didn't reside with myself and how to act around the special people in Brody's life.

"What kind of business is it?" I asked casually instead. Because this was the first time he'd mentioned this. It's not like we'd told each other everything, but the reason why he didn't concerned me. Mostly because the last time I'd heard of this business with his family. He'd been arguing about it with his brother. Though, I guess he didn't know that I knew that as I'd overhead the exchange.

Placing the to-go containers to the side, I fell back and wrapped myself in his arms.

His hands gripped my biceps, his breath a warm constant sound near my ear. He squeezed, kissing my shoulder. "A furniture business. My pop designs things. He's so great at that stuff."

His voice sounded far away and I looked up. When I did, he was smiling a little.

His finger brushed restlessly against my arm. "I remember one year," he said, looking down at me. "Money was shit. Mom had just left a year prior and I'd been at my third school at that point. We moved a lot while Pop looked for jobs and Christmas ended up being in this crap town. The neighborhood was *rough*, but it was all my old man could afford. None of us thought we'd be getting presents that year. Things had just been too hard. Money too tight and though, we knew we'd be coming back to Texas to celebrate the holiday with Gram and the rest of our family later, we never thought the day would be anything special. Pop just didn't have the funds or the means to do it."

"What happened?" I asked him liking this story for some reason. It was his voice I think. He was talking about something sad, but his voice wasn't. It was content, peaceful.

He grinned a little. "A few weeks prior, he woke us up one day out of the blue. Like literally woke our butts up and told us to get in the truck. Pop can be kind of gruff so we all thought our asses were in trouble."

I laughed a bit as he did.

His arms tightened around me. "And we drove. We drove forever. We ended up going to these woods. We got out and all this brush was around, wood for miles. Taking us over, Colton's hand in his, as he was the littlest, Pop told us to pick something out. He told us to pick any piece of wood and when he did, he told us to pretend.

"'Pretend that it's anything you want,'" he paused, deepening his voice. He made it thick. He made it rough with his accent. He smiled. "We asked him what he meant by anything and he said it again. 'Pretend it's anything you want. Pretend it's any toy you want.' And so we did. I chose a spaceship and made the sounds and everything. My brothers being fools, they followed my lead and played. We played in the woods with pieces of wood. We made shooting sounds, guns, lasers, and even did some car noises. That's what Colt chose, a car. It was the best day, and on Christmas? We found those same presents under the tree. Except they were real this time. Pop made them real. They were all wood and wrapped in newspaper and like in the woods, we played for hours. Hours."

He looked at me after he finished and I had seen that contentment over his face before. He wore it while touring his Gram's ranch. He wore it every day there.

"So when the idea came about for a business, Pop naturally went that way," he continued. "Griffin, the one that plays basketball professionally, had been doing well in his starting season and offered to back it. Just a small loan to get things started. It took some nudging at first, but Pop eventually gave in. He hated working under someone else and then there was the stress on him."

"Stress?"

His eyes went away for some reason after that. He laid his hand on his arm. "Um, yeah. He had a heart attack. It was last year. I guess working in construction was too much."

The words literally chilled me to the bone. I couldn't help it, all things considered, all things considering *him* and his own heart condition.

He moved on quickly. "But, uh, yeah. That's what the party is for, the business. The ribbon cutting makes things official, but they've been already operating with private orders. I guess lots of folks need furniture in Miami. My brother has lots of connections since moving there."

That all sounded so great for them, but I still had to wonder something. So many things had me wondering really.

Brody reached across me, taking a drink of his beer, and I watched him. Whatever contentment he had before, seemed to have evaporated and was replaced with thought. They moved over his face like an endless sea.

I dared to figure out why.

"Will you be taking some time off?" I asked him. "You know, to help with the opening?"

His eyes narrowed like he wondered why I asked. "No, they got everything covered. Hayden, my older brother, he's taking care of the marketing and some other logistics on the business side. He has some schooling and Pop of course, has the designs going. He's even using some of my younger brother's stuff. Colton's an art major at Texas State."

He smirked with that, grinning. "I guess if his basketball career doesn't turn out, he has something to fall back on. He's actually pretty talented and Griffin, he's got all the lawyers going and all that legal stuff. Pop has got this thing pretty solid."

But where did he fit into all this? He said this was family business, but he didn't really seem to be a part of it. And then there was that argument, the one with his brother. I never got to meet Hayden that day. He'd already left before I came inside and notified Brody about Elena, but I did see him peel out, his face flushed in his truck. That day, Brody said he had other interests and didn't want to be a part of the business because of them. But he couldn't have meant truck driving, could he have? Did being on the road really make him that happy? I didn't know, but one thing I did know was being around family, being home certainly *did* make him happy and genuinely so.

"Are you a part of the business?" I asked, and though I wanted to hold my tongue. I couldn't. I passed it off with a shrug. "It's called *Chandler & Sons*, right? Aren't you a son?"

His head moved within that candlelight spread around the room. His lashes flickered down and his fingers tapped the beer bottle. "They asked, but it's not really my thing."

"Why?"

He faced me, his lips turned down. He grabbed my hand, the pads of his fingers drawing invisible designs over the back of it.

"You know why, Alexa," he suddenly said, but I didn't, not really. My first thought was that it could be his concerns over his heart, but that couldn't be it. His dad designed. His younger brother did, too, and the eldest did marketing and other things. The one in Miami of course financed, but none of these tasks were physical things. None of these jobs would hurt him or be something he'd have to worry about down the line for his health.

I put my hand there, right over his chest. "You don't have to do anything physical. Doesn't your dad have people that make all these designs for him?"

He considered that, his lashes flickering. "But that's the thing, I was that guy. The physical? The labor? That's what I did. I don't do designing. I didn't go to school. Hell, even Pop did some trade school." His lips went tight, his brow knitted. Breathing, he gazed up and put his hand over mine. "I don't do anything else but what I used to do and I don't want them to have to figure something out for me, to put me somewhere like some kind of special case."

It hurt my heart that he *believed* that. I shook my head. "I'm sure it wouldn't be that way. They know you're limited to what you can do. They'd understand."

His eyes left mine after the words, his lips tight again. I could feel his frustration and for some reason and I... I didn't understand.

Placing his drink down, he turned me by my knees, making me face him. His hands smoothed down to cup my hips and his mouth landed softly on my forehead. He breathed me in and I shuddered, holding his shirt to do the same.

His lips brushed my eyebrow. "You're the only one I've told," he admitted, pulling back. Those eyes softened in the corners, his hand coming up to hold my cheek. "I can't tell them. I can't have them worrying. You didn't see them last year, Alexa. After my pop..."

Reaching up, I braced his cheeks. This made him keep his eye contact when he looked on the verge of taking it away.

He squeezed my wrists. "It shattered my family *for weeks* while he recovered and I can't do that to them."

It all made sense now. Why he pushed himself so hard at the ranch and why his Gram let him do so. He was pretending. He was pretending everything was okay for their sake.

My mouth came forward to close over his jaw and his hands, so strong, moved down to my shoulders.

"But how do you think they'd feel if something happened to you," I asked, raising my head. "If you went down, if you got hurt, and they never knew. If it hit them out of the blue and they never got a chance to understand the reason why or were never given any opportunity to help."

"That's the thing. They can't help. They can only worry and that doesn't help anyone."

"What about you?" I asked. "Support, Brody, is good for the soul. It's just as strong as anything else you could do to take care of yourself. And that healing goes both ways, your family included."

He had nothing to say to that, his gaze following the light

in one of the flickering candles. His arm went around my shoulder and I came into his lap, holding him tight, holding him so long while he held me.

"You should tell your family," I told him. "Because not doing so is keeping you away from them and not just with the business."

"I..." he started, bringing his hand down my back. His mouth warmed the top of my head. "I'd be of no use to them."

I closed my eyes, that hurting me so much. He did have use. He'd always have use. He was the most beautiful person I had ever met and good people like that? They'd always have their place in the world.

Because the world needed them.

Twenty-Nine

BRODY

I TOSSED and turned despite her being with me tonight. I usually didn't do that. Not unless I was on the road and ticking down the countless hours. Whenever I was back home, in bed with my arms around her, I never had a problem finding sleep. Alex allowed me to do that. I had a place of peace with her, but tonight I couldn't find that.

Sitting up, I pulled my feet over the side of my bed. I carried her there about halfway through the night. Usually, we slept in separate bedrooms seeing as how her nephew lived here as well, but since Aiden had a sleepover tonight, I took his aunt right here. We'd both fallen asleep on the floor and I didn't want her back hurting in the morning. She had to teach a couple classes over the weekend and didn't need to be aching or anything. I found my pants on the chair next to the bed and rooted through some other clothes scattered about on the floor. I wasn't the cleanest person sometimes, but Alex had been helping me with that. I picked up a shirt and a warm hand touched my back as I was pulling it on.

Smiling, I turned around and pressed a kiss to that

gorgeous, sleepy mouth. When I pulled away, her eyes were partially closed.

"You okay?" she asked opening her eyes a little more, and when she saw me, she frowned her full lips. "Where are you going?"

"Just for a drive," I said, rubbing a hand down her shoulder. I figured getting behind the wheel would be the quickest way to get my eyes heavy. I used that tactic every day. "I'm having a hard time sleeping. I figured it would help."

"Oh." She made to get up, but I squeezed her shoulder. That mouth turned down again. "I can come."

But I was already tucking her back in and bringing the blankets back around her. I kissed her forehead. "I won't be gone long. You *can* sleep, so don't waste it, okay?"

That made her smile a little, the humor in my voice, I assumed. She lay back, though, it looked like she didn't want to and stayed put, letting me go. I told her I had my phone before I left. I always did and always kept it on for her. She had her sister's phone of course, but didn't feel comfortable using it. She didn't want to keep it busy until she called, which was understandable. That didn't mean she couldn't have her own phone though, and the day we got one for her had been the happiest day. It kept me from worrying about her as much while I was forced to be away from her.

I tried not to think about my job as I got behind the wheel and started in on that drive. I pulled down the street, annoyed already by the bright lights of a tailgate. Folks were up at all hours out here. The people in the street took their time getting out on the road and once clear, I didn't waste the opportunity. My foot hit the gas and I shook my head, heading down the block.

The encounter amped me up. The exact *opposite* of what this drive was supposed to do and I cursed under my breath, maneuvering out of my childhood neighborhood. Some real characters lived around here and I'd like to get out eventually and get Alex and Aiden out with me, of course. We could think about getting a house, but I was just gone so much. I wouldn't be around to enjoy it with them, though, that would never stop me from getting one for them.

I cursed again, a never-ending sea of street lamps and neighborhood road surrounding me. Words filtered through my head and I realized why I was so wired. They were Alex's words. They were her concern and I didn't blame her. I had my own for a while about the decisions I made in my life and every day, I questioned them more and more. As far as tonight, the woman in my life made me see a little bit more why. She put it all out there. She made me face it, which was something I wouldn't do before. I'd been an all-star lately at not addressing certain aspects of my life, my family and myself included.

Tapping the wheel with my fist, I turned it. I cruised a bit and realized the area was familiar to me. How at first, I didn't know, but then I made it down a long road with large homes and wide views of the mountains. The area reminded me of Gram's except nearer to the city. The houses weren't stacked on top of each other and made the neighborhood a part of the vast land surrounding it. It was country meets city, which I suppose was why he chose it, my pop. He had both of his trucks parked in the driveway, his dark Escalade the biggest. It was a gift from my brother once upon a time. If Griffin was one thing, he's generous and that's something I'd forever preach in connection with his name.

I thought about just driving past and moving on. I needed to get back to Alex anyway, but another car was there in the drive. I parked, getting a closer look, and knew right away it was Ann's, as I'd seen it the night we all had dinner at my grams.

I checked the number on the dash, blinking at the hour. So late, it would be morning soon.

So Ann stayed the night...

That surprised me at first, but definitely not in a bad way.

I smiled a little, reaching to put the truck in gear, but some lights froze my hand. They were the lights lining the walkway leading up to the porch.

And they lit up like an airport runway as they turned on.

The lamp outside the door came on next and my heart jumped with it. The door opened and out came a large man, his jeans and flannel t-shirt on and his eyes crinkled no doubt with sleep. Stepping down the porch steps, he approached, and I swallowed, pushing down the passenger side window to speak to my pop.

He stared into my truck when he got there, his eyes everywhere but me at first. They lifted and when they did, he said few words. "You gonna come in?"

I'd been in this place a few times, my pop's new house. He finally decided to make the big move after fighting my brother, Griffin, on it for months. Griffin offered to pay for the two-story home in full of course, but Pop wouldn't have it. I didn't blame him. We made our own way around here. We always did, and well, Pop had been the one to teach us that. In the end, he ended up getting financing himself and that actually coincided with that first big order that came down from Miami from what I heard. More of Griffin Chandler's doing of course.

The bum always got his way in the end, didn't he? It was enough to get Pop out of the trailer we'd all called home for years, though. I was glad the bum always got his way.

Pop settled into his favorite arm chair. That thing had made its way over here, too, and he put it right in front of a brick-laid fireplace. He had it off now, but I could still smell the job it did to the home. A woodsy smell filled the whole place. It reminded me so much of Gram's.

I took my place on the couch, but my back went straight when a feminine face rounded the corner. Ann. In a flannel and jeans herself, she was silent, but Pop didn't even flinch when she placed a hand on his shoulder. He simply settled into it and I'd never seen such a thing. She smiled at me. "Morning, Brody." And she was right. It was getting there. I confirmed that out in my truck.

I nodded, feeling guilty about that. "Morning and sorry about that. It being so early and all that."

She wouldn't hear of it, shaking her head. "You being here is only good. Can I get you something to drink? Water or..."

"Uh, nah. I'm okay."

Bending, she got Pop to face her when she tilted her head at him, a dark brown curly strand from her bun moving over her face. "You, Blake?"

She only got a smile from him, a *smile* and Pop didn't do that. At least, he didn't used to anyway. At Gram's, he had been all smiles. He'd been all kinds of happy and this nice woman made him this way.

He declined her offer, but did so only politely, a calm shake of his head and that pleasant lift of his lips behind his whiskers. Ann left us to our peace after that, leaving a smell of soft flowers in her wake and for a moment, I let the thought flash that I just might be watching my future stepmom leaving the room. I never had much experience with one of those, a mom, but this woman seemed like she'd be a pretty good one.

I smiled a little more. She'd have her hands full with us. No matter how grown we were. I let the thought marinate, but then it fell from my head when I realized she'd left me and Pop alone. The tone went different with her gone and I became well aware of the hour—and the fact my pop caught me sitting outside his home in the dark.

"It's early, Brody," he said simply.

I nodded, knowing that. I pushed my hair out of my face. "Sorry. I hope I didn't scare Ann."

Her name brought something out on my old man's face. He shook blond hair with subtle stands of silver. "That woman don't scare easy."

She didn't seem like she had. She was with my pop and he could be a bit rough around the edges. Rough, but good. My pop was a good man. I rubbed my legs. "I didn't really want anything. I... I was just driving through and..."

He got up before I could finish and I instinctually followed him, moving behind his wide frame through the large house. He stopped in the kitchen and got us both drinks despite both me and himself turning down Ann. I had a feeling he just didn't want to inconvenience her. Again, we made our own way around here. I accepted the bottle of water, cracking it opened as we moved down the hall. Pictures of me and my brothers littered the hallways. He'd taken the best ones to surround himself with. On the windows, curtains were placed with what could have only been a feminine hand. The decorations sprinkled around the house only confirmed it.

"The house is looking good," I said, watching him flick a light on the wall.

He turned. "Ann helped. I'll let her know what you thought."

I nodded, sneaking in a sip of my water. I busied myself with it. Pop unlocked a door and opened it, going down a set of wooden stairs. I quickly found out the stairs led to his garage, but he wasn't using it for that. The entire area was filled with woodwork crafted only by a fine hand. If Ann handled the interior, my pop definitely had his stamp out here. He had toy boxes and even a few sets of dress drawers. The best was his rocking chairs, though. He took one, giving me the other, and I ran my hand down the wood. The work was polished, fine.

"We can keep our voices down out here," he said, and I acknowledged that with a nod, understanding.

Bracing the arms, I sat back in the rocker, testing it, and my pop smiled.

"You made all these?" I asked him, knowing the answer. Of course he did, the job too fine for anyone else.

He confirmed that when he lifted and lowered his chin. "They're for the business. I make the originals, so the boys have something to go by."

I was sure he did. He was probably in that shop breaking his back with guys half his age. That was just my old man, tough. He had a heart attack and he still pushed himself. That was just his way.

The thoughts had me in mine and I rocked, still busying myself and Pop watched me, not saying a word. The depth of his hard gaze I felt immensely, but didn't dare address it and like I said, he didn't either. I idly wondered how long the pair of us could sit there, both unspoken, and I would admit, a bit tense—at least on my end.

Why had I come here?

The urge to leave moved through my legs and made my hands fold around the rocking chair's arms. I gripped them, giving in.

"You can keep that one," Pop said, surprising me. He tipped his whiskered chin in the direction of the rocker. "If you want it, that is. You don't have to if you ain't got no place for it. It's up to you."

My hands moved on the chair. I looked up. "Thanks. I think I will. I've got room."

A husky, "Mmhmm," sounded from his throat with his acknowledgement. His gaze travelled away, but a buzz got his attention. His cellphone. Pop shifted his body and then proceeded to do something that blew my mind.

He texted someone.

My eyebrows raised. "Everything all right?" The question came partially from the fact it was so early and because hell, when had I ever seen Pop text, and though, he did it with a little fumbling, hunting and pecking with a single finger, he was doing it.

His eyes shown from under the wrinkle of his brow. "Eh, uh, yeah," he said, messing with his phone more. He tapped slowly, determined to get his message out. He raised and lowered a shoulder. "Just my shop manager. Name's Dean. Him and the boys are pulling some early hours. We're wanting to get a big order done before the opening."

Nothing about what he said should have surprised me. The early hours and pulling them to get things done. Like I said, Pop broke his back to get the job done, but what surprised me was he wasn't there himself. What even surprised me more was the presence of this guy Dean and his need for him.

"Your shop manager?" I asked. I couldn't help it. Pop was just the type of man that did all things himself. He cracked the whip himself.

Finally, he finished the labor over his phone. He reached back, slipping it into his pocket, and folded his hands over his stomach after he did. "I hired him a few months ago to oversee production in the shop. It was your grandmomma's idea, so I wasn't in there doing all the work myself. I really didn't find the need at first, but Dean makes things easier. I guess it doesn't hurt having help."

So many things I never thought I'd hear or *see* from him today, but that? That was a new level.

After a moment, his brow lifted. "But don't tell your gram that. I'd never hear the end of it."

I couldn't help it. I smiled. I lifted my hand. "Code of silence."

His chair started to rock again, a *creak*, a *crack*, and in those sounds of soft leisure something impulsed me. Something made me.

"Did it," I started, trying to push through. A tight ball had suddenly formed in my throat. I swallowed it. "Did it hurt you?" I asked. "Me not doing this with you? The business?"

He glanced around at all the pieces in the room, to the craftsmanship. His jaw ticked a little and I thought I might have pissed him off, but not by what I'd asked. I might have upset him by addressing it and making him voice his opinion. My pop wasn't really a sharing guy and really, I wasn't either, but a conversation not too long ago hadn't been sitting well. It was the one with Hayden, the day Alex's sister left.

He blew out a breath and I didn't think he'd answer until, well, he did.

"It didn't hurt me," he said, his voice low, concentrated as if he was choosing them carefully. It was as if he was trying to find them. He stopped rocking. "I think it more so confused me and I guess it did disappoint me a little."

It disappointed him.

Why did that tug at my chest more?

"You know I never mind what y'all boys are into," he said. "I'd never stop you from doing what you want to do."

I did know that. He'd been real supportive with Griffin and Colton. He even put in the extra hours to send Hayden through school until my brother left, realizing it wasn't for him.

His thick fingers tapped the chair. "But you," he said, and when he did, he smiled a little. "You and I have always been on the same wavelength and I couldn't get you to veer off of it for nothing. I send y'all off to summer camp and you're wanting to stay home, worried about the trailer and how everything is going to get done while you're gone. You get off the bus from school, the first thing you do is the chores, and then make sure the others are doing their homework before you even start on yours."

He shook his head after that. "It was something else. You worked just as many hours as me when we all worked *Carter's* if not more, and the only way you were able to keep any money for yourself instead of putting it all towards the bills was because I *made* you. I guess with the business taking off, I assumed you'd be there, too, pushing it with the rest of the boys in the shop."

He was right. I would have been. I still wanted to.

I just couldn't.

"And maybe, that had been my mistake," he went on. "I assumed you were like me and maybe you felt some pressure because of that."

Every word made me want to rage out of myself, crush something, curse or something, but I couldn't. I had to keep it together, so I fought the urge. I fought the explosion racing within me.

My hands shaking, I clasped them, staring down.

"You should tell your family... Because not doing so is keeping you away from them..."

Pop leaning forward took me out of my head and his own hands came into his lap, his own hands clasping themselves. "If I made you feel that way, I'm sorry and I apologize for everyone else, too."

His voice cracked, cutting off a little on the end and he sat back. He faced away from me and I almost said something then. I almost admitted everything in one sweep. I wanted to tell him how much I wanted to be there. I wanted to tell him I'd do anything, *anything* just to have a chance to do that. But most of all, I wanted to tell him I was scared. I was scared not for my health, but with what I was limited to now, I was scared

I'd never be able to help my family in ways I always had before. I didn't have money like Griffin. I wasn't creative like Colton, and definitely didn't have what Hayden had. He was real smart, my brother, and didn't even need a college degree to tell him that. Those things about my brothers, I just didn't have and never would and *that* was my greatest fear. That I added no value to any of them anymore.

That I couldn't take care of them like I used to.

Pop's hand moved over his face and I knew the moment had passed. The time for all those words had evaporated. I let what I knew to be pride get me again.

He pressed his hands on his legs, standing. "Let me help you get that chair out."

And so we did, together. Pop had the tethers and tossed them to me, the two of us working alongside each other like we used to. It only took us a few minutes, but outside of my time with Alex, it had been the most content I'd been in a long time.

I let that pass and got in the truck. Pop hit the passenger door, bidding me off, but came back when I rolled the window down.

I breathed. "You weren't wrong, you know?" I said nodding. "You weren't wrong about me. I am just like you. I am and I'm proud of that."

That small smile he had before, reappeared and broadened. He put a hand on the velvet of the window. "You do what you need to do, boy, and we all trust in that. We'll all be at peace with that."

He pushed off the side of my truck and headed toward his house. The door opened before he did and he went back to that kind woman waiting in the doorframe for him.

Thirty

ALEXA

I COULDN'T FIND IT, my hands flailed. It was dark. I was alone and I was pretty sure I was screaming a little, too. Slapping over the oak dresser, my eyes clouded with tears. The phone continued to ring and I thought I would miss it. But then hands came, strong ones in the dark. Brody made an appearance out of nowhere. Dipping down, he found the ringing phone on the floor. He turned it on and pressed it hurriedly to my face, my saving grace.

"Baby?" I called into the receiver. I put my hand on my face, pushing it into my hair. It was late, and if he was calling this late...

He wasn't ready.

I breathed. "It's okay. I'll come pick you up from the sleepover. I just got to get my shoes on and—

"Alex?" came a light voice, soft and hesitant. It lacked confidence. It lacked aggression and I pulled the phone from my ear. This wasn't my smartphone.

It was Elena's phone.

The phone returned to my ear by my hand and I heard her voice again.

"Alex, it's me," she said. "Alex, is everything okay? Is Aiden okay? Why would you need to pick him up? From where?"

The questions came in rapid fire like we spoke every day about her child. Like she hadn't left both him and me.

Is this really her on the phone? Did she really call?

The bed dipped down beside me. An arm came around my waist, Brody's, and I let my body fall into the hard ridges of his side. When he returned, I didn't know. He'd been gone for hours, but somehow he happened to come back when I needed him. He was always there when I needed him. He had to know who was in my ear right now. He'd been the one to find the phone.

"Alex? Alex?" sounded from the voice again. It was no longer soft. It panicked, and I had half a mind to let it continue on. I had no idea how I'd be on this day. In fact, before now, I *wanted* her to call. I treasured her phone. I kept it safe for her so we'd always have a link. But now that she had, my own hesitance buzzed around in my chest and resentment followed close in my wake.

Brody's hand reached up to squeeze my shoulder. I doubted he'd make me say anything to her. I bet, knowing him, he'd fully support my decision to keep her completely out of all our lives.

I dampened my lips. "Elena."

"Alex, is everything okay? Where's Aiden?"

I pushed my hand into my hair. "He's fine," I told her, and now, I knew he was. He'd gotten past our checkpoint. My watch went off earlier, but he never called like I told him he could. He'd made it. My baby was okay.

"And he's at a birthday party. A sleepover," I went on. "I just thought he was calling maybe wanting to be picked up early."

A breath sounded into the phone, chilling out and even. "A sleepover?" she said. "By himself and he didn't call."

I didn't have to tell her anything, but I chose to. "Yes."

"That's great," she said, and I nearly heard a smile in her voice. "How…" she started. "How are you? Him?"

Such a loaded question she asked. Yeah, we were fine physically, but emotionally we all still carried the weight of her; of Nathan.

I put the phone on speaker and let my head fall to Brody's arm. He didn't say a word, just brushed his fingers across the top of my shoulder.

"We're surviving," I said to her, because we were. Our tight little unit was making it, and we were doing it all without her.

"I knew you would," was her only response, and I had no idea if she'd say anything more. She went so quiet so fast.

I made her talk. I made her own up. I made her *hear* me like a kind woman at a ranch told me to one day not so long ago.

"So you're back," came from my mouth, a bit cold, a bit hurt. "You're back now?"

I waited a long time for the next words and honestly? I didn't know how I felt about them when I finally heard them.

"I am," she said. "I am."

So many days later, we sat in Brody's truck. The day should have been happy. The day should have been one felt with no anxiety, but it was—because of her.

Gazing up, I watched my nephew play through the wide windshield of the four by four. Brody and I said he could play on the playground as long as he stayed within distance. Aiden couldn't believe his luck today. Time at the park and then dinner on Ms. Rose's ranch later that evening, almost too much for him. Brody and I told him about the dinner reservation after we picked him up from the birthday party and he took that excitement with him into the week.

I had no idea that same day Elena would want to meet.

I could have told her no. I *should* have told her no, but I couldn't. I wanted to hear what she had to say. I wanted answers to all my questions. She said she just wanted to talk and that's all I would let her do. That talking, though? That wouldn't include her son. I had been clear on that on the phone. He'd be within my eyesight, though. He'd be here at the park with the man I loved.

He sat with me now, his hand rubbing down mine on my jeans. "You don't have to do this," he said. "If you're not ready."

When would I ever be ready for this? I had a feeling if I let today go, I might always do so.

My fear and anxiety of the unknown kept me in the truck despite my need for answers. I could feel it. It coursed through my veins like a oncoming storm. That's when Brody took my hand. He pressed it to his lips, his soft perfect mouth, and he played with my mood ring with a thick finger after he did. He smiled at it and I couldn't help smiling at him. That little thing seemed like the start of us. It knew we'd be together I think before even we did.

"Remember our talk?" Brody asked, lowering my hand to his lap. "And how I left the night your sister called?"

So much had happened that night, but I didn't fail to notice how once again my issues had taken the forefront. After it had all been said and done, Brody chose to keep to himself the details of that night. I hadn't pushed him on it because I never did. We knew how the other operated. Pushing never worked, only openness, and then later acceptance.

"I went to see my pop," he said, chasing the line between my index finger and thumb with his. His hand was so much larger. He looked up. "I really didn't know why. I just found myself there, but I'm glad I did. I think I needed to know how he felt. I think I just needed to talk to him." He laughed a little. "I think I just needed to talk—period."

I pushed a leg under the other. "What did he say? What did you say?"

He sat with his thoughts a moment before he spoke. "We talked about the family business, but it's not what we said that stuck with me. It's what I ended up finding out. The pair of us, we're real similar. We don't like bothering folks with our issues and never like saying when we need help."

I definitely got that from him, but also respected that about him, too.

He laced our fingers. "I'm going to tell everyone today about my condition. I figured dinner tonight will be a good time. We'll all be there and it will just be out there, you know?"

I squeezed his hand, fully supporting him on that. His family should know. They should know everything.

"We'll be able to figure out what's next," he said swallowing. "And where I fit in now that I have this issue."

That's where I had to cut him off. I kissed the back of his hand. "This isn't just your issue. I think you believe it is, but it's not. Your family will be there for you and you know you have me."

His eyes crinkled in the corners. He glanced away toward the playground, toward Aiden playing.

"This will all be... different for me," he went on. "Letting people help and even harder adjusting to what I'm now limited to do for my family, for the business."

Hearing that on the end made me smile. He both needed and wanted to be a part of his family's business. To actually take action had to be up to him and when *he* felt he was ready. I was glad he finally believed what I did and what his family no doubt had since the beginning. We all believed in him.

"But I can do it," he continued. "And you? I know you can do what you're about to do. Your strength, Alexa, gives me strength. It makes me believe in any and everything. It lets me know it's going to be all right for both of us. For all of us."

He lifted our hands, kissing the back of mine before kissing me. I had to believe in his magic again. I had to believe in his words.

She looked up when I came into the cafe and she looked so, so different. Her hair had gotten a little longer and her face fuller, no bags under her eyes. Elena looked awake. She looked alive and something else, too.

She didn't look so unhappy anymore. In fact, not at all, though a bit anxious, the unease patting her fingers lightly against the hard plastic table.

My uneasiness matched as well, my strides taking me toward someone I was starting to question if I'd ever see again, but there she was, Elena, my older sister.

Her gaze traveled the length of the room and when she spotted me, she stood, her hands clasped in front of her.

I closed the space with small steps, the words exchanged with me outside my driving force. Brody, he gave me strength, too.

I got to Elena quickly. The room had been small. The whistles and aroma of warm coffee beans moved through the air, surrounding us, but they couldn't distract. We had too much between us. There was too much unsaid.

Elena's hands gripped the hem of her blouse like she didn't know what to do with them. A blouse. She wore a pretty blouse with flowers on it, the petals reaching for sunshine. She tugged it. "Hey," she said, chewing on her lip a little and what else could I say but, "Hey" in return.

The two of us sat by my lead. Elena already had a lidded cup in front of her, asking quickly what I wanted.

I raised my hands. "It's okay. I'm fine." I refused to say I had no intention of being around here long. I'd let her say what she needed to say, then I planned to take the time *I* needed to go over it. This was all a lot for me and I wasn't the only party involved.

Elena acknowledged my decline, a subtle dip of her chin. Her head tilted ever so slightly afterward. She glanced behind my shoulders and every which way and I knew she was fully aware I wasn't the only party involved in this conversation. Just as quickly, she gave up, realizing that party wasn't with me and I didn't fail to notice she didn't address what and who she'd been looking for.

I had so many questions, but started by stating something of the obvious.

"You look good," I said, because she did. She looked well. She looked healthy.

The compliment only pleased her a little. Her smile was tight. "Thanks. The getting there was what it was, but I'm glad I did it. I feel good, so thanks."

"So you're clean?" I asked her. This had been something I needed to know off the bat. If she wasn't, there was no reason for this conversation to continue. There was no reason for me to stay.

"The treatment was ninety days," she said, tapping the side of her coffee. She cupped it. "Ninety days and I completed every one of them, Alex. I'm clean now and over a hundred."

Over a hundred. One hundred. I couldn't remember her being sober past a handful of days since we were teens, but what she said didn't add up.

I slouched back, my shoulders dropping. "But you've been gone four months, Elena." They'd been four months in which I had to repair wounds, fleeting days of holding her child while he cried into the night. Some of those nights had been my own. Some of those the man I loved had to *help me through* my own.

Her arms moved over her chest and I recognized the body language. I did it myself when I was uncomfortable.

"I had some things to take care of," she said, her gaze escaping me. Her fingers played at her arm. "I had to track down Nathan."

My back up, my hands gripped my handbag. It never made it off my shoulder, sitting in my lap. Maybe something told me to never take it off.

I rose from my seat, but her voice stopped me.

"I had to end it," came her words, and when I turned, her hands were on the table. Midair, she was standing. She was pleading. "I had to track him down to end it. To end everything."

"You went to see him?" The very thought chilled me. So toxic, he'd have my sister right back where she was in a matter of moments.

But she said she was sober...

Elena shook her head, her ponytail moving over her shoulder, and that's when I sat down. She didn't go back to him. She didn't see him.

Watching me, she retook her seat as well, placing her hands flat on the table. "I didn't see him, but I needed to find him. It was the only way I could make all of this stop and get him out of our lives for good."

What she said didn't make sense to me. "How did you end things if you didn't see him?"

Her fingers came together. "I made some calls. From some friends, I found out he wasn't far from where I stayed."

He was probably watching for her, *waiting* for her like the creep he was.

She went on. "Once I knew that, I made a call."

"To who?"

"The police," she said.

I had to say, my brow jumped. "The police?"

"Yes, I filed a report and I had enough evidence for them to make an arrest."

My arms moved over my own chest now, my skin lining in gooseflesh at my next question. "An arrest for what?"

"Domestic abuse. Among other things. Drugs and his contacts. He kept a stash not far away and I fed them everything. Then there was Aiden. He hadn't touched him, but he was present when Nathan laid hands on me. I had enough. I gave the cops everything."

"How did you prove the domestic abuse?" I asked. Any injuries that occurred had to have gone away by the time she was out of treatment, her arm healed.

Out of her pocket, she pulled some pictures. They were printed out on computer paper like they'd been uploaded. The first glimpse of a black eye had me sitting back, my sister bruised and battered. Seeing my reaction, she folded them, pushing them to the side of her coffee.

"Aiden's teacher knew what was going on," she said. "I used to pick him up from school, so I was sure his whole school did. One day, she pulled me aside. She did her talking like women do. 'You need to report him,' she'd said. 'You need to say something.' At that point, I had been sneaking around with Nathan. Aiden didn't even know he was back and I passed off the bruises with lies. I fell. I dropped something on my legs. I burned myself."

The bile in my throat summoned by the dread. He burned her. He hurt her and she was wrong about Aiden not knowing. Aiden knew his voice when he called that day. He knew. He was smart.

Elena sat back. "His teacher told me to take pictures. I didn't have to do anything with them, but at least take them so if I did decide to act, I would have them. I don't know why I listened, but I'm glad I did."

I wouldn't say it, but we shared that; that gratefulness.

She carried so much information here, not only was she clean, but she removed Nathan. She'd rid herself from him, no doubt, permanently this time. He'd been paroled for abuse, *my abuse*, and wouldn't come back from this easy.

My anxiety of today lifted in ways I didn't think could happen. I realized quickly it had been closure. I needed closure of him.

"So he's arrested?" I asked. I needed to know for sure.

"They were preparing before I left, told me they had everything, and they'd keep me in touch. I came straight here after that. Pretty much drove all night."

She'd driven all night. Before she left, she said she had to make everything better, but I never held stake in those words. Elena had never given me a reason to. She'd never taken care of me and barely had provided for her son or herself.

Her fingers gripped over her knuckles, her hands fisting. Tense, she sat there in silence, but eventually, could no longer hold back.

"Is he okay?" she asked. She didn't need to say who.

My bag finally fell from my shoulder, resting in my lap. I nodded. "He is and he's attending school here. We got him enrolled shortly after you left. He's doing well."

That brought happiness out in her face again. "So you're still with that guy? Brody?"

And that? That brought out the happiness over me. Brody had that way. I smiled. "Yes, we're together. He's over at the park now with Aiden. He's been great."

"Can I see him?" she asked "Aiden?"

This question I knew lingered over today. Would she want to see him, but worse, would she try to take him? The sea of dread washed over me, but I fought it down, trying to be strong.

I played with my fingers. "That depends. What do you intend to do after you do?"

We both knew I had no rights to her son, but that was on paper. The connection Aiden and I had ran deep. It fused through both of us and she knew that. We also both knew her history. If I didn't want her to have Aiden, I could make it so.

Her hands opened up, wide on the table as she titled her head at me. "I don't want to take him from you, Alexa."

"Then what do you want to do? What's your angle, Elena? What's your motive? You're clean now, but so what? What about tomorrow and the next day?"

"It will be a step by step process. The program taught me that and I understand that."

I still wasn't convinced. I still didn't *trust* her. How could I when she did nothing but bring chaos in her wake. I pointed my finger on the table, shoving it down. "I won't let you come back in here and undo everything I've done. He *just* stopped crying, Elena. He just started to... To..."

I didn't want to say it. I didn't want to say move on from her, because he never could. But he could heal and that's what he was starting to do. And me? I was finally starting to get some of that, too. I was starting to *heal,* too.

I sat back. "Things are starting to get better. Aiden likes living here, Elena. He likes his school. He likes his friends."

"And he'll keep that," she stressed, her face so flushed. Her hands still remained where they were on the table, but they reached, almost pleading in their way. They looked like they wanted to do more and eventually, they did.

Sliding across the table, Elena grabbed my hands, and when she did, I didn't let go. I found... I didn't want to let go.

Her hands went tight on mine following the lack of resistance and soon, she squeezed. She squeezed so hard.

Her eyes flickered up and a smile like mine told me we shared more than our eyes.

"I know I have a lot to prove," she said, and a cloudiness hovered over her brown eyes. She wiped the mist away. "But I'm willing to put in the hard work to do it. I wasn't lying when I said I wanted to be better for him. I wasn't lying when I said I wanted to be better for you."

My own tears lingered at the precipice, my throat locking up to clear them. I swallowed, pushing through them.

"But how can I trust you?" I whispered. I meant to say Aiden, but when the words came out, they ended up being about myself.

Reaching up, she pushed away a tear from underneath my eye. She hadn't done that since I was a little thing. She hadn't been my big sister in so long.

Raising my hands, she kissed the back of them, shaking them in hers. "I could do a thousand things right and never fix what I've done. I can *never* fix what I let happen to you, Alexa. God knows if I could go back..."

She sniffed, bringing our hands together. "I'm sorry I wasn't there for you. I'm sorry I didn't protect you and though, I can't go back, there won't be a single day forward where you won't have me, where I won't try for you, Alex. I'll try every day and that's something I can promise you."

My tears dotted the table and she wiped them away again. Soon enough, the table no longer separated us. She brought me into her arms and when she did, I held her. I held her like my life depended on it and maybe a little part of me did.

"I love you, Alex," she said, bringing her hand down my back.

I buried my face in her neck. I could try. I could try for her, too.

～

Brody

She'd been in there for so long and I started to worry. I stood, glancing over my shoulder from my position at the park bench. Only the casual traffic of the cafe moved in and out, but no Alex.

Are you all right? Are you okay?

"Brody, can you push me?"

His voice made my grin come out before I even turned. Aiden sat in his swing, gripping the metal chains with that carefree air about him that all children had at the park. I was happy he'd somehow kept it through all the things in his life.

"Sure, buddy," came from me as I made my way over. I stopped in front of him, grabbing above the chain. "You sure you need my help though? You were pumping like a champ."

He rolled his brown eyes. "I know, but I want some air. I want you to push under."

The bravery of this kid caused me to step back, mocking in the fashion. "You sure you can handle that?"

Those eyes lifted to the heavens again. Turning, he pulled his backpack around. His action figure, Joe, had his head poking out the back. He went everywhere with that guy. Though, I did notice his appearance less and less. He used to hold him nearly every moment of the day, but now he rarely left Aiden's bag.

I definitely call that a sign.

Aiden slid the bag off his back.

"I don't want Joe to fall," he said, setting him down to the side gracefully and after that, he got himself ready. His tiny fists held on the chains of the swing, the most determined look on this nine-year-olds face.

Getting behind him, I took up my position. "All right, but you better hold on, now. I don't want you falling out."

"I'll be okay, Brody. Just push."

I wouldn't go to full height. If I did, he *would* go flying, but I did pull him back pretty far. When I drew forward, I squatted a bit going under. He went about half the height he could have, but I didn't think he noticed. His laughter, his glee, filled the air and I think I accomplished the job I set out to do. He asked me to push him again, so I did a couple of times. My phone buzzed before the third, so I took a break to see the text.

"She wants to see him," Alex said, then two seconds later. *"She said it can be when I'm ready. Should I today?"* And I really didn't know what to tell her. This was her call and she had every right to do what she felt was best for her nephew.

"I think you should do what you feel you need to do for his sake," I said to her, and I firmly believed that. We all had our journey and it shouldn't be rushed. Everything would still be there when she was ready and the world would wait until she was.

A few seconds passed then another text came in. It said, *"We're coming over,"* and that sent me peace because she finally had hers.

More calm settled when I realized I would have my own tonight, my own peace after talking with my family about things and though, anxious, it wasn't my nerves. The anticipation had me ready for the future. It had me hopeful for the future. I gazed up to go get Aiden. I wouldn't tell him what was going on, but thought it best we head to the picnic tables or something to wait. My study of the swings left me empty, though. The swings, they were there, but he wasn't in them. The one he'd been in swung haphazardly like he'd recently left it.

I stepped out, eyeing the playground and found him quickly. He chased after another kid, a boy, and the little snot had Aiden's backpack. Laughing, he ripped Aiden's action figure out of the bag, calling Aiden names like "baby" and some other profane shit that shouldn't be leaving kids' mouths. Aiden was handling it like a champ, though. He didn't cry, but his lip was pouting a little.

My strides took me that way and I got to watch as the boy threw Aiden's toy. It landed with a *thunk* on the sidewalk and I yelled, "Hey!" in his direction.

The little kid darted off like he had fire under his feet and I shook my head. Kids could be real dicks sometimes, but Aiden, this kid was strong. He picked the toy up without missing a beat.

I smiled and started to head that way when some talking got my attention. I could hear her voice in a crowded room. Alex walked across the street and she did so with her sister coming out of the cafe. The last time I'd seen Elena, she hadn't looked great. She'd been injured more than just physically and that shown all over her face. Now, she both looked and seemed on the road to recovery.

The pair stopped when they saw me before crossing and I lifted my hand, waving a bit. Aiden was about ten feet away from me and I opened my mouth to call to him, to get his attention, but something in the distance got my attention, a white car. It was a Corolla, old and beat up, and it only got my focus because of the speed. It was accelerating, getting faster and faster and soon enough, it took possession of two lanes. It made a beeline and as it got closer, I made out the driver.

His hand raised, Nathan pointed a finger. He pointed it sure. He pointed it true, and pointed it right at me. But there was a little boy. There was a little boy only ten feet away. Aiden was too close. Nathan would have to hit him to get to me.

I ran, the car coming closer and closer. Its bald rubber tires cut onto the side walk, cruising down it. I grabbed Aiden.

A scream hit the air from the boy in my arms and a screech took to the wind from the vehicle I knew was too close. It was still too close.

I rolled, Aiden in my arms and we hit. We hit something hard, something metal that knocked the wind straight out of me, and sent me clear on my back.

I heard another scream then, my girlfriend. I'd hear her voice anywhere.

Thirty-One

THEY TOLD me his heart stopped that day. It ceased rhythm after he fell and I couldn't believe it. I just heard it. I…

Something that powerful, something that strong just didn't stop. *He* didn't stop. He couldn't.

They told me he died. He *died*, and I did, too, because we were linked.

I'd die forever.

Thirty-Two

BRODY

I didn't remember much from that day. I remembered the car coming, old and fucked up, and I remembered dodging it. I remembered slamming into the playground to get away from it and I also remembered that motherfucker. I remembered him crashing. I had been on the ground at the time, Aiden underneath me crying. But he wasn't crying because he'd been hurt. He cried my name, shaking me, and then another cry sounded, too. I saw her face, her crystal tears in her eyes as she hovered over me. Behind her a white Corolla went up in flames. It had hit a tree.

Good riddance.

The world went dark.

My memories fleeted, my awareness. Sharp smells I never wanted to breathe in again surrounded me. I was in a hospital. My first thoughts went to my family. They'd see me here so soon after the scare with my pop, but not only that. They'd see me die here. I would die and they wouldn't know why.

The fight began after that. I fought to breathe, *to live*, and when I saw those tears again, they welcomed me out of the fray.

Alex sat beside me, her hand on my cheek, and a mash up of everything lined those gorgeous eyes. She had fear there, worry, but also happiness. She was happy.

"Hey, darlin,'" I breathed. Doing so stabbed at my ribcage and I was grateful for the pain. It meant, I was still here.

The tears flowed, filling her eyes, and she stood, covering my mouth with hers. I kissed her back, touching her hip though it hurt to shift.

"It's okay," I told her. "It's okay," but she wasn't listening, and the salty flow got caught between us. Eventually, she rested her forehead on mine, saying all kinds of things. She said, "I love you." She said that so many times. I told her I loved her too, and when I finally got to see her face, touch her, I asked about the little guy with me during that terrible day.

"He's okay?" I asked. "Aiden?"

Her tears touched my hand. She pushed them away with a nod and I was grateful for yet another painful breath.

"Thanks to you," she said, pushing her thumb over my cheek. "He's here because of you."

I smiled, shaking my head. "That boy is here because of himself. I just helped him out." It hurt to joke, talk, really everything, but her laugher made it worthwhile.

Bending, she kissed me again. She pushed a little hard and I cringed a bit. Her hands had the nerve to go delicate, but I grabbed them. She moved them to my ribs then.

"You broke two," came from her lips, her hands moving down them. She placed one on my heart. "And it stopped. You stopped."

I had a feeling. I couldn't really explain it, but I did. I put a hand on her cheek and she moved it into my palm, clasping it.

"What about *him*?" I asked. I didn't really want to say his name. She knew who I meant.

Her face went hard, cold, and when she told me he didn't make it, the world just seemed to come to full circle. I didn't wish death on anyone and never would no matter how bad they were, but the world now being minus one asshole like that? It wasn't a bad thing. Alex went into more detail after that, how her sister turned him in before coming to Texas, and how he'd followed her here after seeing the police. Both the girls figured he was coming after Elena and though that might have been true, some of that intent, *that rage*, definitely had been reserved for me. Not long after she finished, I looked around.

"Is my family here?" I wanted to see them, all of them, no matter how the visit would end. I was done running. Done.

My hand slid down her arm when she stood and she gripped it right after. "They've been here in and out since I have. Two days."

Two days. I'd been out for two days. The ribbon cutting... The store opening...

What had I put them through?

The reality coursed through my body and seared like an angry burn. Everything I'd tried to prevent, their worry, caught up to me anyway and not only that, I made it far worse.

Alex kissed my lips again, breathing me in, and I held her there for strength. I needed hers and mine. She backed away, holding my hand. "I'll tell them you're awake. They're all here but the one in Miami."

"Griffin?"

She nodded. "There was bad weather, flights delayed."

Shit. Not only was I stuck in here, but he and Roxie were stuck down there. Everyone must be a mess.

Alex's lips touched my hand before she left the room. I

had maybe seconds to come up with something to say. Maybe I should start with sorry. I was sorry I kept my condition from them. I was sorry for being weak.

The first that came in was Gram, followed by my Aunt Robin, a large hat on her head, and my greatest fear came to fruition. Their stress, their trauma.

My aunt had a tissue to her face and my Gram's face all tight, scared, and everyone else that came in matched. My brothers looked a wreck; Colton's face red and even Hayden had a flush. His wife, Karen, didn't bother hiding her tears. They flowed freely down her face as she held their oldest, my niece, Sarah, and Hayden their youngest, Crissy. The scene matched that of my pop, everyone in distress, everyone shattered, and then there was Pop. He'd been the one in the hospital bed back then, helping us all keep it together as he'd been the one ill, but here, now? Even he couldn't escape the emotion in the room. His lips were tight, hard in a line, and Ann, kind Ann, held his hand. He squeezed hers so hard his own was pale white.

I opened my mouth to say something. I opened my mouth to apologize, but the words never came. They didn't because I was surrounded, a hug, a hand. They didn't stop and when one person left another just took their place and they all said the same thing. They told me they loved me and they thanked God I was okay.

I had so much to own up to. I'd done so many things wrong, but for some reason, I got these peoples' forgiveness. I got their compassion and love and I also got their understanding no matter how undeserved. I guess that's why they call it family. They love you. They stick by you no matter what and all the hell you put them through. And I definitely had put them through that.

"You put yourself through more," my gram told me later that evening. Alex had left to take Aiden and her sister back to my place. They both visited with me for a long while and that made me happy to see that Aiden actually had been all right. He really was strong, that little kid. They stayed with me all day like Alex said they had the last couple.

I let Gram's words sit with me. She'd said a lot in our time alone together, but never once had she guilted me. Her words were cherished, comforting as much as I needed to hear them. I took value in them, every one, and when Pop finally came to me, I did the same. I had been sleeping a little, resting off those pain meds when he came in, but even still, I straightened up a little in his presence.

In all honesty, I thought he might lay into me, at least a small amount. It would be deserved. But he didn't. He just sat with me. He pulled up a chair, turned on the TV, and we watched a game together. Basketball, of course. We couldn't get enough of that stuff.

"I'm sorry," I told him, turning. I'd found out they had to push back the ribbon cutting because of this, yes, but I was sorry for so much more and I told my pop that. I told him everything; my fears and not wanting to disappoint him and how that fear kept me from the business. My pop, he didn't sugar coat his feelings, telling me he wished I'd been more open, but again, he never guilted me. I think because he understood. He'd been in this bed himself not too long ago, and well, like he'd said—I was like him.

"I'd still like to help," I told him later after it was all said and done. We'd been between game quarters. "With the business? That is, if you'll still have me."

His eyes drifted a little, his hand on the remote. He sat

back, his arms folded across his chest, and I wondered if he would say anything. Maybe he just didn't know what to say to that. The thought crossed my mind that I had separated myself from the business for so long that maybe he didn't *want* me to be a part of it anymore. But then, he asked me what I had in mind and wanted to do and he did it with a smile while watching the TV.

"Um, Brody?"

Alex's voice led her in, but she looked hesitant, lingering by the door.

I rose up a bit. "You know Pop, Alex." They'd met in and out today and of course, I was sure while I was out of it.

That same smile lined Pop's face when he tipped his chin to her and her sunshine radiated into the room just the same. She didn't need to linger by the door, though. I waved her in, but she didn't move.

She grabbed the door. "I just wanted to make sure you were still awake," she said, then widened the door and in came a face, I didn't expect to see tonight. They'd said his flight was delayed.

Griffin came in and had a look I'd seen far too much today. Eyes red and cheeks flushed to match. He had his wife's hand in his, and Alex left, closing the door behind them both.

Fuck, he looked a mess, his hair messy and all over the place. His clothes wrinkled, he seemed all out of sorts and Roxie had a similar look. She wore her hair up messy-like and had these big glasses on. They both had the air about them that screamed lack of sleep and I wondered how much they got. Alex had said they'd been having issues with flights and the thought they might have had to stay in the airport came to mind.

And then there was all this with me.

Roxie approached me first, because Griffin? Well, he stood there. He only came because she did, his hand still in hers. She put an arm out and I went in when she went to hug me.

"You're okay?" she asked, pulling back.

I smiled, settling back into the bed. "Yeah, I'm good. Everything turned out all right."

"Thank God," she said, but her husband, he still didn't move. Not only that, but his nostrils flared, his eyes narrowed like he was heated. Like he was angry. I hadn't been yelled at today by anyone. Even Pop had let things go, but I knew that wasn't deserved. I had screwed up, royally, and maybe now, I'd be answering to that. But then my brother came forward. He did and I didn't think we'd ever shared a tighter hug.

"You big, stupid motherfucker," he said in my ear, and I laughed a little. I laughed even though it hurt like hell.

I gripped his back. "Hey, Griff. You good, too?"

He pulled away, his hand on my shoulder. "Yeah," he said. "Yeah, long day. Long few days."

It had been that for all of us, but I had a feeling we'd all pull through. We always did. The pair of them talked with me for a little while and I did find out that they'd spent the last twelve or so hours in an airport. Their layover in Chicago got delayed due to engine trouble and then all their issues with even getting a flight due to the weather where they lived. Griff chatted with Pop after a bit and that's when Roxie let me in on something.

"He's been real upset," she said. "Real worried about you and then all the flight fiasco. He took it hard."

I had a feeling. I gazed over at my brother, glad he was good now, as he was watching the game with Pop in two chairs.

"Thanks for handling him," I told Roxie, grateful for her. She'd been Griff's rock when Pop went through his heart attack last year. She was my brother's heart and we all knew that.

She grinned a little. "I had help. If Alex, Alexa?" she paused, eyeing me for confirmation of the name. I nodded. "Yeah, if Alexa hadn't spoken to him first, I don't know how together he'd have it. She knew everything and gave us details over the phone. It really calmed him down."

I had to admit: I loved that girl more than a little.

Thirty-Three

ALEXA

"THE WHEELCHAIR really ain't necessary, guys." Brody eyed his hospital transportation like it had an infectious disease, his hands braced on the mattress while he sat on the side of his hospital bed. He shook his head. "I can walk just fine."

He went to stand, but cringed the moment he pressed his hands to the mattress to stand. He placed a hand to his ribs and his Aunt Robin scoffed. She'd been standing over his bag, packing it up so he could go home from the hospital today.

She placed her hands on his hips. "Like hell, boy," she said pushing a finger in the direction of the wheelchair his Grandma Rose had brought in. "Now, you get your butt in that chair and quit fooling around. You're just as stubborn and hard headed as your poppa."

She'd said that so much and each time Brody's dad had laughed a little whenever he had been around to hear it. Brody had because it wasn't him this time getting it from his aunt.

His little grandma came around the chair, tilting her head of snowy-white hair at him. "Darlin', can you just be coopera-tive with us? We don't want you getting hurt no further."

Sighing, Brody sat back down to the bed with a huff, but

didn't look any closer to getting in that chair. He still had a hand on his ribs and I placed my hand on top, frowning at him.

"Will you just use it please?" I asked him, sighing myself. "They're right. You don't want to exert yourself unnecessarily."

He had been so hard headed like his aunt said, but I guess I understood why he was so stir crazy. He'd been in the hospital for nearly a week and Lord knows, Brody Chandler didn't take being fussed over very well. He had me, his aunt, and his Grandma Rose fretting over him, and then there was the rest of his family floating in and out over the past few days.

Blowing out a breath, Brody's large hand moved to grip mine, his lengthy blond lashes flickering up at me. Lifting our hands, he touched my cheek with the tip of his thumb. "I understand y'alls concern. But really, Alex, I'm fine."

Yeah, he was fine on paper, his doctor giving him the a-okay to go home today, but how would he get to be one hundred percent if he kept fighting us all the whole way toward recovery? My nephew, who had overhead the whole exchange, uncrossed his legs. He got up from the chair he sat in near my sister, the two playing at the makeshift activity table that had been Aiden's idea for himself and the small kids. My nephew only left the hospital when he had to this week, wanting to "keep any eye on things," he'd said. He wanted to be here for Brody.

He got up, coming over to my stubborn big man. Brody's gram squeezed his shoulder with a smile when he got near the bed.

"Can you use it, Brody?" he asked, chewing his lip. "Please?"

That little face could get him whatever he wanted when it came to me and it only had the same affects on Brody.

A small smile pushed into the corner of Brody's mouth.

"Okay, bud. Okay," he said, and with that, the matter was settled. I helped push Brody out of the hospital and on the way; Brody's Aunt Robin drew an arm around Aiden's shoulders, tucking him into her cushy side.

"I'm recruiting you, youngin'," she said, grinning. "We could use some of that to wrangle these stubborn-headed boys around here."

And the Chandler men were definitely something. Massive blonds ranging in six-foot-plus inch frames traipsing around the hospital like gods among men. They definitely could intimidate, especially, Brody's dad. The man was a colossus, but I knew him to be nothing but a sweetheart. He'd been so nice to me, a stranger amongst all this kin and extended family and that had to be where Brody got it from. His goodness came from that man, the backbone of the entire family. He held them all together and led by example. These last few days had been tough, but Brody's dad made sure everyone kept their head on and the way these men all treated their women *had* to be from him. There had been so much care between him and the woman always by his side, Ann. He constantly had a hand on her, tending to her, and I saw the same with Brody's older brother Hayden and his small family.

The basketball player, Griffin, had been the same way. He and his wife were inseparable and once Griffin knew Brody was okay, Roxie had his attention. The youngest, Colton, I didn't see around much as he kept mostly to himself, but even he had a sweet air about him. His big body folded up, he sat with the kids in the waiting room when we'd all first arrived, playing alongside them with Legos and other things there. Aiden had joined in on that and Colton had kept them all laughing.

Brody's fingers laced with mine when we made it outside the hospital doors, and when the cavalry arrived in the form of trucks with members of the Chandler family sticking out of them, Brody palmed his cheek again. They had signs, balloons, and happy grins of arrival on their faces. Brody looked to have his own personal parade to escort him on his way home.

He shook his head. "These folks are going to be the death of me," he said, though he definitely smiled a little when he said it.

That evening consisted of backyard barbeque at Brody's trailer, though Brody's diet definitely consisted of applesauce and other foods on his approved list for his heart. Ann, the woman Brody's dad was with, ended up being a nurse and made sure to get a good list going for him. He grumbled, but a few harsh gazes from his gram and Aunt Robin had him shutting up quickly. They sentenced him to more bed rest, but he wouldn't have that. He sat on his couch with his brothers and dad, watching sports and the whole thing made me feel some kind of way. This family was so huge, so warm and full of love, and on the floor sat my little man. Aiden had his back to the couch, taking in the game with the rest of the men and that had me smiling so hard. In the kitchen, the women cleaned up from the barbeque Brody's dad had made for us all, but I noticed the kitchen was minus one.

I left the area of clanking dishes, moving around little Sarah, Brody's niece, as she played on the floor. Her sister slept in a traveling crib set up in one of the trailer's spare bedrooms. The boys were of course were enjoying the game and I bent, shaking Aiden a little. He looked up at me.

"Where's your mama?" I asked him, rubbing my hand on his head. Even still, his gaze didn't leave the television. I smiled.

He shrugged a bit. "I saw her go outside earlier. Probably there."

Outside? Had she gone to smoke? Standing, I went to go that way, but a hand shot out.

Brody's fingers slid down my wrist. He maneuvered a bit.

His eyes crinkling a little in the corners and I knew moving took him some effort.

"Everything good?" he asked, and I lowered, sitting on the arm of the couch.

Turning my head, I stared across the living room and over the bar into the kitchen. There, the women of his family laughed, tossing their heads back as they conversed with each other and in the living room, there was a similar setting. The boys drank beer, jostling each other, and Brody's gaze followed me to both places. He smiled and I brushed his arm.

"I think you know the answer to that," I told him, actually physically feeling all this support, his family around him. I squeezed his arm. "I'm just going to check on my sister. Aiden says she went outside."

He nodded, watching while I stood. In front of me, Roxie passed and went to her husband, Griffin, in the armchair. He made room for her, allowing her to sit in the space between him and the chair. She ended up being partially on his lap and she definitely didn't mind that, her head moving to tuck underneath his neck. Brody looked up at me.

"Hurry back," he said, letting my wrist go. "Because I'm thinking I'm trying to do some of *that*."

He winked at me, making me feel all kinds of warm. All this love and affection I could definitely get used to. Definitely.

He let me go and I found my way out front. Elena was there, but she wasn't smoking, no. She sat to herself on the mobile home's steps, arms crossed over knees. Her head turned, eyes glancing over her shoulder when the door snapped behind me. Her lips moved into a small smile and that was something else I could get used to, my arrival doing that to her, making her happy. She made room for me on the step and I asked her what she was doing when I sat beside her.

She shrugged, playing with her hands. "Just chillin' I guess," she said, watching the neighborhood.

Others out here were doing the same as we were, grills lifting smoke into the air. We sat together for quite a little bit before we spoke again.

"I see where you fit in here," she said suddenly, her lashes flickering my way. She smiled again. "You fit right in with them inside. You guys just make sense."

It was funny she said that, because I felt the same way, too. It was something about Brody's family. It was just something about *him*.

"Even Aiden has found his place," she went on, nodding. Her shoulder lifted. "I guess I'm just trying to see where I go from here."

That seemed like quite an easy solution to me, and I brought my arm around her, bringing her in.

"Anywhere I am," I told her, because I had a feeling with as big as Brody's family was, as big as their hearts seemed to be, they wouldn't mind making room for one more.

Epilogue

ALEXA

"Brody!" I giggled, stumbling forward. I couldn't do anything else with his hands over my eyes. My foot caught on something. Grass, I assumed since we were outside. I giggled again. "Where are you taking me? We're going to be late."

We literally had minutes, *minutes* before we had to be clear across town. His childhood church was quite a drive, a cute little white chapel and it was cute. I'd seen it both decorated and without.

Brody spun me around and his face replaced his hands, his lips on my mouth.

Giving in, I slid my hands up a broad chest and over thick material I knew to be fine lapels. He was so handsome today. Well, he was handsome every day, but this one in particular. I should get him to wear a suit more often. His mouth grinned against mine.

"You trust me?" he asked, his voice light, excited. "I know we don't have a lot of time, but we won't be late. I'd never hear the end of it."

No, he wouldn't. His family, his dad, would kill him. I sent my own nephew over there early to hold down the fort in our absence. Well, I guess he'd be there anyway, as he was in the ceremony. He went down to the church with Brody's sister-in-law, Karen, and her kids. Elena drove with them, my eyes and ears. We shared that role now. We relied on *each other* now to care for our family and I was right about something. The Chandler Family?

They definitely had room for one more.

My eyes still closed, I nodded. I trusted Brody with everything, my life and so much more. Since his accident, he regained his physical strength, but really, it had never really left him.

He popped a kiss on my mouth, but didn't put his hands back over my eyes. He asked me not to cheat and keep my eyes closed, so I did.

Thick fingers laced through my hands and he tugged, turning me to guide me around. We continued on by his lead off grass and then onto something harder, sidewalk. I hit his body a bit when he stopped, but not hard. His hand went to the small of my back, his fingers laying delicately on the chiffon dress that hit just above my knees. He told me to wear yellow today. He loved yellow on me. He said it brought out the sunshine even more.

He said the most wonderful things.

Holding onto me, he brushed his fingers along my back. "Almost there."

I grinned again, able to do nothing but listen. I heard a click, then a creak, and I was pulled once more.

"Watch your step."

I did as told, off the concrete down and on something different. The flooring clicked under my heels and I drew in a breath, trying to find any indicator as to where I was. I smelled nothing but air, a bit stale, but nothing more.

His hand clasped around mine and then he took both, squeezing. "You ready?"

I laughed. "Not sure," and that sent a laugh from him, deep and hearty. I could bask in it.

"Open them," he said, and I did, my eyes adjusting to the dim room. Only the sunshine lit it and I let go of Brody's hand, walking through. To my left was a ballet barre, it went on for a few feet and was surrounded by wide mirrors. The sun in the room gleamed off them, bouncing and shining on the hardwood floors. And it was wood, solid with a thin layer of dust. My heels left tracks and I turned, seeing more mirrors and barres.

"What...?" I didn't understand, turning around, but Brody did. His hands in his pockets, he came over to me, just as handsome and beautiful as when I'd last seen him outside. A yellow tie complimented my dress and matched wedding colors and his dark suit formed over the broadest body, and the thickest shoulders. He grabbed my hand, pulling me to him.

His eyes lifted to the room. "Do you think you can do something with it?"

I gasped, trying to find breath, trying to understand. "Do what? What do you mean?"

His hand left mine now, spinning on the heel of his leather shoes. The sunlight did all kinds of things to his golden locks, caught every varying shade of dirty blond he had slicked back. I would never see him this clean again, but that didn't matter. He did debonair well, but he did messy sexy even better.

He grinned a little. "I got a good deal on it if you want it. If you want to teach in it. It's your call, but if you want it? You can have it."

I could have it. I could have *this;* mine. I went up to him. "Brody, I could never afford this. I could never pay you back." My hours had been cut even more at the gym and my savings was non-existent since we moved. We'd moved into a house, a place for me, him, and my family and it had been great so far. It had been *amazing* so far.

"You're right," he said, sliding our fingers together. He raised them in the air, bringing me to him by them. "*You* can't afford it. But *we*," he paused, lifting a finger and gesturing between the two of us, "can. You've been wanting to get out of that gym, Alex. You can teach classes here and be your own boss."

He'd been so full of dreams lately; being a businessman now himself seemed to bring it out of him. He took charge of the delivery unit of *Chandler & Sons Furniture Co.* recently. Who better than the best driver this side of El Paso?

And he cracked the whip on those boys, too, like a boss.

He was right. I did want this. *This* was a dream, but what if I wasn't like him? What if I couldn't run a business?

But I was willing to try.

"You'll help me?" I asked, beaming up at him. "I don't know anything about being an entrepreneur."

"Mmm, well that," he said, his lips getting closer, so close. "We can both muddle through. We can both learn along the way. We can grow along the way."

We would grow, wouldn't we? We'd done nothing but since we got together. We pushed each other. We leaped together.

His full lips found mine and we did something else together. We kissed in *our* new ballet studio.

And still made it to his dad's wedding on time like champs.

Click the link below to download book four of The Found by You series!

Download on Amazon

www.ingramcontent.com/pod-product-compliance
Lightning Source LLC
Chambersburg PA
CBHW051204220726
48293CB00014B/1885